Advanced Reviews fo

MW00983918

This is a beautifully written, yet heart-rending tale. I highly recommend this book for anyone who seeks to understand, for this just might be one of the most important novels of our time. **Mary Jo Thayer,** award-winning author of *Close to the Soul*

Ellen Gable tells a very personal and difficult story, *Where Angels Pass*, with such gentleness, love, and heartfelt honesty. What I expected to be an uncomfortable story ended up being a love story of a daughter for her father. This is a deeply moving story that will surely touch readers in a profound way. **Jim Sano,** author, *The Father's Son*

Incredible book, magnificently done. This is a story with uncompromising honesty that offers humanity hope despite one of the worst sins of all—the corruption of innocence. **A.K. Frailey,** author, *The Road Goes Ever On*

The greatest tragedy that could befall the Roman Catholic Church is for a child's innocence to be stolen by a priest. Told by Ellen Gable, as only she can tell it, with candor and faith, this story sheds light on the darkness of a case of clerical abuse. A moving and heart-breaking read that will change your life and strengthen your faith!
Elena-Maria Vidal, author, *My Queen, My Love: A Novel of Henrietta Maria*

In the unfolding of the story — with the inevitable fury and sorrow that surfaces along the way — we are finally brought face to face with Jesus' call to forgive those who harm us. A feat that Ellen shows us is not impossible, for nothing is impossible for those with God on their side. This book will change, teach, and inspire. Every Catholic should read it.
Veronica Smallhorn, author, *A Channel of Your Peace*

Ellen Gable has done a great service to our Church, the victims of this dreaded abuse, and particularly to their families whose suffering has gone virtually unnoticed. She has done a masterful job mixing fact with fiction.
Michael Seagriff, author, *Pondering Tidbits of Truth* and *I Thirst for Your Love*

Ellen Gable addresses the darkness of sexual abuse and the resulting lifelong wounds with delicate finesse.
Michelle Buckman, award-winning author of *Rachel's Contrition* and *Death Panels*

I couldn't put this book down, so don't let the topic deter you. The story, told simply and honestly—and without sensationalism—will draw you in and have you rooting for these characters long after you close the book.
Victoria Ryan, author. *I'm Listening: Praying with Art and Story*

A powerful story that helps Catholics better understand the long-lasting damage that this type of abuse creates.
Carolyn Astfalk, award-winning author of *Stay With Me* and *Ornamental Graces*

Where Angels Pass

A Novel

By Ellen Gable

Full Quiver Publishing

Pakenham ON

Copyright 2021
Ellen Gable Hrkach
Published by
Full Quiver Publishing/Innate Productions
PO Box 244
Pakenham ON K0A2X0

This one's for you, Dad.

I look forward to our reunion in eternity.

Books by Ellen Gable
Great War Series
Julia's Gifts, Finalist 2019 IAN Awards
Charlotte's Honor
Ella's Promise, 2020 International Book Awards
and 2020 Finalist IAN Awards

O'Donovan Family Series
In Name Only winner, IPPY Gold Medal, 2010
A Subtle Grace, finalist, IAN 2015

Emily's Hope, IPPY Honorable Mention 2006
Stealing Jenny (Amazon bestseller)
Come My Beloved: Inspiring Stories of Catholic Courtship
*Image and Likeness: Literary Reflections
on the Theology of the Body* (with Erin McCole Cupp)
Dancing on Friday, The Story of Ida Gravelle
Remembering Mom

Contributor to:
Word by Word: Slowing Down With The Hail Mary
edited by Sarah Reinhard
Catholic Mom's Prayer Companion
by Lisa Hendey and Sarah Reinhard
God Moments II: Recognizing the Fruits of the Holy Spirit
God Moments III: True Love Leads to Life
edited by Michele Bondi Bottesi
*After Miscarriage: A Catholic Woman's Companion to
Healing and Hope* edited by Karen Edmisten
Motherhood Matters Study Guide
(editor and contributor) By Dorothy Pilarski

'Neath wings of tarnished bronze they pass,
Our wary pilgrim youth,
Through archways firm, near tiles of glass,
Consoled by guardian truth.

But, beyond the halls of stone and oak,
Our seeds of hope descend
Midst wolves adorned with pale white yoke,
Who'll help them to their end.

James Hrkach

"Beware of false prophets, who come to you in sheep's clothing, but underneath are ravenous wolves." Matt 7:15

Based loosely on actual events

Prologue
Evie
Saying Goodbye
Runnemede, NJ
April 1982

The shock of losing her father felt like someone had dumped a pile of bricks on Evie Gallagher. She just couldn't wrap her fifteen-year-old mind around it. Evie and her family walked around on autopilot, stunned.

This happens to other families, not ours.

Her world as she knew it had ended, and yet the birds continued to sing. Everybody outside her family went about their business, and life carried on despite her father's death.

Aunt Flora, Mom's oldest sister, stayed with them for a few days. If her aunt had one job to do, it was to keep the kids busy so that they didn't think too much about what had happened to Dad. Of course, Evie's brother Mitch and her sister Deb, both over eighteen, probably didn't think they needed someone to distract them. Her aunt didn't seem to care and ushered them all to the mall. Evie welcomed the distraction. She found herself smiling at a cute toddler running around the mall. Then she felt guilty for smiling. Her father was dead. She had no right to be happy.

Two days after Dad's death, while Mom had an appointment at the funeral home, Aunt Flora took Evie, Deb, Mitch, and her younger brother Hank to lunch at the diner across the street.

"You know, kids, death is just another part of life. Your dad won't be the last person close to you to die."

Evie appreciated Aunt Flora's sentiment, but until now, Evie had never lost anyone so close. As she stared out the window at the traffic crisscrossing the road, she bit her lip. Maybe if she had rushed home from school, she could've gotten there before he passed away. She'd known her father had been drinking. She should've just stayed home with him. Her eyes clouded over when she thought of one of the last things her dad had said to her.

"Eve, you need to find a guy about my size because you fit so perfectly to me."

Evie sighed. *I would be happy just to have you, Dad.*

Of course, her father's life had been far from perfect. He'd had a nervous breakdown when Evie was a toddler. Struggled with alcoholism. Attended Mass sporadically. But she'd always thought of him as a kind and devoted father who had so much more life to live despite everything that had happened to him. Regardless of his difficulties, her father had incredible value.

Evie's stomach churned, and she lost her appetite, despite the juicy hamburger sitting in front of her. She pushed the plate away. She'd have no more Christmases with Dad. No more Thanksgivings. Dad would never walk her or her sister down the aisle someday or get to know his grandchildren. She shrugged. Then again, she'd never dated or kissed a guy, so maybe marriage wasn't even in her future.

***

At the private viewing the following Wednesday, Evie lingered in the corner of the fancy room at the funeral home, hesitant to approach the casket.

Mom knelt for some time by the casket. Then she got up and motioned to Evie and her siblings. "Come here, kids."

They all followed her to the open casket and stood together, staring down. *Dad looks like he's sleeping.* The sparkling blue rosary that Dad's parents had given him lay draped on his hands. Evie touched his arm, finding it hard and cold. So lifeless. Unable to hold the tears in, she wept.

Deb followed, and even her brothers began to cry.

Mom cleared her throat. "The mortician did a great job. He looks really good."

Baffled, Evie stifled a sob. How can any dead person look *good*? They're dead, aren't they?

Then she studied him more closely. No worry lines. No scowl. He didn't actually look like he was sleeping because even in sleep, his expression was always one of turmoil. Now, her father seemed truly at peace. At that moment, Evie felt tremendous relief flow through her. Dad would no longer have to deal with his alcoholism or his mental illness.

The funeral director had dressed her father in a suit. Dad rarely wore a suit. Why couldn't they have put regular clothes on him?

Her youngest brother, Hank, named after Dad, asked, "Do you guys remember what Dad looked like last summer when he wasn't working? A button-down shirt, Bermuda shorts, and dress shoes with black socks."

Evie wiped her eyes and laughed. *Dad has no fashion sense.* Maybe he should've been buried in his summer outfit.

Had no fashion sense. It was going to take some practice speaking about him in the past tense.

Evie knelt and said a prayer for her father's soul. She thanked Jesus and the Blessed Mother for inspiring her father to return to Confession and Mass.

The rest of the evening visitation passed in a blur. Hundreds of people showed up to express their condolences. Evie didn't even know most of their names. Some of her and her siblings' classmates from school came, as did her father's friends and fellow letter carriers.

They all woke early the following morning to get to the funeral home for the last visitation before the Mass of Christian Burial at St. Maria Goretti Church.

When the visitation period ended, Mom called her and her

siblings to the casket. "It's time to say goodbye to your father." Mom leaned over and kissed him. Then Deb kissed his cheek, then Aunt Flora, Aunt Tess, Grandmom. Evie stood back and waited. Finally, Evie, at only four feet six inches tall, approached the casket and tried to lean in, but the kneeler had been taken away, so she couldn't reach him. She tried to hoist herself onto the casket. Suddenly, hands came from behind her; her brother Mitch picked her up. Evie leaned over and kissed Dad. She knew he wasn't really in there anymore, that it was just his body, but she didn't want to think of him buried in the cold, hard ground.

Would her shattered heart ever be whole again, or would it feel like this forever?

***

At home in their living room, Evie, her siblings, and her mother sat quietly. Her dad's high school yearbooks lay scattered across the coffee table. Evie picked up his freshman yearbook. She searched for his picture and found it. Her father appeared to be the shortest in his freshman class. She squinted and tilted her head. He looked much younger than fourteen years old.

Chapter 1
Hank
First Day of School
Philadelphia
September 8, 1954

Fourteen-year-old Hank Gallagher lifted his head and peered at the main entrance of the high school he would be attending for the next four years. Above the door, a bronze statue of St. Michael the Archangel sat perched above a monstrous Satan, who lay crushed underneath the mighty angel. The statue had turned pale green after being exposed to the elements. Above it, a clock tower stretched to the sky.

Hank pulled at his necktie and opened the top button on his uniform coat jacket. It was supposed to be the end of summer, but at 8:15 a.m., the sun's hot rays beamed down, and it had to be eighty-five degrees. Homeroom didn't begin until 8:45 today, but Hank wanted to make sure he knew where he was going. Besides, only a few boys remained outside.

Nervous, he straightened and strolled through the doors. He stepped into the foyer of the clock tower and made his way to the arched doors of the entrance to the school's main building. It was cooler in here. Hank stared, mouth open, at the high ceiling, wide marble staircase, and enormous statues that filled the area above the stairs. He had passed the school several times but had never stepped foot inside until today.

Holy Archangels High School for Boys hadn't been Hank's first choice. He had wanted to attend St. John Vianney High School because three of his buddies were going there. But his parents insisted, especially his mother, that he must go to

13

Archangels because it was closer—and the tuition less expensive.

Shoved from behind, Hank lurched forward and fell, his hands slapping onto the checkered linoleum floor. Scowling, he glanced up to see two older boys snickering, "Stupid midget freshman."

As the boys walked off, Hank stood and dusted off his pants. He lifted his chin and fixed his gaze upon the statues overhead: two large angels holding swords—Raphael and Gabriel?—on either side of the staircase and a larger one— St. Michael, who gripped a much longer sword.

His schedule listed Room 105 as his homeroom. He turned left down the hall and scanned the room numbers: 101, 102, 103, 104. There it was, 105. A glance at the wall clock showed that he still had twenty minutes. When he reached the door, he turned the knob but found it locked.

Leaning against the wall, he waited.

As the minutes passed, more students arrived. Soon twenty-five boys stood with him, waiting outside the door of Room 105. Hank checked his watch. 8:45.

The bell rang, and the boys still waited. Finally, the hurried tapping of shoes made the group turn toward the direction of the sound. A young priest dressed in a white habit raced toward them. Hank's parish had one or two Dominicans over the past few years, so Hank presumed this young priest was also a Dominican.

Hank's schedule indicated this was Brother David McCallum, O.P. His youthful looks suggested he was straight out of the seminary. Two years ago, when he was an altar boy, Hank thought he might have a vocation to the priesthood. Now, though, he was pretty confident he didn't.

"Sorry, gentlemen, for my tardiness." Brother McCallum unlocked the door and opened it wide for the boys to enter.

Hank stepped inside the classroom. Sunlight streamed in through tall windows and fell on neat rows of desks, but the odor of fresh paint and the stifling warmth nearly overwhelmed him. It had to be about as hot as hell.

"Quickly, boys, help me open the windows. It's stuffy in here."

Wanting to make a good first impression, Hank volunteered, but he was too short to help with the windows. As he gave up trying, someone behind him snorted, "Shorty."

When he turned, he couldn't see anyone glancing in his direction, so he headed to the back of the room and claimed his seat.

The young brother stood in front of the green chalkboard. "Welcome to Homeroom 9 G. My name is Brother David McCallum. Right now, I'm a brother, but in two years, I'll be ordained a deacon, then a priest. I'll be your homeroom and probably your Religion instructor here at Holy Archangels High School."

After prayer and the Pledge of Allegiance, as Brother McCallum passed out forms and permission slips, he asked the class, "What do you call a sleepwalking priest?"

Brother McCallum waited for a beat, but no one answered. "A Roamin' Catholic." Then he roared with laughter.

Hank shook his head. This almost-priest was a bit strange.

Before the bell rang to change classes, Brother McCallum chatted about how he was new too, and they could all "learn the ropes" together. As he spoke, Hank studied his schedule. His next class was English in Room 218 with Fr. Timothy O'Reilly, O.P. Each class today would be only thirty minutes, then noon Mass and early dismissal since it was the Feast of Our Lady's Nativity.

Overwhelmed by the heat again, Hank tugged at his tie and opened a button on his shirt. He wiped the sweat from his forehead and face with his handkerchief.

The bell rang, and he joined the flow of students in the hallway. He darted and dashed in between the throngs of boys heading for the stairs. This was where it came in handy to be short.

As he climbed the marble staircase, he stared again at the St. Michael, St. Gabriel, and St. Raphael hanging statues above him. Soon a mob of boys filled the stairs, everyone pushing and taking Hank along with them. He stumbled out onto the second floor and searched for Room 218. He followed one of the students from his homeroom, hoping he might also be going to Room 218. He caught up to the boy, a redhead, slightly taller than Hank. "Are you going to Room 218, Fr. O'Reilly's class?"

"Yup," the boy answered, pointing to a classroom down the hall.

Chapter 2
Hank
English Class

Hank followed his new acquaintance into the classroom and sat down at a desk beside him in the last row. "My name's Hank. What's yours?"

"Colin Farrell. But everyone calls me Red."

"Nice to meetcha, Red."

"Likewise."

Hank now considered the day a success. He'd made a friend!

The priest stood with his back to the class as he wrote his name on the green board, the course title underneath it. He wore a white habit, but judging from his bald head, he was older than Hank's homeroom teacher. Finally, the bell rang to signal the start of class.

A slight breeze traveled in through the windows, which someone had opened wide, and a large fan stood at the front of the classroom. It was still warm but a lot less so than his homeroom.

Fr. O'Reilly turned around. A wide smile stretched across his face, and the palm of his hand lay flat against his chest. "As you can see from the blackboard, my name is Fr. Timothy O'Reilly, and this is English 101. Class, I always enjoy getting to know new pupils for the semester. First, though, I'd like to start with this young man. Please stand, sir."

The lanky boy stood and eyed the priest warily. "Students, I'd like to give you a lesson in what you see is not necessarily what is true."

Fr. O'Reilly pulled a coin from inside his habit. "Can you tell the class what this is?" He handed it to the skinny boy.

"Um…it's a quarter."

"Thank you," said the priest, "you may sit down."

Fr. O'Reilly flipped the coin back and forth between his hands. Suddenly, it disappeared into thin air. Oohs and aahs came from the class.

The priest leaned over to the now-sitting, thin student and pulled the coin from behind the boy's ear.

A few students clapped, so Hank joined in, already impressed with this new teacher.

"Now for introductions. Starting with this young man here," the priest waved his arm like a kangaroo's tail at the fellow to the right of the skinny student. "Please stand, introduce yourself, and tell us from which parish school you graduated."

Hank's pulse quickened, and the thumping of his heart pounded in his ears. He despised public speaking. He didn't know any of these kids, except for Red, and he had just met him.

In a few moments, he would have to stand and introduce himself. *This is fine. All you have to say is your name and the school from which you graduated.*

"Mr.…uh… Gallagher?"

Hank's hands trembled. "Y… yes, Father?" Hank stood, and a few students snickered. One boy whispered, "Dwarf."

"Students, quiet. Go ahead, Mr. Gallagher."

Hank cleared his throat and avoided eye contact with Fr. O'Reilly. "M—my name is," he cleared his throat again, "Henry Gallagher, and I graduated from St. Barnabas School."

"Thank you, Mr. Gallagher."

Hank sat down and slowly and quietly blew out a breath.

He studied Fr. O'Reilly. He was probably in his forties, bald except for a round patch of hair, and with kind eyes that peered out under bushy eyebrows. His mouth always seemed to be on the verge of a smile, and he used his hands as he spoke.

Once all the introductions had finished, Fr. O'Reilly got down to business. First, he asked for volunteers to pass out the English textbooks and, although Hank had raised his hand, Fr. O'Reilly chose two tall, muscular boys.

"All right, class. These books are to remain here at the school. Turn to page one of *Grammar Basics*. This should be an easy review for you all. A sentence has two parts: a subject and a predicate."

As Hank followed along with Fr. O'Reilly's recitation of the parts of the sentence, he allowed his mind to wander. He wondered if Pop or Uncle Edwin would take him and Billy down the shore this weekend. It was still hot, and they could get another day of swimming and searching for unique seashells.

The bell rang, and Hank closed his book.

"Boys, please leave the books on your desks for the next class."

He and Red parted company as they were in different third-period classes. Hank had Physical Education for third period, and his teacher, Mr. Romero, proudly told the class that he had been on the USA rowing team in the 1936 Olympics. He explained that they would be participating in baseball, field hockey, and basketball this semester. When Hank heard "basketball," he groaned. He didn't expect to get a good grade in that sport.

Hank had three more classes to attend: Algebra with Fr. Smith—a very elderly priest—Religion with Brother McCallum, and finally, Social Studies with Fr. Bonneville, a stern-looking fellow.

Of course, the elderly Math teacher gave homework the first day, which Hank had expected from his older teachers.

At Mass, Hank met up with Red, and afterward, they ate lunch together before taking different public buses home.

Chapter 3
Hank
Home Life

The first day of school completed, Hank returned to his row house, where he opened, then slammed the screen door shut.

"Hank, is that you?" his mother asked from the kitchen.

"Yeah, Ma, it's me."

"What'd I tell you about slamming the door?"

"Sorry."

The aroma of pork chops and sauerkraut wafted through the balmy house. Hank dropped his books on the coffee table in the living room, stepped through the dining room, and entered the cramped kitchen. His mother stirred something in a pot on the stove. Ma wore her usual attire: a gray short-sleeve dress with a flowered apron over it, and her brown speckled-with-gray hair pulled back. The woman had bigger biceps than Hank. But that's about all that was big about her. When she wore heels, she stood taller than Hank, but she wore flats today.

"How'd the first day go at Archangels?"

"All right, I guess." He leaned in to kiss her cheek.

"Any homework?"

"Yes, ma'am."

"Do your chores and homework. Then you can go out and play or read the comics."

"Yes, Ma."

Above his mother on the kitchen wall hung a framed picture of the Holy Family. Hank had always thought it was strange to have a holy picture in the kitchen. After all, the rest of the house had plenty of crucifixes and a few statues of the Blessed Mother. He shrugged.

Hank emptied the ashtrays and took the empty bottles to the basement, passing his mother in the kitchen.

Then he tackled his math homework. He didn't have much because it was the first day of school, but he wanted to get into the good habit of finishing his homework. That way, his parents would be more open to him getting a job after school.

His older sister, Helen, had a job after school, so she wouldn't be home until suppertime. His kid sister, Tessie, was not quite seven and in first grade. His kid brother, Billy, was twelve and in seventh grade, and people outside the family always thought Billy was the oldest because he was taller.

Hank had stopped growing. He was not quite five feet tall, while everyone in his class was at least four inches—or more—taller. It burned him up, having to wear hand-me-downs from his younger brother. Whoever handed out the tall genes must've skipped Hank.

After changing out of his school uniform, Hank sat on the couch and placed the newspaper flat on the coffee table. He carefully turned each page until he got to the comics. His favorites were *Flash Gordon*, *Beetle Bailey,* and *Steve Canyon*. He wished he could draw as well as the men who created these comic strips, but he was lousy at drawing. Writing was a different story. He enjoyed creating tales of faraway lands and even tales of ordinary people. One of his fiction pieces, the story of a boy and his dog, won an honorable mention last year in eighth grade.

He wished Ma would allow them to have a dog, but she complained that animals were too messy. Even after Hank promised to take care of a dog, she remained firm. No pets.

The door opened and shut quietly. Hank lifted his chin and glanced at the door.

Tessie skipped in and giggled at Hank. Hank should've known his baby sister would remember not to slam the door.

Billy was supposed to walk Tessie home, but Hank suspected Tessie sprinted ahead of him.

"Whatcha doin'?"

"Homework."

"Sister Marie Cecilia is nice." As she turned around, her ponytail flopped back and forth.

Hank couldn't resist. He leaned up and pulled her hair.

"Ow! Mommy, Hank pulled my ponytail!" she yelled and strutted off to the kitchen.

"Hank, what'd I tell you about tormenting your sister?"

"Sorry, Tess."

His sister pranced into the living room. "You should be."

"Ah, go on, Tess."

The door opened again and slammed shut. Billy swaggered through the open doorway like he owned the place.

"Billy, is that you?" Ma yelled from the kitchen.

"Um, no. It's the milkman."

His mother's sigh from the kitchen told Hank that Billy was about to get an earful—and maybe a slap—from Ma.

She stomped into the living room. "What'd I tell you about slamming the door, Billy?"

"Sorry, Ma."

"And what'd I tell you about being a wiseacre?"

"I was just—"

He was interrupted by Ma slapping his leg with a kitchen towel.

"Gee whiz, Ma, I was only fooling around."

"Fool around with someone else." Ma scoffed and returned to her duties in the kitchen.

Billy dropped his books on the coffee table and picked up the Wiffle bat and balls. "Come on, let's go to the back alley."

"Do you have any homework?"

"Who are you, my mother? I'm still in grammar school, remember? No homework the first week."

A short time later, Hank yelled to his mother that he and Billy would be playing out in the back alley. Their neighborhood of rowhomes was separated by wide alleyways where most people parked their cars. The Gallagher rowhome had a small back porch, from which his mother could look out and watch the boys. Ma rarely did that now that he was fourteen and Billy was twelve.

The back alleyway smelled of a combination of a warm summer breeze, Italian gravy (what his mother called spaghetti sauce), and a mild hint of garbage.

As Billy hit a pop up, Hank positioned himself under the ball and caught it easily. They played for an hour before he heard a honk from a car horn behind him. He turned and saw his father pulling up in their 1951 Ford Country Squire. Kind eyes peered out from under Pop's hat. Henry Francis Gallagher, Sr. almost always smiled, unlike his mother, who seemed to have a permanent scowl etched on her face.

The older man stopped the car and pulled into their parking spot under the back porch. Hank and Billy met him at the driver's side. He got out, removed his hat, and reached into his pocket. "Just one for each of you to enjoy after your supper." He held out his palm, revealing four Dum Dum root beer lollipops.

"That's swell, Pop," Hank said and swiped one from his palm. "Thanks!"

"Thanks, Pop," said Billy, taking another.

"Oh, and Hank?"

"Yes, Pop?"

His father leaned into the car and picked up a small brown package. "This is for you since today was your first day of high school."

Hank felt a lightness in his chest. "Can I open it?"

"You bet."

Hank tore off the paper, finding inside a small leather book with blank pages.

"I know you like to write stories, but you can also jot down what's going on in school."

"Gee, it's great, Pop. Thanks."

His father ruffled Hank's hair. "I hope you get good use out of it." He glanced at the back door. "Is Tessie-Bess home?"

"Yep, she's inside with Ma," Hank offered.

When their father was out of sight, Hank and his brother tore open the lollipops and started sucking on them. Within moments, the boys crunched and swallowed.

They played more Wiffle ball until Hank heard the door open again and Ma's voice. "Boys, time for supper. Come in and wash up."

Hank and his brother raced toward the back stairs and into the kitchen.

***

At the supper table, Hank's mouth watered at the savory aroma of the pork chops and sauerkraut.

His father made the Sign of the Cross, so the rest of the family did the same. "Bless us, O Lord, and these thy gifts which we are about to receive, from thy bounty through Christ our Lord. Amen."

Hank cut up his pork chop, then stuck his fork into one of the pieces and took healthy scoops of mashed potatoes, sauerkraut, and his Ma's homemade baked beans. *Your mother is the best cook this side of the Mississippi*, his father always said. As he ate, he listened to his sisters, Helen and Tessie, chatter about their first day of school.

"And Sister Marie Cecilia is really nice. I was 'fraid she might be a mean nun. But she's nice. I like her."

Helen scooped food into her mouth, swallowed, then said, "I had her as a teacher in fourth grade, Tess, and she was pretty nice then too." Helen took another bite of food then continued, "Ma, I need new shoes. All the girls at Hallahan have brand new saddle shoes, and I'm still wearing my old ones."

Ma shook her head. "I polished your old ones, and they're fine. No need to get new ones. Besides, you have a job. You can pay for your own shoes if you want them."

His sister was as short as him, but it wasn't so bad to be short if you were a girl. Helen went on about her after-school job at the library. Hank wondered if his parents would let him have an after-school job. He was, after all, fourteen years old, soon-to-be fifteen. Maybe he could deliver newspapers.

After he finished his supper, Hank asked to be excused to go outside. By now, the Italian boys in the neighborhood would be out back. They always ate their dinners early.

Billy said, "Wait, Hank. I want to go outside with you."

Hank watched Billy shovel the rest of his food inside his mouth and also ask to be excused.

He and his brother raced through the small kitchen, out the back door, and down the steep staircase into the alley.

Carlo Carpaccio and Dino Franchetti were playing stickball.

Hank approached them. "Hey Carlo, how'd your first day at South Catholic go?"

Carlo responded, "All right, I guess. What'd you think of Archangels High?"

Hank shrugged.

"You guys wanna play?" Carlo asked.

"Sure," Hank and his brother replied.

"Hank, you're on my team. Billy, you're with Dino."

"All right."

Hank and Carlo lost to Billy and Dino, but then again, Hank and Carlo weren't the best stickball players. Carlo was only a bit taller than Hank, so Carlo never called him Shrimp or Shorty.

It felt good to be with kids who didn't call him names.

They played until Ma called them. "Hank, Billy, it's getting dark. Come inside."

Hank hopped onto his bunk bed. The previous night, he couldn't sleep. Now, he could barely keep his eyes open. He drifted off, thanking God that his first day of school was over.

Chapter 4
Evie
Missing Dad

The Saturday after Dad's funeral, Evie missed her father so much that she went down to the dirty clothes pile in the basement to find one of his post office shirts. Her family would think her insane if they saw her sniffing her dad's shirt because she missed him. It still smelled faintly of him and his Old Spice aftershave. Hugging the shirt to her chest, she sat cross-legged on the basement floor, next to the dirty clothes pile. This was all too much to bear. How could he go from being on the wagon and fine to falling off the wagon and dead?

And the manner of her father's death had been under scrutiny. Initially, the insurance company refused to pay out the money for Dad's death because they said he "committed suicide." Evie knew that had to be wrong. Her dad had issues, yes, but he would *never* have killed himself on purpose, not if he had been thinking rationally. He loved his family too much—and his Catholic faith.

When Mom was on the phone with the insurance people a few days ago, she'd yelled a few swear words, slammed the phone down, and ordered a copy of the autopsy report.

Late that afternoon, Evie sat back against the pillows on her bed. She picked up her diary and wrote another entry.

Dear Diary,
I keep thinking that this is all a bad dream, and I'm going to wake up, and Daddy is going to be fine. But that's not going to happen.

Mom has asked me to sleep with her at night because it's been so long since she's slept alone in a bed. I feel a bit weird about it. Every night before we go to bed, Mom says something about Dad and how much she misses him.

During the day, Mom consoles us, but at night, I console Mom. All I can do is rub her back until she falls asleep.

Almost time to go to Mass.

Evie changed from her jeans to black pants and a light sweater. Downstairs, she opened the door to leave, and her mother stopped her. "I'm going to Mass with you, Eve."

Evie's eyes widened.

"Your father's sudden death made me realize that I've been lazy. I want to go to Confession and Mass with you."

Two weekends in a row, Evie had one of her parents attend Mass with her. She was thankful that Mom decided to return to Mass but disappointed that it had taken Dad's death for her to do so.

When they returned home, Mom asked Evie to help her sort through her father's things. Evie wondered aloud whether it was too soon to do this, but her mother insisted.

Her father's life was a mystery in so many ways. He had rarely spoken about his childhood, except one time when Grandmom was visiting, he said, "Hey, Ma, remember when you tied me to a chair and beat me with the eggbeater because I stole candy from Pearcy's?" Then they'd both laughed.

Evie didn't find that funny at all. She couldn't picture Grandmom doing that to her kids, but she was glad that Dad didn't seem to hold any grudges for the beatings.

Evie opened her father's nightstand to find it empty. "Did you already go through this one, Mom?"

"No, Mitch and Deb took some things from that drawer, a

file containing Dad's stories and a few other items."

"Right."

As she watched her mother reach up into the high closet, Evie wondered how she ended up at four feet, six inches tall, given that Mom was five feet, six inches tall. Deb stood a few inches taller than Evie, but both her brothers were in the five-ten, five-eleven range. The girls had obviously inherited Dad's genes for height, and the boys inherited Mom's.

Evie was not quite sixteen, so maybe she would still grow another inch or two.

Mom pulled down a large box labeled "Hank" from the closet and placed it on the bed. Evie peered inside. There were mementos from his years in the Marines and a bunch of envelopes as well as an old saltwater taffy box.

Evie picked up the box. "I wonder what this is."

"I think it's where Dad kept mementos from his childhood and early adulthood."

"Would it be okay if I keep this, Mom?"

"Sure."

That night, Evie held the box in her hands. She opened it up to discover seashells, baseball cards, and a deck of cards. She also found an old name tag from Eastman Chemical. Her grandfather had been a supervisor there, and her father had worked there too. The name tag said, "Henry Gallagher, Jr. Office."

When the postmortem report arrived the following Monday, Mom read it carefully. "Now I have proof! The coroner indicated your father's death *was* accidental."

Mom dropped the paper on the end table and went right to the kitchen phone to contact the insurance company.

Evie picked up the report and quietly read it aloud. "The body is that of a middle-aged white male measuring five feet, five inches in length. The hair, brown and gray, the eyes,

29

hazel. Rigor mortis and posterior liver mortis are noted."

Evie's eyes filled with tears. This report was cold. Her father was so much more than this indicated. He enjoyed watching television and playing cards. He had an infectious laugh. He loved his wife and children. He loved his Catholic faith.

When Evie heard her mother hanging up the phone in the kitchen, she returned the paper to the end table. Mom probably wouldn't be happy knowing that she'd read it.

"Well, the insurance company relented and, thankfully, will be issuing a check. I still plan on working at the courthouse, but I'll be typing from home for the next few months."

Evie returned to school the next day. In English class, they had just finished reading *On the Beach* by Nevil Shute, one of the most depressing novels she'd ever read. Next, they would be studying *Moby Dick* by Herman Melville, not the kind of book she usually liked to read. Give her a Jane Austen novel or a Mary Higgins Clark mystery, and she could devour those books in a day or so. However, any book had to be less depressing than one about radiation killing the world's population.

Back at home, she sat on the couch and read the next few chapters of *Moby*. Fluffy, their dog, jumped up and snuggled beside her. She recalled the times when her father sat in this same spot, Evie next to him and Fluffy, trying to situate herself between the two of them.

Her eyes clouded over. She placed *Moby Dick* on the side table and turned on the television.

Chapter 5
Hank
A Job Opportunity
1954

Hank and Red met at the door of their homeroom the following day. Red shared with Hank that he had also been on the receiving end of some name-calling. The same crowd that called Hank "Dwarf" had also called Red "Orange Boy." Red's hair *was* bright orange, but Hank was in awe. Orange hair was cool and different.

Brother McCallum arrived on time for the second day of school. Hank studied the youthful almost-priest, wondering if he was old enough to shave.

Brother McCallum said, "I've got a joke for you. Why were Adam and Eve the happiest couple who ever lived?"

The boys exchanged glances with one another. Hank tilted his head, thinking it over. He couldn't think of the answer.

"Because they didn't have in-laws!" Brother McCallum guffawed.

Like yesterday, the boys responded with a few pathetic snickers. Hank didn't quite get the joke, but he liked that Brother McCallum wanted to make the class laugh. Perhaps he needed better jokes, though.

The almost-priest cleared his voice. "All right, class. I need to take attendance." He paused. "Abbott, William?"

"Here."

Once he finished with attendance, Brother McCallum passed out the religion textbooks. The almost-priest reviewed the first chapter and gave the students homework.

The bell rang to signal the end of class. Hank and Red

made their way to Fr. O'Reilly's room. As they climbed the stairs, Hank couldn't keep his eyes off the marble statues above them. They had to be the most enormous statues he had ever seen. And strangely enough, he felt protection from those angels wielding swords whenever he passed under them.

The two boys stood at Fr. O'Reilly's door and waited as other students hurried back and forth. A click alerted them that someone was behind the locked door.

Opening wide the door, Fr. O'Reilly stepped aside. "Just what I like, boys who are punctual." He waved his hand in a sweeping gesture to invite the boys inside the classroom. They sat down at their desks, and other students piled into the room. Hank wondered whether Fr. O'Reilly would do more magic for the class.

Fr. O'Reilly sauntered to the blackboard and picked up a piece of chalk. "The next two weeks, we'll be reviewing some of the basics of English grammar and composition, then later in the semester, we'll be reading *Moby Dick* by Herman Melville." He had such fluidity in his motions that Hank wondered whether the priest had ever been a conductor for an orchestra. On the board, he wrote, *"Write a short theme about an exciting event that happened this past summer."*

Hank straightened. He knew what he would write about in his essay. His family had gone to Willow Grove Park in July. He had anxiously anticipated the visit for months, but when the day finally came, the rain pelted his bedroom window so hard that his heart sank. His father had only one day off, so they decided to go anyway. Disappointed, Hank watched raindrops on the window during the entire ride to the park, and when they arrived, he just about cried. A big "closed" sign hung on the front gate. He was glad that Ma hadn't accompanied them on the trip. They waited in the parking lot for an hour, Tessie whining and Billy punching his arm. But his father remained cool and calm as they waited. "Let's give it an hour and see if it opens." Pop had sounded so sure of himself, as if he *knew* the park would open soon.

Within forty-five minutes, the rain stopped completely. Hank craned his neck to see when they would open the gates, and sure enough, five minutes later, the gates opened.

A day that started off as the worst day of the summer turned out to be the best because the park was like a ghost town for the first hour, and they had been able to get on every ride—even the roller coaster—without waiting.

The priest set the chalk down, clapped his hands of the chalk dust, and turned to face the class. "I'd like you to work on this during class, and tomorrow, each of you will read your theme out loud to the class."

Then the priest looked in Hank's direction.

Hank's heart stopped.

"Mr. Henry Gallagher, what is the definition of a noun?"

His throat closed. He knew the answer, but he hated speaking in front of the class. As he stood, he cleared his voice and willed his heart to stop pounding. "Uh." Hank avoided eye contact.

"Go ahead."

"A noun is a person, place, or thing."

Hank flopped back down and blew a breath out.

"Good, Mr. Gallagher." He turned to write on the board just as the boy behind Hank shoved him in the shoulder and said, "Brown-noser." Then the boy slapped Hank's head with a ruler.

The snap made Father turn around. "Mr. Simmons, please go down to the office and tell the principal that you hit another student with a ruler."

Behind him, the boy grunted and left.

Hank couldn't believe it. First, that a teacher had caught

the boy in the process of hitting Hank, but secondly, that Father had also reprimanded him. Most of the time, the teachers remained oblivious to the shenanigans of the students. Yes, Hank was going to like Fr. O'Reilly.

Father erased the board, wrote four more questions, and then chose Red and a few others to give the answers. Red did a good job, but the other boys responded like they'd never been to school before.

When the priest finished choosing boys to respond to the questions, he erased the board then clapped his hands free of chalk dust. Fr. O'Reilly turned. "Now, you may begin writing your theme."

Hank couldn't believe how easily the words came to the paper. In only ten minutes, he was finished and checking his essay for mistakes.

When the bell rang, Fr. O'Reilly called Hank and Red up to the front.

They quickly made their way to the priest's desk.

"Boys, I'd like to see you after school for about fifteen minutes."

"Certainly, Father," Hank said, and Red nodded.

Before they went to different classes, Red said to Hank, "I wonder why Father wants to see us after school."

"I don't know. We certainly didn't do anything wrong."

"Right. See you."

Hank stood in front of his locker, tossed his English book inside, and retrieved his Math and Religion books. *Maybe Fr. O'Reilly wants to give Red and me a special English assignment.*

The rest of the school day dragged by. After lunch, Hank went to Religion Class with Brother McCallum but found it hard to concentrate. He kept wondering why Fr. O'Reilly wanted to see them.

When the bell signaled the start of class, Brother

34

McCallum asked, "Did you hear the one about the crook who stole a calendar? He got twelve months!" The almost-priest bellowed, while the other boys in the class either groaned or stared at him.

"Very well, students. Today we're going to review the Catechism."

Hank liked the young almost-priest, but his class was about as dull as watching paint dry, and Hank found himself nodding off a few times.

When the bell rang to change classes, he was glad he had only one class left to attend: Social Studies with Fr. Bonneville. Hank liked Social Studies, but Fr. Bonneville spoke so quietly that he had to strain to hear the man speak. Thankfully, the priest wrote everything on the chalkboard, and Hank copied it.

At the bell, Hank jumped up and went to his locker. He took only the books he needed for the weekend then sped up the stairs to Fr. O'Reilly's room. Hank met Red there.

"Come on in, boys," Fr. O'Reilly called to them from his desk at the front of the classroom.

Hank and Red walked in and inched toward him.

"There's nothing wrong, boys. No need to be nervous." He motioned for them to take seats at the two desks closest to him. "I need two reliable young men for an after-school job for the rest of the school year."

Hank and Red exchanged glances.

"Now, I can only pay you boys a buck fifty a week. I know that's not minimum wage, but..."

Red blurted out, "Father, you don't have to pay us at all. We'll help you out for free."

Hank was about to say the same thing.

"Nope. You haven't yet had me as an employer. I can be tough." He paused, folding his arms across his chest. "So, what do you think?"

The two boys nodded. Beaming inside but trying to maintain a serious, responsible expression, Hank said, "You've got yourself two new helpers."

"Marvelous. Most of the work will be organizing and carrying boxes downstairs to the basement of the rectory. I might also send you to the store to buy pens and supplies for the class."

Hank felt like he was on top of the world. "We're happy to be able to help you, sir—uh, I mean, Father."

He handed them each a piece of paper with the typed words, *I, the parent of _____, give permission to my/our son to work for Fr. O'Reilly every day after school, in exchange for 1.50 per week.*

"We'll start next week so you can get permission from your parents. Make sure one of your parents signs this, then return it to me before we start on Monday."

Hank and Red stood. Hank felt like he was standing on air.

"Dismissed, boys. You may want to race downstairs so you don't miss your bus." The priest gestured toward the door.

They both nodded and dashed down the steps and to the area where the busses waited. As Hank climbed onto the bus, he heard, "Dwarf." But he didn't care. Those boys could say anything to him now. It wouldn't spoil his good mood.

He sat down and felt the sting of something hitting his head. Rubbing the back of his head, he turned.

Jack Simmons sat behind him, glaring at him through beady eyes. "You jerk. You made me get detention during lunch."

"*You* were the one hitting me."

"Oh, yeah? Well, *you* were the one brown-nosing the teacher."

Hank sighed. "You hit me again, and I'm going to tell the bus driver."

"Oh, so you're a brown-noser AND a tattletale. You better just kill yourself now."

Hank clenched his jaw and got up and sat down next to another boy.

"He's a sissy too." Simmons and his friend laughed.

Chapter 6
Hank
Permission or No Permission:
That is the Question

Hank clicked open the door, then breezed through the entrance and closed the door quietly. The aroma of roasted chicken greeted him, and his mouth watered. He hadn't realized how hungry he was. He dropped his school bag on the coffee table. Maybe Mom would allow a small snack before dinner.

"Ma?" he called.

"Yeah, Hank, I'm cleaning upstairs."

He wandered into the dining room. A plate of chocolate chip cookies—he hoped they were warm—sat on the table.

"May I please have one of the cookies on the table?"

"Go ahead, but only one. You'll spoil your dinner."

He picked one off the top—finding it blessedly warm—and popped it whole into his mouth. Thirsty now, he stepped into the sun-drenched kitchen and grabbed a bottle of milk from the icebox. He was tempted to just drink from the bottle, but if Ma caught him in the act, there'd be a whipping, for sure. So he grabbed a glass from the cupboard, thankful he could now reach the one with the glasses. Warm chocolate chip cookies and a cold glass of milk—life couldn't be better. Ah, and an after-school job.

Hank couldn't wait to tell his folks, but he planned to wait until Pop came home. Pop would more than likely give his permission. If he asked Ma now, she'd say no. His mother knew that Hank wasn't a straight-A student (like Helen), and he'd have to prove that he'd do better with homework.

Hank sat on the couch and placed his homework on the coffee table. It was only the second day of school, and the teachers were thankfully light on homework. Besides, he wanted to ensure he got it all done, even the assignments that weren't due for another week. That would demonstrate to his parents that his schoolwork wouldn't suffer.

As he finished his Algebra, his mother tromped down the steps, a bucket under her arm. "Can you boys please aim better when you're in the bathroom? I can tell you that Helen and Tess don't leave such a mess around the toilet."

Sure, Hank thought. *They don't leave a mess because girls always sit down.* "Yeah, Ma."

Turning his attention back to his paper, Hank checked it over then shoved it into his schoolbag. He glanced at the wall clock. Four in the evening, Billy would be walking in soon, and perhaps they'd go out back and hit pop balls.

The back door swung open, then closed. His father usually came in from the back. Hank got up and stepped near the kitchen, tilting his head. *Yes, it was Pop!* Pop kissed Ma on the cheek.

"You're home early. What's the occasion?" Ma asked.

"Going to a meeting in Harrisburg early tomorrow. The boss encouraged me to take the evening off."

"Someday, you'll be the boss."

"Maybe."

"Hey, Pop!"

"Hey, son." He came out of the kitchen and approached Hank. "Your brother's not home yet?"

"Nah. Any minute, though."

"Well, no sense in making you wait." He reached into his pocket and pulled out a Tootsie Roll. "Here you go…" Then he whispered, "Don't eat it before supper, or your mother will have me by the ears."

"Yes, sir."

"Now, I best get washed up before supper."

Before Hank could say anything about the permission slip, Pop glided up the stairs, taking two at a time. His agile father was a great dancer; his mother, well, her abilities in the kitchen were more known than her dancing skills. Of course, Pop tried to teach her from time to time, but she still kept stepping on his feet, so the only time he danced was at weddings and other receptions.

Hank continued watching his father climb the stairs when the front door opened then slammed shut. *A missed opportunity to ask him to sign the permission slip.*

"Whatcha gawking at, Hank?"

He turned to find Billy smirking at him. "Wanna go pop some balls, Billy?"

"Nah, cranky old Sister Rose Bernadine gave us homework. Gee whiz. It's only the second day of school, and she's giving us homework."

Hank inwardly smiled. He was hoping that Billy would get Sister Rose Bernadine. It wouldn't be fair if only Helen and Hank had had to contend with the crotchety sister. She was so old that she needed bottle glasses and a magnifying glass to read. Every day after lunch, she'd have the class fill in workbooks while she nodded off for five or six minutes.

Hank picked up his schoolbag and hung it on the hook near the railing. He ascended the staircase two steps at a time, just as Pop had done. At the top, Hank nearly tripped, and Billy's laughter floated up. "What a klutz," he said.

The boys' bedroom was situated at the top of the steps, the girls' bedroom beside it. The bathroom was further down the hall, the only room on the second floor with no windows except for a small glass opening with a screen in the ceiling to let out steam. Pop and Ma's sizeable bedroom was at the front of the house.

Inside his room, Hank climbed to the top bunk of their

bunk beds. Uncle Edwin, Pop's younger brother, built it for the boys when they were about seven and nine. Billy's feet always stuck out beyond the mattress and wooden slat, but Hank still had lots of room before he'd grow too big for his bunk. He sighed and picked up the comic book beside his pillow. His eyes caught sight of the journal Pop had bought for him. He hadn't written much in it, but he promised himself he would soon.

He opened up his box of treasures. In the box, an old James Salt Water Taffy container, he kept comic books, seashells, a few of his prize baseball cards—Willie Mays and Ted Williams—and a deck of cards.

Hank took out a Batman and Robin comic book and shut the box. Last he left it, Batman and Robin were battling the Riddler. Hank enjoyed escaping into Gotham City for a while.

"Hank, it's time for supper."

He blinked and sat up on the bed. He must've dozed off.

Tessie was talking up a storm at the table, so Hank had little opportunity to get a word in. When she paused, Billy jumped into the conversation, and then Helen picked up from there. Hank pushed his food around his dish. Tomato-based beef stew with dumplings was not his favorite meal, but he ate it because there were starving kids in China, or so his mother said.

The phone by the banister rang, and Helen got up to answer it. "Yes, he's here, Father. Pop, it's for you." She handed him the phone.

Did Helen say, *"Father?"* Was his dad speaking to a priest? He listened. "No, no problem, Father. Yes, I understand. You want him to start on Monday? Sure, that sounds fine."

Starting on Monday? Him? No, it couldn't be.

Pop hung up the phone and returned to the table. "Hank, do you have a permission slip from Fr. O'Reilly?"

Hank's heart nearly stopped. "Uh, yes, sir, I do. I was going to tell you about it. I have the paper in my bookbag."

"What's this all about, Henry?" asked Mom.

"That was his English teacher. He asked if Hank could work after school with him every day, and he's going to pay him a buck and a half."

"What? No, I don't think so. You're too young to work after school."

"Look, hon, Fr. O'Reilly is a priest, and he wants Hank to work for him after school every day. What harm could there be in that?"

"He won't have time for his schoolwork."

Helen reached across the table for another dinner roll. "Mom, I'm older than Hank and have more homework than he does, and *I* can get my work done. Certainly, Hank can do it."

Hank wanted to kiss his sister. *Thanks, sis.*

"I don't know. Hank's still so young."

"Come on, Ma, I'm fourteen, turning fifteen this year. Helen was fifteen when she started working."

His mother's shoulders relaxed. "Right, I keep forgetting you're older than Billy."

Billy snickered, so Hank shoved him in the side with his elbow.

"Mom, please. I *really* want this job, and Fr. O'Reilly is nice. And I want to help him. He's a priest, after all, right?"

"I suppose it's all right, then. But if your homework suffers…"

"It won't!" Hank jumped up, reached into his school bag for the permission slip, and handed it to his father, who signed it. He took it from his father and dropped it back into his bag. This would be his first real job with one of his favorite teachers. Best start to the weekend, ever.

Chapter 7
Hank
First Day on the Job

That Monday morning, Hank woke before his alarm clock went off. He lay on the top bunk bed, listening to the birds outside. They sounded happy about something. Then he heard an early plane taking off from the Philly airport. Hank enjoyed modern technology. Maybe he would be a pilot someday.

Hank rolled onto one side and took a deep breath. The sun shone through the opening in the curtains as a cool breeze blew them in and out. The breeze also carried the smell of bacon and fresh-baked bread. Ma would have breakfast ready soon. Yes, this was going to be a good day.

Later, when he hopped off the bus in front of the school, two upperclassmen knocked into him. He ignored it.

In English class, Fr. O'Reilly winked at him as he entered the classroom. *He's so kind.*

When he read his essay in class, the priest patted him on the back and said, "Well done, Mr. Gallagher, well done indeed."

Hank approached the gym. On the wall hung massive posters that said, "Go, Angels Football Team!"

Someone smacked him on the side of the head. Hank turned to find a group of senior jocks laughing. They wore "Angels" athletic jackets.

"Don't you belong in grade school?" one of them said in a high-pitched voice as if trying to sound like a girl.

"Do your parents work in the carnival?" another one teased.

"Leave me alone." Hank clenched his fists and

43

straightened. "Leave...me...a...."

"Is everything all right, Mr. Gallagher?"

Hank looked up to see Fr. O'Reilly frowning at Hank's tormentors. "You know, fellows, when you wear jackets bearing the name of our school's team, you represent our school. And every boy who attends Holy Archangels is an 'Angel' whether they're on a sports team or in a club or merely a student."

The bullies said nothing.

"I expect you to treat this young man as an equal. Do I make myself clear?"

Hank now stared at the older boys, who were exchanging looks with one another but said nothing.

Fr. O'Reilly cleared his throat. "Did one of you boys lose your wallet?"

A tall, broad-shouldered senior checked his front and back pockets. "Hey, where's my wallet?"

"Leave Mr. Gallagher alone." Fr. O'Reilly circled the group. "If I hear of you boys teasing Mr. Gallagher or any other students, I'll report you to the principal."

"But where's my wallet?" the big guy asked.

"Check your pocket again."

The guy shoved his hands into his pockets and, this time, he pulled out his wallet. *How did Fr. O'Reilly do that?*

The boys finally shuffled away. On the one hand, he was thankful that Fr. O'Reilly showed up, and he liked that he performed magic on them. On the other hand, he wondered if it would make the bullying worse. He glanced up at the priest and mouthed, "Thank you."

Fr. O'Reilly patted his shoulder and nodded.

In his next class, Hank kept glancing at his wristwatch, anxiously anticipating the end of the school day and his first day of work. Finally, his last class ended, and he met Red outside Fr. O'Reilly's classroom.

The door swung open, and Fr. O'Reilly's smiling face appeared. "Come in, boys. Ready to get started on your first day?"

They both nodded.

Fr. O'Reilly said, "First, Mr. Farrell, I'd like you to alphabetize these files." He pointed to a stack of file folders on a desk in the first row. Fr. O'Reilly put his hand on Red's back and gently nudged him forward, keeping his hand on his back until the boy was seated. Hank admired the priest. He never lost his temper and always seemed to be in a good mood.

Turning to Hank, Fr. O'Reilly said, "Mr. Gallagher, since you have such excellent penmanship, I'd like you to copy these notes for me." He then placed a hand on Hank's back, pointing with his other hand, until Hank sat at the desk closest to Father's desk. "If you don't understand my scribbling, just let me know."

Hank nodded, picked up a pencil, and began to write. The penmanship on the notes was excellent, so Hank wondered why Fr. O'Reilly would want him to copy them. He shrugged and kept writing.

Within what seemed like minutes, Fr. O'Reilly said, "Okay, boys. All done for the afternoon. Good work. See you tomorrow at class and after school."

Hank stopped writing and placed the pencil in the holder. For the past few days, he couldn't stop thinking of the incredible magic tricks the priest had performed. Hank had to ask. "Father?"

"Yes, Mr. Gallagher?"

"How did you do that magic the other day and today, where you make the coin and wallet disappear?"

"Now, now, Mr. Gallagher. A magician never reveals his secrets."

Although Hank was disappointed, he nodded.

45

"By the way, I won't need you boys on Wednesday because that's when the newspaper staff works on the school newspaper."

The school newspaper? Since Hank liked writing, maybe he should volunteer for the newspaper. "Um, sir, could I help out with the newspaper too?"

Fr. O'Reilly's grin slowly stretched across his face. "Of course, Mr. Gallagher. We're always in need of eagle-eye proofreaders."

When the boys stood up, the priest placed a hand on each of their backs and accompanied them to the door. Fr. O'Reilly cleared his throat. "Since we'll be working so closely together, I think we can be on a first-name basis after school. How does that sound to you both?"

"Um," Hank stuttered, "so you want to call us by our first names?"

"Yes, and you can call me Father Tim."

Red shrugged. "Sure, but don't call me Colin. Everybody calls me—"

"Red, I know," said Father.

"And you're called Hank, correct?"

"Yes, Father."

Hank liked that Fr. O'Reilly felt comfortable enough to be so familiar with them. Yes, he was going to enjoy this after-school job.

Chapter 8
Evie
Finding Ways to Keep Connected
June 1982

Summer vacation brought more time to relax, but Evie could only dwell on her father's passing. The shock had eased, but the grief still weighed heavy on her heart. Her father was now at peace in eternity, and Evie would have to find a way to adjust to life without him.

Evie slept for the first time in her own bed since Dad's death. For two months, Mom had asked Evie to sleep with her. Some nights, she'd hear her mother quietly cry herself to sleep. Evie would rub Mom's back until she heard her snoring, then Evie would allow herself to fall asleep.

It was only the third day of summer vacation, so Evie spent her time either reading romance novels or watching old reruns on television or walking up to the corner store to buy flying saucer candy. Her favorite treat had a hollow wafer on the outside and multicolored jimmies on the inside. The wafer tasted like the wafers used for Holy Communion.

Back in the living room, she turned on the TV. Just about everything reminded her of Dad. Above the TV hung two wall pieces that resembled a king and queen. Dad had purchased them with his Raleigh cigarettes saving stamps, just as he purchased the coasters on one end table and a frame on the other.

Evie spied the Parcheesi game on the floor beside the couch and the deck of cards on the end table. Dad liked playing Rummy, and Evie had become proficient enough to win a few times.

She turned off the television and made her way down to

47

the unfinished basement. If she couldn't stop thinking about her father, then she might as well explore the cellar. Mom had stored several boxes of Dad's things down there.

Fluffy followed her down the stairs and wandered to the left, toward the heater. To sniff out interesting scents, Evie supposed.

The washer and dryer were also to the left, and a large upright freezer stood against the far wall, a set of folding chairs beside that. To the right was a ten-by-ten area where she and her siblings often played marbles or board games. Of course, that was years ago. No one had played games with her during the past year except for her father, as her siblings had lost interest in card and board games.

A metal shelving unit that held marked and unmarked cardboard boxes lined the right wall of the ten-by-ten area. She took a folding metal chair and brought it to the shelving unit. Even with the chair opened, she had to stand on tiptoes to reach any of the boxes, the chair creaking beneath her, but she finally pulled an unmarked one down.

Evie sat on the folding chair, opened the box, and pulled items out. This box appeared to hold a bunch of income tax returns and invoices for her mom's transcription work—nothing too interesting there.

She stepped up onto the folding chair again and returned that box to the shelf. The few containers near that one were marked "Christmas," so she left those alone. Evie dragged the chair to another group of unmarked boxes. As she reached up to the shelf, the chair wobbled, and she nearly toppled over. That wouldn't have been a good way to start summer vacation.

Evie folded the chair and returned it. Then she searched for something sturdier to stand on. Fluffy came by and sniffed around where Evie stood, and then she trotted back up the stairs.

Evie strolled around the cellar. She spied a metal stool near the oil tank. She picked it up, and it seemed sturdy. Good sign, although the rust covering it said it had seen better days.

She placed it on the floor near the shelving unit and carefully stood on it. It wobbled but not nearly as much as the folding chair.

Standing on tiptoes and reaching as high as she could, Evie grabbed a box. As she pulled it from the shelf, it slipped out of her hands and fell onto the floor. *I hope there's nothing breakable inside.*

Thankfully, from the sound it made hitting the floor, it was light. The top had opened, and an off-white fabric became visible. Evie jumped off the stool and peered inside. Mom's wedding gown! While the dress was slightly yellowed with age, she recognized it from her parents' wedding album.

Holding the dress in her hands, Evie marveled at the detail. It had a scoop neck with a wide collar that went right around to the back, a lace bodice, and a wide satin skirt. The forty silk-covered buttons on the back must've taken forever to fasten when her mother had put this gown on.

Evie pictured her parents nearly twenty years ago on their wedding day. In their photo album, which Evie had recently perused, their smiles radiated an inner joy and an unawareness of the troubled life they would have together.

She packed up the dress and returned the box to the shelf.

The next box she chose was much heavier. She opened it to find a bunch of different magazines: *National Geographic, Life* and *Time*. Some of the magazines dated to the early '60s. At the bottom of the box lay an old, leathery book.

Evie took it out and opened it, her fingers tingling. She'd had a feeling the book was special even before she saw her father's name scrawled on the inside cover and the date: 1954-55. After putting the box of magazines back on the shelf, she raced up to the den, where her mother was typing. When not working at the courthouse, Mom took freelance transcription jobs she could do at home. Mom had earphones in her ears and didn't seem to notice Evie come into the room.

As Evie approached, she heard the muffled voice of the court reporter reading his notes. "Question, where was the package when you arrived interrog, answer, it was on the desk, period." Evie found it strange that the court reporters said the punctuation aloud, but she guessed that's the way they did it.

Her mother stopped typing and glanced up, noticing Evie standing there. She removed her earphones. "What have you got there, Eve?"

"I think it's Dad's journal from his high school years."

Her mother took it from her and paged through it. "Wow, this *is* old. Your father was always doodling and writing on papers. It's odd that there isn't much in this journal."

Evie leaned towards her as she perused the book with her. "I wonder why Dad didn't write more."

"I don't know."

"May I have this, please?"

Mom handed the book back. "Sure." Then she put her earphones back on.

Evie took Dad's journal to her bedroom and read through it. His handwriting was a bit more polished compared to when he was an adult. He'd written a short entry from Christmas of 1954. He was so excited that he received a transistor radio. After that, he'd written only one short story. He enjoyed writing, so why hadn't he written more in this journal? She read the tale, *The Apprentice and the Magician,* aloud, but in the end, the apprentice wound up in a dungeon. *Depressing.* Even so, she treasured this book.

She wished that her father had saved more items from his childhood. Evie had his treasure box of seashells and baseball cards, but their family only had one or two photos of Dad from when he was little. She had asked her mom why they didn't have more. Mom said it was because Uncle Edwin and Aunt Miriam had most of those photos since Grandmom and Grandpop didn't own a camera when the kids were growing up.

Almost in answer to her wish, later that afternoon, Uncle Edwin dropped off a box of photos and albums. Evie surmised that Mom had called Uncle Edwin to bring them over, and she was thrilled. Evie loved history, but she became obsessed with finding photos of her father. Evie and her mother sat side by side in the living room, studying one picture after another. She had never seen any of these pictures before. A few were from his graduation from high school, some from when he and his siblings were younger, and more from the shore near Atlantic City.

One photo was of her grandfather, her father, Uncle Edwin, and Uncle Billy at a baseball stadium. She turned it over to find the words, "Last home game, Edwin, Hank, Hank Jr., and Billy, September 1954."

Chapter 9
Hank
First Crush and Confession
September 1954

A home game between the Phillies and the Giants was the highlight of the last Sunday in September. Pop and Uncle Edwin brought Hank and Billy to the afternoon game. It had become one of Pop's annual traditions to attend the final game of the year.

Unfortunately, the Phillies lost. But Hank was always in awe at Connie Mack Stadium. That place could fit tens of thousands of spectators. And his father always treated them to a hot dog, soda, and a soft pretzel.

The following Monday after dinner, Carlo came to the door and asked if Hank and Billy could come out and play tag with the neighborhood kids. Hank yelled for Billy, and they joined the other kids on the street in front of their house.

Hank recognized most of the other kids, like his neighbor Chet, but he'd never seen the girl among them, a girl with dark, curly hair. She was short, so she was probably younger than Hank. When the girl turned around, Hank's eyes just about popped out of his head. Despite her stature, she had an hourglass figure, dark eyes, a flawless complexion, and a beautiful smile.

Carlo stepped forward. "Hank, this is my cousin, Linda."

Hank couldn't speak.

"Nice to meet you, Hank," Linda said.

Hank nodded.

Carlo patted his cousin on the back. "She attends Hallahan High School." Turning to Linda, Carlo asked, "You know Helen Gallagher, don't you?"

"Yes, I do. She's a sophomore. I'm only a freshman." Her voice could melt butter.

Throughout the tag game, while kids raced through the streets, Hank kept stealing glances at Linda. She had to be the most beautiful girl he'd ever met.

That night, Hank sank into his pillow, and his mind turned to Linda. What would it be like to kiss her?

Hank lay next to Linda. Oh wait—she wasn't wearing a shirt! Hank trembled. They lay so close together, side by side. Oh no—what happened to his pants? Linda was touching him, the feeling so intense that he thought he might die.

He woke up, his heart pounding, and he couldn't resist. A moment later, as he cleaned himself, he wondered if this was what the priests meant by "impure thoughts."

As he tried to fall back to sleep, feelings of guilt weighed him down. He was pretty sure what he'd done was wrong.

The following week, on Thursday, the school children prepared for noon Mass for the Feast of the Most Holy Rosary. Before Mass, priests filled the confessionals on either side of the church, so Hank went into one. "Bless me, Father, for I have sinned. It has been three weeks since my last confession. These are my sins: I said two swear words, and—" Hank cringed. He didn't want to say it, but he had to. "I had a dream where I was naked and woke up and touched myself to finish. I think it might be wrong."

"Is that you, Hank?" Fr. Tim said.

Hank stuttered. "Y-yes, Father O'Reilly," his face burned as he realized he knew the priest.

"Well, my boy, you know there's nothing wrong with having dreams, and whatever you do in the dreams is not morally wrong."

"I guess so, Father."

"Keep in mind, Hank, that you're discovering all these new feelings, and it's perfectly natural to finish once you've started. So I would say at most, it was a venial sin."

Hank's shoulders relaxed. *It's only a venial sin. Good.*

"But try to avoid masturbating in the future."

That was a strange word for it. Masturbate?

"For your penance, since this is the Feast of the Most Holy Rosary, pray a decade of the Rosary."

"Thank you, Father."

"Now go ahead and say your Act of Contrition."

He whispered the Act of Contrition and shot out of the confessional, feeling so much lighter than he did before.

At home, Hank opened then quietly closed the screen door. Ma sat on the sofa—something he rarely saw her do—and Uncle Edwin sat upright in the armchair next to the staircase. His hat was in his hands.

"Hey, buddy," said Uncle Edwin, giving him a quick wave.

"Hi, Uncle Edwin."

Uncle Edwin had never married. Hank wondered why. Uncle Edwin worked hard, cared about everyone, and loved spending time with the family.

Ma spoke up. "Hank, Uncle Edwin would like to take you and Billy fishing down the shore this weekend. Would you like to go?"

"Would I? Sure!"

"You'll have to get up really early, Hank," Uncle Edwin warned.

"Aww, that doesn't bother me. It might bother Billy, though. He's not very nice in the mornings."

"Well, you leave that to me," Ma said. "I have ways of getting boys up in the morning."

His mother told the truth. One morning last year, Hank slept through his too-quiet alarm clock, and Ma woke him by putting two pot lids together and clanging. Even minimal sounds woke him now.

The following morning, Hank roused before his alarm and

finished packing his bag. He wanted to be ready when Uncle Edwin picked them up tomorrow morning. He tried to wake Billy, but Billy slept through Hank's attempts to get up for school.

Hank went downstairs. His mother stood over the stove, making bacon and eggs. Tessie sat at the table, her legs swinging. She scooped scrambled eggs into her mouth. Helen stepped into the small kitchen, took a plate from the counter, and held it out so Ma could put bacon and eggs onto it.

"Your brother up yet?" Ma asked Hank.

"No, ma'am."

Ma turned the element off, wiped her hands on her apron, and reached into the cupboard to retrieve two pot lids.

Hank couldn't help but crack a smile. Billy was in for a bad start to the school day.

Pop came into the kitchen just as the lids clanged together. Gee whiz, it sounded loud even to Hank one floor below. Hank heard Billy start to cry.

Tessie said, "I'd cry too if Mommy did that to me."

Hank shrugged.

Pop chuckled. "Your mother has an interesting way of waking you fellows. I'm just glad she never did that to me."

"You bet." Hank paused, an idea coming to him. "Hey, Pop, why don't you come with us to the shore tomorrow with Uncle Edwin?" Hank loved when Pop came along, but he rarely joined them.

Tessie interrupted. "Can I go to the shore with Uncle Edwin?"

Hank responded, "No, Tess, you're too little. And we're going fishing. You don't even like fishing."

Pop chimed in, "Hank's correct, Tessie-Bess. I'll take you somewhere special on my next day off. All right?"

Tess pouted. "I guess so." She finished the last bit of her eggs.

55

"So, can you come, Pop?" Hank sat up straight, hoping.

Pop cleared his throat. "I can't, Hank. Sorry. I've got to work tomorrow."

"But it's a Saturday," Hank whined, knowing he sounded like a baby, but he didn't care. It wasn't fair.

"I know, but I have to work because I'm a supervisor."

"Darn it."

"Darn it indeed." Pop smiled sadly. "I'd much rather go fishing down the shore with you boys and Edwin than go to work on a weekend."

Chapter 10
Hank
Pep Talk

Only one more day till the weekend and the shore. It hadn't been a bad week, but today the bullies came out of the woodwork to taunt Hank. Didn't they have anything better to do with their time?

Just before he entered English class, someone shoved him and said, "Midget." Not bothering to look behind him and identify the culprit, Hank stepped inside the classroom and sat down at his desk. From the corner of his eye, he saw Fr. Tim coming forward.

"Mr. Gallagher?"

"Yes, Father?"

"Sticks and stones can break my bones, but words will never hurt me," the priest sang.

Hank couldn't help but smile. Fr. Tim was a nice man but couldn't sing in tune. Of course, neither could Hank. "Yeah, I've heard that before. But words *do* hurt."

"Well, you need to let them drip off you like water. Boys who call other boys names are often being mistreated either at home or at their job, so they feel like they need to mistreat someone else."

"I suppose."

"You are a marvelous young man, Hank," he whispered. "Don't you forget that."

"Thank you, Father."

One of the things he liked best about Fr. Tim was how he made it seem like you were the only one in the room when he spoke to you. He cared *that* much.

The bell rang, and students stampeded into the room and

dropped their books on their desks.

"All right, Angels, quiet down. Today we're going to take a well-deserved break from schoolwork."

All the boys yelled, "Yeah!"

This was another reason Hank liked Fr. Tim so much. At least once a week, he didn't teach English, and instead, they all participated in fun activities. What sort of activity would they do this time?

Fr. Tim reached under his desk and pulled out three Scrabble game sets.

I love this game!

"We're going to split up into three groups. Each group will split in half, and no, you don't get to choose which team you're on. That's for me to decide."

The priest walked up and down the aisles between the desks and counted off. Once each student had their number, he said, "All right. Numbers 1, 7, 13, 19, 25, and 31 are in Group 1." Hank was number 7, so he was in this group.

They spent the entire forty-five-minute period playing Scrabble. As much as Hank enjoyed the game, the boys Fr. Tim put him with were not proficient players. But at least Hank had gotten a triple word score with a "Z" to bump their number up to 124. Still, the winning team had 250 points.

He'd had fun, though, and playing Scrabble made this one of the fastest classes ever.

In gym class, they ran laps outside.

After lunch, during Religion, Brother McCallum started the class with another corny joke. Hank liked this teacher, but he wished he'd stop with the jokes.

They were still in the middle of reviewing the Catechism. Brother McCallum went over the first sentence of the Apostles' Creed.

"So we're talking about our belief in God and His omniscience. What does it mean that 'God is omniscient?'

Hank, do you want to read what that means?"

He didn't like reading aloud, but he cleared his throat and managed to say, "God is omniscient means that He knows all things perfectly and from all eternity; He knows all things past, present, and to come, even our most secret thoughts."

"Excellent, Hank."

Hank wasn't sure that he liked the idea of God knowing our most secret thoughts. But, then again, He created us, so maybe that was His right.

After school, he and Red made their way to Fr. Tim's classroom. They clapped the erasers outside and then organized the books on the priest's shelf. Fr. Tim gave Hank and Red their money in an envelope and told them to have a good weekend.

Hank was happy that his week finished on a high note, and the weekend would begin with an even higher one when Hank, Uncle Edwin, and Billy went fishing.

Chapter 11
Evie
First Thanksgiving
November 1982

Thanksgiving Day would arrive tomorrow, and her family would be celebrating with a turkey dinner, even though her father had only died six months previously.

Evie stayed up late, helping her mother cut up celery, onion, and fresh parsley for what Mom called the filling, but what other people called stuffing. *Quincy, M.E.* with Jack Klugman blared on the TV in the kitchen. Quincy was trying to figure out how a young, healthy football player had died of a heart attack.

The best thing about TV was that it allowed Evie to forget her sadness.

When Evie woke up the following day, she couldn't find her mother anywhere. She searched the basement, the kitchen, and the bedrooms. The car was parked in front of the house. The turkey was in the oven. The Gimbels Thanksgiving Day Parade was booming on the TV. But no Mom. *Where could she be?*

Just as Evie started to worry, Mom came through the front door.

"Where were *you*?" Evie asked, trying to push down her anxiety.

"Taking a bike ride." Mom, dressed in a blue sweatsuit and a white jacket, kicked off her sneakers by the front door.

"A what?" Evie's hands went to her hips.

"A bike ride." Mom turned up the volume on the television and stood in front of it.

"You haven't ridden a bike in years. You could've hurt

yourself. You've got to let someone know where you are."

"Honey, I only went up the street and back."

"But you're older now. It's too dangerous to ride a bike." Her voice came out high, her throat tight.

Mom stopped watching the TV and turned toward her. "Evie, I'm only forty-four. And once you learn to ride a bike, you never forget. I was fine."

"But what if you weren't?" Evie kept trying to push the anxiety down, but it pushed back even harder. She couldn't bear to think about losing her mother.

"Don't worry, honey. I'm not going to take unnecessary risks." Mom patted her shoulder, a twinkle in her eyes. "If I tell you I'm going to ride a motorcycle, then you can worry."

The anxiety Evie felt inside must've shown on her face because Mom said, sounding more serious now, "I'm not going anywhere." Then she took off her jacket and lit a cigarette on her way to the couch.

A cigarette? Eve stared for a moment before blurting, "Can't you quit smoking? Smoking causes all kinds of diseases, doesn't it?"

"I'm still young." Mom patted the couch, inviting Evie to sit next to her. "I'll be fine."

Evie and Mom watched the parade on television. Just before noon, the parade ended with Santa on his sleigh—or at least a guy dressed up as Santa.

Her youngest brother, Hank, walked into the living room, hair messed up and still in his pajamas. "Hey, Mom, I need to talk to you about something."

"Oh? Sure."

Hank glanced at Evie then back at Mom. "Maybe we can talk in the den."

"All right," Mom said.

Her brother and Mom left the living room.

Evie thought it funny how most people outside the family

thought Evie was the youngest since she was the shortest. Young Hank was only fourteen but had reached five feet ten inches to Evie's four feet, seven inches.

Suddenly, she heard Mom shout, "What? You're kidding! That son of a—"

Now, Evie sat straight up, her ears perking. What was going on with her brother?

Then her mother's voice again. "That's the last time I'm ever going to allow you to attend that youth group."

She didn't hear her brother's response.

But her mother said a few curse words, then, "I'm glad Walt punched him in the face."

Walt punched someone in the face? Why would Mom be happy about that?

Finally, it was quiet. Her brother returned to the living room.

"What happened, Hank?"

Hank hesitated and glanced away. When he turned back toward her, he said, "Fr. McGinley tried to touch Walt in the bathroom, and Walt punched him in the face."

Evie blinked, not sure she'd heard him right. "Wait a minute. Fr. McGinley tried to touch Walt?"

"Yeah. Walt went to the bathroom, and Fr. McGinley was in there, and he tried to touch Walt." Hank's grimace turned into a grin. "Then Walt socked him in the face." He made a fist and demonstrated. "Chuck and I heard him yelling, so we ran in there and found Fr. McGinley on the floor, holding his eye. Walt was shouting, 'Try that again, and you'll get more than a black eye.'"

Evie's mouth hung open. She couldn't believe it. Priests were holy men of God, not predators. Could Walt have been mistaken about the priest's intent?

Mom came into the living room. "I hope his mother reports that priest to the diocese."

Hank said, "I hope so too. Fr. McGinley will have a real

shiner. It'll be interesting to hear how Fr. McGinley explains his black eye to the other kids in the youth group."

Evie remembered going to Confession a few times with that priest. He seemed nice enough. She couldn't fathom how something like this could've happened. It must've been a misunderstanding.

***

Earlier that week, Evie's mother told her and her brothers and sister that Thanksgiving would be a small affair with no company. On the one hand, Evie was glad she'd spend the day with only the immediate family. On the other, she missed her cousins, aunts, and uncles.

At supper, Evie, her mom, and siblings sat down to a plentiful Thanksgiving dinner with all their favorites. Dad always said the grace each Thanksgiving. This year, Mom asked Evie to say the prayer.

Evie felt honored, although she was sad too. After making the Sign of the Cross, Evie said, "Bless us, O Lord, and these thy gifts, which we are about to receive from thy bounty, through Christ, our Lord. Amen."

"So, Evie, do you want to go Christmas shopping with me tomorrow on Black Friday?" Mom grabbed the carving knife and studied the golden turkey. Dad always did the carving too.

"I'd love to."

"Let's go into Center City and watch the light show at Wanamaker's."

"That'd be great, Mom." Her siblings disliked shopping with Mom, but Evie loved spending time with her. And she hadn't seen the light show at Wanamaker's since her father took her there when she was about nine years old. She stared at his empty place at the head of the table and said a prayer for his soul.

Chapter 12
Hank
Christmas is Coming
1954

Just before Christmas, Hank slept in on a frosty Saturday morning.

He was doing well in his classes, but the highlight of each school day was that time after school, working for Fr. Tim. On a few days during the past week, Hank had helped Fr. Tim bring boxes down to the high school's cellar storeroom. It had a dirt floor and stunk like mold and old shoes. It was cool, though, because it had beams made of tree logs and walls made of large stones. The small windows, which had dulled with age, were probably the original windows. Hank's job was to stack the boxes onto the long metal shelf lining a stone wall underneath one window. Hank could see his breath in the cold air as he worked. He was thankful that Fr. Tim had thought to get his coat and help him on with it before they went to the cellar.

Hank may not have gotten Billy's tall stature, and he wasn't as bright as Helen, but he had something better: an after-school job with the best teacher in the world.

He leaned against the pole at the bus stop. Now that he was in high school, his mother allowed him to take the city bus to Center City. Even though Hank had his own job, Pop gave him five dollars for helping him collate business papers for the past two weekends. He'd use that money to buy presents for his family.

Hank spent the day Christmas shopping and enjoying the decorations at Wanamaker's. With a huge, decorated tree, red ribbons, and twinkling lights everywhere, no store did

Christmas decorations better than Wanamaker's.

He returned home late that afternoon by bus. When he walked through the doorway, he was surprised to find Fr. Tim in their living room, speaking with Ma and Pop.

"Father Ti-O'Reilly! Is, uh, everything all right?"

"Hello, Hank. Sure, everything's fine. I was in the neighborhood and decided to drop by and visit your parents."

Ma and Pop sat next to each other on the couch, grinning from ear to ear. Ma was so pretty when she smiled. Hank wished she'd smile more, but Pop said her disposition had something to do with Ma's mother dying when she and her twin sister were babies. And Ma's father wasn't the nurturing type.

"If you don't have other plans, Father, why don't you stay and have supper with us?" his mother asked.

Hank's eyes widened. She'd never invited anyone to dinner except family. Hank was pleased. Now his parents could get to know Fr. Tim the way Hank knew him.

Fr. Tim monopolized the conversation at supper, asking Helen, Billy, and Tessie questions but mostly speaking with Ma and Pop. The priest couldn't seem to say enough nice things about Hank, and, for that, he was grateful. Fr. Tim performed a few magic tricks, which Billy and Tessie watched with wide eyes. He also complimented his mother more times than Hank could count. While Pop often told her she looked nice, having a priest say it probably made his mother's day. When Fr. Tim finally left, it was evident that everyone finally understood why Hank enjoyed working for the priest.

As he lay awake in bed later that night, he overheard his parents in the hallway speaking about Fr. Tim.

"That Father O'Reilly sure is a wonderful priest," said Ma.

"Yeah, he seems to be. There's something about him I can't quite put my finger on, though."

"What do you mean?"

"I don't know. It's like he's playing a role. I mean, no one can be that affable one hundred percent of the time."

His mom replied, "Says someone who's friendly all the time."

"Well, you know what I mean."

"Hank says he's never seen the priest lose his temper, and he constantly has a smile on his face. I don't think I've ever met a kinder priest."

Hank couldn't hear his father's response. What did Pop mean when he'd said there was something about Fr. Tim? Pop wasn't usually suspicious, especially of priests. After all, priests were the closest thing to God, weren't they? And Fr. Tim was certainly the holiest priest he knew. Maybe Pop was tired from work. That's the only reasonable explanation.

As he drifted off to sleep, Hank said a prayer of thanksgiving for Fr. Tim. After all, the priest was making it possible for Hank to buy a new transistor radio. Every week, he'd go to the local radio store and give them another dollar towards the radio. So far, he had paid almost half. It was expensive at $49.95, but he figured he'd have enough by March so he could listen to ball games and music at night with the headphones.

Chapter 13
Hank
A Peculiar Touch
January 1955

The thermometer on the outside of the kitchen window showed that it was seven degrees Fahrenheit. *Did it have to be so darned cold on the first day back to school after Christmas holidays?*

He picked up his journal. He hadn't written anything in it since the beginning of the school year. However, he *had* to write about his favorite Christmas.

This is the journal of Hank Gallagher, December 1954.
My Favorite Christmas
This has been the best Christmas I've ever had! Pop and Ma got me the transistor radio I've been saving for! It's like a dream come true to be able to listen to sports and music in my own little world.

Hank still couldn't believe they had gone to the radio store and paid the rest of the money to purchase his transistor radio. Hank was pretty sure that had been his father's idea because Ma never would've thought of it herself. And they rarely spent that much on Christmas gifts.

Either way, it was like a dream come true. For the past week or so, he'd been listening to Christmas songs by Ella Fitzgerald, Rosemary Clooney, and Bing Crosby. He fell asleep most nights with the headphones in his ears and music softly playing. It had been his best Christmas *ever*.

Hank stuffed his hands into gloves. Despite the cold weather, he was ready to return to school. He loved being with Fr. Tim and couldn't wait to see him again.

After school, he and Red met at Hank's locker and proceeded up the stairs under the Archangel statues. Even after seeing the statues every day for the past four months, he never ceased to be in awe of these massive representations of the Holy Archangels.

Strolling down the hall toward the classroom, Red turned to him. "I have to leave early today. Broke a tooth eating too much Christmas candy. Might have to have it pulled. My dentist appointment is in forty-five minutes."

"All right."

"Yeah. The fact that I never brush my teeth might have something to do with it breaking." Red gave him a goofy look.

They stopped in front of the door to Father Tim's classroom, finding it closed. Red tried the knob, but it didn't turn. "It's locked."

"Gee, that's weird," Hank said.

"Yeah."

"Maybe he's just delayed getting here."

"I can wait for a bit"—Red glanced at his watch—"but I still have to catch the bus to make my appointment."

Five, ten, fifteen minutes passed with no Fr. Tim.

Finally, Red bid him goodbye and left. Hank wondered whether he should leave too, but five minutes later, he heard someone's footsteps racing down the hall. He turned to see Fr. Tim.

"Hank, where's Red?" Fr. Tim's bushy brows lowered over his eyes with a look of concern.

"He had to go to a dentist appointment."

"Well, I'm so glad *you* stayed. I was detained with...a...medical...um...never mind. Shall we get to work?"

"Sure."

Fr. Tim unlocked his classroom door, and the two stepped inside. Fr. Tim closed the door behind him as he said, "Would you please erase and clean the chalkboards?"

Hank nodded and proceeded to the front of the classroom. Red usually cleaned the boards.

Once he started erasing, he realized he was too short to reach the top of the board. So he did what he could first, then he turned to scan the room for the stepstool. He couldn't see it anywhere.

"Need the stepstool, Hank?" the priest asked.

For a minute, Hank wondered whether Fr. Tim was teasing him, but the priest would never do that. "Yes, sir."

The priest picked up the stool from the closet and carried it to the front of the classroom. He placed it on the floor beside Hank. "There you go. All set."

Hank got onto the stool and finished erasing the blackboard. He was about to step down when he felt a grip on his pant leg. Was that Fr. Tim's hand? Every part of his body went still.

After what seemed like moments, the priest finally said, "Come on, I'll help you down."

Hank breathed a sigh of relief. "Thanks, F-Father."

Hank moved the stool and climbed up to finish erasing the middle section of the blackboard when Fr. Tim's hand again gripped Hank's pant leg. This time, the priest held onto Hank's legs with one hand on each leg. "Don't want you to fall, Hank."

Once Hank finished erasing that section, Fr. Tim assisted him down. Hank moved the stool to the far end of the board and stood up to erase the rest of the chalk writing. He felt weird about the priest holding onto his legs, so he quickly cleaned off the board.

When he was almost done, Hank felt Fr. Tim's hand go from around his pants, up underneath his trousers, and stroked his bare leg above his socks. Instinctively, he shook his leg free of the priest's hand.

Fr. Tim cleared his throat. "Here you go, Hank. I'll help you down."

"Uh…what job can I do now, Father?" He tried to shake off the odd feeling, ready to move on.

"Let's get you settled over here at this front desk, and you can put these files in alphabetical order." The priest pointed. "Oh, and I've got Christmas chocolates on my desk. You're welcome to take some if you'd like."

"Sure." Before Hank sat down, he took a healthy handful of the Whitman's sampler chocolates. He unwrapped one and wolfed it down.

While Hank worked on the alphabetizing, Fr. Tim acted normal, as if nothing had happened. Well, nothing *had* happened. The priest had simply put his hand on Hank's leg. Sister Rose Bernadine had done worse when she slapped his leg with a ruler when he'd ignored the recess bell and remained in the schoolyard. It had stung like the dickens.

"You okay there, Hank?"

"Yes. I'm fine."

That night, Hank pulled the covers up and shivered. His bedclothes were cold.

He reflected on the day, his thoughts turning to Fr. Tim standing beside him while he was on the stool. He couldn't stop thinking about it. But of course, the priest was just trying to keep Hank steady. What other reason could he have?

Fr. Tim was always putting his hand on Hank's shoulder or back. Heck, he touched Hank more than his mother or father did most days.

Hank put his headphones on and turned the radio to the sports channel airing the Philadelphia Warriors against the Syracuse Nationals basketball game.

He drifted off to sleep, dreaming of spring, hot dogs, and Phillies games.

Chapter 14
Evie
If At First, You Don't Succeed
June 1983

Cheerleading tryouts arrived for next year's squad. Dressed in shorts and a tee-shirt, Evie wrote her name on the clipboard at the front of the gymnasium and joined the other girls gathered near the bleachers.

Some of the seasoned cheerleaders sneered at her as if questioning why she bothered trying out when she wouldn't make it anyway. Evie didn't disagree with them, and she wouldn't have come at all if not for her friend Kate's support and encouragement.

Plus, she kept reminding herself of her primary motivation. It was not the cute uniform or even the cheering. Those were definite perks to being a cheerleader. However, her primary motivation was boys. If she made the cheerleading squad, then the boys would *have* to notice her. All the cheerleaders had boyfriends. To Evie, it seemed like the only way to get a boyfriend.

She wanted to get on the squad so badly that she had prayed a Rosary. Although she was pretty sure she wouldn't make it, Evie had the skills: she could do a split, jumps, aerial cartwheels, and round-offs, and she knew most of the cheers.

Everyone knew that the cheerleaders who had been on previous years' squads would make it. So, for someone new to try out during her last year of high school was unusual.

Evie bit her lip and tried to avoid eye contact. Every other day leading up to this one, she'd informed her friend Kate that she would *not* be trying out for cheerleading after all. It

71

made her too nervous, and Evie didn't want to experience rejection, which she expected would happen. Then Kate would remind her that she'd never make the squad without at least trying. Of course, then Kate mentioned how her father would've wanted her to try out for the squad, whether she made it or not.

Now, as she listened to the whispers and snickers of a few of the experienced cheerleaders, she scolded herself for even showing up.

Cheerleading coach Mrs. Schaeffer retrieved the clipboard with the signup sheet. She studied it for a moment before calling the first name. "Evie Gallagher."

Evie's eyes opened wide, and she gasped. Her name was not the first on the list. Why would she be called first? She wished Kate was with her now, but only the girls trying out were allowed to be in the gym.

Mrs. Schaeffer motioned for her to come to the center of the gym floor.

Evie stood in front of the four teachers who acted as judges, and Mrs. Schaeffer told her she could begin. But she couldn't move a muscle or say a word. *God, please help me.*

Inside, she heard her father's voice. *You can do this, Eve.*

The giggling and snickers of the other girls didn't help.

Mrs. Schaeffer, who was about the same age as Mom, smiled. "Why don't you start with the jumps, Evie?"

Evie nodded. She went to do a toe touch jump but tripped and fell to the floor before she even got to the jump part—more laughter from the bleachers.

"Try again, Evie," said Mrs. Schaeffer.

Waiting a moment for her heart to settle, she readied herself. This time, it was a perfect toe touch. Then she did a Herkie and a pike jump flawlessly. She sighed with relief—no more giggling from the girls.

Evie then performed two cheers and finished with a flying

split leap onto the gym floor. When the judges clapped for her, the girls in the stands also clapped, albeit less enthusiastically.

Relief washing through her, Evie beamed. She had now completed her first cheerleading tryout. She had gotten over her fears and had done it. Still, did she have a chance of making the squad?

Evie sat through the rest of the girls' tryouts and clapped for those who weren't especially very good. If they were anything like Evie, they needed the encouragement.

After everyone finished, Mrs. Schaeffer announced that the names of the Junior Varsity and Varsity Cheerleaders would be posted on her door tomorrow at 8:00 a.m.

Kate met her outside the gym and walked her home. Evie excitedly told her how everything went.

"It sounds like you just might make the squad, Eve!"

"Well, I haven't allowed myself to hope as much, Kate, but I think I did well enough."

***

Evie tossed and turned all night before getting up and heading for school. Kate offered to go with her to Mrs. Schaeffer's door to see whether her name was on the list.

They waited behind the crowd at Mrs. Schaeffer's door. Some of the girls cried; others squealed with happiness. When the group thinned, Evie hesitantly approached the door, her heart pounding so loudly, she thought she'd have a heart attack.

When the two girls got within reading distance, Evie could not bear to look, so she turned her head. Then Kate squealed, "You made it, Evie! You made the Varsity Squad!"

Evie turned and read her name. She couldn't believe it. She had made the Varsity Cheerleading Squad.

"See, I told you!"

She squeezed her friend in a joyful hug. "Yes, you did."

Chapter 15
Hank
The Cold Cellar

The weather finally returned to normal, so that by the Friday of the third week of January, temps were averaging in the 30s and 40s. Not warm, but not too cold.

After school, Fr. Tim asked Hank if he wanted to work in the cellar for half an hour. The basement creeped Hank out. Nevertheless, he said yes. He waved to Red, who was busy working on a card file.

"Take this, Hank." Fr. Tim handed him a cardboard box with a small metal box on top of it. He placed the key to the cellar on top of the metal box. Hank took the boxes and headed out of the classroom. He went down the stairs under the Archangels statues and into the main lobby, then he turned under the stairs to the cellar door.

After setting the boxes on the floor, he unlocked the door, opened it, and pulled the chain to turn on the old-fashioned bulb light. Then he picked up the boxes and stepped carefully as he descended the wooden steps. He pulled a chain for another light fixture at the bottom of the stairs, but the bulb was dim, and the large room remained primarily dark. It was only 3:30 p.m. and still light outside, but the dirty windows allowed little light in. At least he had the dull glow of the fixture, so it wasn't pitch-black. His brother would tease the heck out of him if Hank ever admitted to being afraid in this cellar.

He straightened. He was fifteen and shouldn't be frightened of stupid stuff like this.

He placed the cardboard and metal boxes on the shelf and turned to go back upstairs when Fr. Tim bounded down the stairs with more boxes.

"I'd like you to take these boxes..." He pointed to the dark area behind the gigantic heater.

Hank followed him, squinting at the floor and hoping no rats lived down here. Just the thought made him squirm. Shoulders back, he stopped when Fr. Tim stopped and let his eyes adjust to the area. An ancient wardrobe like the one in *The Lion, the Witch and the Wardrobe* stood like a sentinel with what Hank guessed were old, covered religious statues beside it.

The priest opened the doors. Hundreds of old files filled multiple shelves inside the wardrobe. "Most of these files can be trashed. However, I'd like to keep everything that pertains to 1940 and onward." He paused. "Do you think you can do that, Hank?"

Sounded easy enough. "Sure, Father."

"Then I'll leave you to it."

"Can I move these files to where the light is?"

"Of course. I may have a portable light upstairs you could use. Would that work?"

"I think so."

From the sound of it, the priest raced up the stairs and shut the door behind him.

Hank stared at the file folders that filled the wardrobe. He squinted and counted five shelves. Looking at the top shelf, he winced. He'd need help getting to that shelf, but maybe Fr. Tim would have him working on something else at that point.

He took an accordion folder out and held it toward the light behind him. On the front was written, "Holy Archangels High School, Sports Stats 1924." He tilted his head and read the different tabs: Football, Basketball, Baseball, Swimming.

The door opened, and Hank heard Fr. Tim stomping down the steps. For a guy in his forties, he seemed incredibly agile.

"Here you go, Hank." The priest held a rectangular metal box with a round light at the top of it. He clicked it on, and it shone so brightly it nearly blinded Hank.

The priest placed the light on an old metal stand and pointed it in the direction of the wardrobe.

With all the light, Hank could now see spider webs galore and a few moving spiders. He tried not to shudder.

"You should be all set, Hank."

"Thank you, Father."

"No, thank *you*, Hank." He turned to go, then stopped. He picked up a metal trash can and brought it to Hank. "You can put any files that are pre-1940 in here."

"Sure, Father."

The priest skipped up the stairs and shut the door.

Hank tried to ignore the cobwebs and to focus on the task at hand. He tossed the 1924 sports file into the trash can. Any files that were post-1940, he stacked on a table near the light. When he removed the last file on the third shelf, a spider jumped out at him.

Hank shrieked and swatted it away.

Now that he had finished the bottom three shelves, Hank reached up and felt around for any files on the second-highest shelf above him. He found none, but as he slid his hand along the shelf, he grasped onto what felt like a piece of paper. He pulled it down, surprised to find a graduation photo. He squinted, studying it. The boy in the picture seemed vaguely familiar, but before he could place who it was, the bulb from the portable light flickered a few times. Then it shut off.

He blinked, letting his eyes adjust again, then stepped in front of the furnace for some light. After studying the picture a moment more, it hit him. This was Fr. Tim when he was in high school! Cool. He seemed pretty much the same, except his glasses were a bit bigger now, and he was going bald. In the photo, Fr. Tim had a warm, wide smile, and if they'd gone to high school at the same time, maybe they'd have been friends.

He placed the photo on the table near the now-dark light and returned to the wardrobe. Admittedly, he was glad for the dim light because he'd rather not see any more cobwebs. Unfortunately, cobwebs meant spiders.

As his eyes adjusted, he reached up to feel for anything else on that second-highest shelf, and his hands touched a few more photos. He slid them off the shelf, then studied them. These were pictures of boys he didn't recognize.

With all the shelves done except for the dreaded top shelf, now he had to find something he could stand on. He found a small metal pail on the other side of the furnace. It was only about a foot high, but that would be enough for him to reach up and grab anything on that shelf. He placed it upside down in front of the wardrobe. As he stepped on the pail, he glanced to where he had put young Fr. Tim's photo. Then as he turned toward the shelf, he straightened. His mind flashed back to Fr. Tim putting his hands on Hank's leg. That *was* weird, but the priest was just trying to keep him safe.

He reached up, praying he'd encounter no more spiders. All of a sudden, Hank felt a presence behind him. Was there another spider on his back? Just then, something brushed against his backside. He swatted at his lower back, and his hand smacked the soft fabric of a priest's habit. He heard someone gasp.

Hank turned around and drew in a breath.

"Oh, sorry, Hank. I bumped into you. I couldn't see you." It was Fr. Tim.

"I thought there was another spider on my back."

Hank hopped off the pail, his heart racing, and faced the priest.

"No spiders here. I came down because I need you upstairs. Let's get to that top shelf another day. Red had to leave, and I have one more job for you."

"Sure, Father." His heart still pounding, he followed the priest up the stairs and to the classroom. When Hank finished a writing task, the priest said, "See you tomorrow, Hank."

He waved and bid Fr. Tim farewell.

That night in his bunk, Hank put in his headphones and turned the dial to WIBG to listen to music. As he listened to "Sixteen Tons" by Tennessee Ernie Ford, Hank recalled the spider incident and Fr. Tim brushing up against him. Why hadn't he heard the priest coming down the stairs? Why didn't Fr. Tim say anything on his way into the cellar? Well, Hank figured the priest must have had a reason.

Billy kicked the bottom of his bed, so he pulled off his headphones. "What?"

"You're humming too loud. I can't get to sleep."

"Sorry." Hank didn't realize that he'd been making noise. He turned off his radio and put it and the headphones next to his pillow.

Chapter 16
Hank
Chocolate and Whiskey
January 1955

Red met Hank at the entrance to the school the following day, and they walked to their lockers together.

"Hey, why did you have to leave early yesterday? Another bad tooth?"

"I didn't have to leave. Fr. Tim said I could go home."

Hank blurted out, "But I thought—" Before he disclosed his thought, Hank decided not to tell his friend what Fr. Tim had said. *Why would Father say Red had to leave when he'd asked him to leave?*

"And he also told me he wouldn't need me today after school."

That was odd. "Oh?" Hank paused, wondering.

In English class, Fr. Tim seemed to be floating on air. He was someone who always smiled, but today he seemed especially happy. The priest kept whistling the theme from the movie *Halls of Montezuma*. While Fr. Tim couldn't sing, he could whistle quite well.

Then he shared with the class how much he enjoyed the novel they were studying. Hank thought *Moby Dick* was a fair story, but nothing to write home about.

"Mr. Gallagher, would you please collect the homework assignments?"

"Yes, Father."

Hank went from student to student and collected papers. When he placed them on the desk, Fr. Tim touched his hand. "See you after school?"

"Uh, yeah, I guess so, Father." He glanced to the back of the classroom at Red then leaned toward the priest. "Why did you ask Red not to come?"

"Oh, sometimes Red can be a bit clumsy. And we'll be working in the basement today. Meet me at the cellar door."

Hank nodded and returned to his desk. He had to agree. Red was very clumsy and often tripped over his own shadow.

After school, Hank stopped at his locker to drop off his books and get his jacket. He then proceeded to the cellar door under the staircase in the main lobby. Hank heard someone's footsteps coming down the marble staircase. He craned his neck to see Fr. Tim with a stack of files in his hands, the hood of his habit in midair as he flew down the stairs.

"Ah, Hank," Fr. Tim said. "Punctual as always."

"I try to be."

Fr. Tim handed the stack of folders to Hank. Then the priest unlocked the door, opened it, turned on the overhead light, and indicated for Hank to go down the stairs in front of him.

Hank descended the wooden steps into the dank cellar. Fr. Tim rested a hand on his shoulder, urging him forward. When they reached the bottom, Fr. Tim stepped ahead of him and pulled the chain for the other light.

Hank remained where he was at the foot of the stairs, buttoning up his jacket and staring at two very worn armchairs facing each other.

Fr. Tim turned. "How do you like it?"

"Like what, Father?"

"This is for you and me." Fr. Tim pointed to the chairs. "After we get a few small jobs done, then you and I will celebrate your hard work for the past six months."

"Um, sure, Father." Hank was disappointed that Red couldn't be here. He'd worked hard too.

The priest took the folders from Hank and placed them on

the metal shelves against the outer stone wall below one of the tiny windows. Hank had already cleaned out the shelves, so the wardrobe was empty.

For the next thirty minutes, Fr. Tim and Hank worked behind the large, noisy furnace. Fr. Tim handed Hank folders and books to place into the old wooden wardrobe.

Fr. Tim tried to maintain a conversation, but the furnace kept going on because it was cold. Hank thought Fr. Tim might've said something along the lines of the oil furnace being less work than a coal furnace, but Hank didn't know much about furnaces either way. His home had cast iron radiators, and although Ma kept the heat down—even in winter—it was always warm enough in their home.

"Hank?"

"Uh, yes?"

"I think we've done enough work for one day. Let's move over to the chairs."

"Sure." Hank felt strange about Fr. Tim inviting him to sit in the chair.

Fr. Tim sat in the chair facing the stairs and motioned for Hank to take the other chair. Then he reached under his chair and pulled out a bottle and a small bowl of chocolates.

"This, my boy, is a reward for all your hard work."

Hank took a few chocolates and consumed them. They were rich, peppermint-flavored chocolates.

Hank glanced over Fr. Tim's head to a shelf near the corner of the basement, where an old statue of St. Michael stood, its face chopped off. Weird that he hadn't noticed that creepy statue before.

As he chewed, he squinted to read the label of the bottle. *Jameson Irish Whiskey*. It kind of looked like a big bottle of the stuff Ma gave him when he was sick. What was that stuff called? Paregoric? "What's this?"

"It's the finest whiskey this side of the Mississippi."

81

"Whiskey?"

"Yes, son. And I've seen how well you work, how conscientious you are, and how grown-up you are, regardless of your stature." He paused, opened the bottle, took a swig, and handed it to Hank. "Wouldn't those boys who call you names be green with envy right now?"

Hank had no idea how to respond to that, although those bullies might be envious. He gripped the bottle but hesitated. What would be wrong with taking one sip of whiskey? His father let him taste his beer a few times. He brought the bottle to his lips then took a small sip. It burned his mouth and tasted like gasoline.

"Hank, come on, take a manly gulp."

He nodded. This time, he took a long, hard gulp but then nearly spat the liquid out. His entire throat and mouth were on fire. He coughed and choked.

Fr. Tim laughed. "Believe me; someday, you won't cough like that."

The priest offered another swig, then another, all the while throwing in a few words. "What about our Varsity Angels Basketball team winning five games in a row? Mackey scored 44 of the 94 points. That's nearly half of the winning score."

Hank's face numbed, and he was lightheaded. He and Red had only attended one basketball game. When Hank recognized two players as the bullies who called him names, he had no desire to return.

Fr. Tim rambled on about *The Lone Ranger*, a dog, and sledding, offering Hank another swig of whiskey.

The heater went on and drowned out whatever Fr. Tim said next. But the priest offered him more whiskey, and he obligingly swallowed.

The priest's words became a jumbled mess of strange words he'd never heard before. His head lolled to the side.

When Fr. Tim offered him another swig of whiskey, he pushed the bottle away. He thought he was going to throw up.

Now the dank cellar was tipping and spinning. Hank slumped back in the chair and closed his eyes, everything spinning around him like on that ride at Willow Grove Park.

As the world spiraled around him, he heard something about "magic" and "love." He heard, "I know you want this, Hank." Then it felt like Fr. Tim was unzipping his trousers. What the—he lifted his eyelids open enough to see Fr. Tim's head in his lap—*oh, God, what's happening?* He squeezed his eyes shut.

***

He didn't remember much of the bus trip home, only that he was sure that every single person stared at him, suspecting what had just happened. Hank bit his lip so hard to keep from sobbing that he finally drew blood. It still felt like the entire world was spinning. His heart burned. His head pounded. When he arrived at the bus stop two blocks from home, he shivered as he got off.

It was a short walk home, but too many thoughts swirled around. *No one will believe you anyway. I'll tell them you wanted it.* The priest's words echoed in his mind. *Ma will know I've been drinking.* How would he remove the stench of alcohol? His mother could smell alcohol on someone's breath from a mile away.

He opened then quietly closed the front door. Billy glanced up from his books at the coffee table and tilted his head. "What's wrong with *you?*"

"Don't feel good." He scanned the living room, not finding Ma. *Good.* Probably in the kitchen. As he moved toward the stairs, he said, "Ma, I'm home."

"Oh, Hank, you're a bit early," she called from the kitchen.

"Yeah, had... to leave early... not feeling so great. Going

up to lay down for a bit."

"All right."

He tried to race up to the second floor, but even the steps moved out from under his feet. Slowing down, he made it to the second floor, down the hall, to the bathroom. He closed and locked the door. Hank brushed his teeth, then took out his mother's Listerine and gargled with it. Feeling an overwhelming urge to throw up, he knelt by the toilet bowl and spilled the contents of his stomach.

"Hank, you all right in there?"

"Yeah, Ma, just threw up."

His mother jiggled the knob. "Unlock the door, honey. Let me in."

"Just a minute, Ma." Hank flushed the toilet, grabbed a towel, and wiped his mouth. He'd just gargled with Listerine, and that was mostly alcohol. That, and the stink of puke, would hopefully cover up any stench of alcohol.

He dropped his pants and cleaned his private area, groaning inwardly. His whole body smelled like the priest's aftershave.

"Hank?"

He wouldn't have time to take a bath now, but he *would* later. Hands shaking, he unlocked and opened the door.

"Good Lord, Hank. You look awful."

"Feel awful too."

She put her hand to Hank's forehead. "You're not warm. You're ice cold. Let's get you into bed." His mother started to escort him to his bedroom, but he shook his head.

"I'll be okay, Ma. I can walk. Just need to sleep, that's all."

"Very well. I'll bring some soup up to you later."

"Please don't. I won't be able to eat anything."

In his bedroom, he closed the door, stripped off his clothes, and changed into his pajamas. He hopped onto the top bunk and pulled the covers up over his entire body. Then he rolled toward the wall and stuffed part of the blanket in his mouth to muffle his sobs.

This was supposed to be a normal day, but it wasn't.

I know you want this, Hank.

If I wanted it, why do I feel so disgusted?

Hank switched on his transistor radio and turned the dial to WIBG. The song "Sh-Boom," was playing. He didn't hook up his headphones. He was on the verge of tears and wanted the music to cover up any sounds he made.

He just couldn't believe what had happened. Hank couldn't fathom a holy priest doing *that*. Sorrow overwhelmed him. His bed wasn't the same. His home wasn't the same. His family wasn't the same. *He* wasn't the same. Yes, everything was different.

Then, with The Crew-Cuts singing, "Life could be a dream," Hank wept.

Chapter 17
Hank
Afterward

Hank woke to the squeaking of his bedroom door and the song "Mr. Sandman" playing on his radio.

"Son?" his father asked.

Hank cleared his throat and turned down his radio. "Yes, sir?" He kept his back to his father.

"Your mother tells me you're sick."

"Just the stomach flu. I'll be better in a few days."

"Sounds like you have a cold."

That could be because I fell asleep crying. "Yeah, may have a cold too."

"Well, I'll let you get some rest. I was worried about you."

"Thanks, Pop."

"At least you have your transistor radio to keep you company."

"I do. Thanks, Pop."

His father's firm hand patted him on the back, and he tried not to wince. How could he explain to his father that he didn't want to be touched right now...by anyone? The door quietly shut.

He felt dirty and could still smell the priest on him. Unable to take it for another minute, he whipped the covers off, hopped off his bunk, and went to the bathroom. He locked the door and filled the tub. He stripped and put his foot into the tub. The water was too hot, but he lowered himself into it anyway. Maybe the heat would burn all traces of the priest from his body.

His eyes filled with tears. Why did he feel so bad? Because he'd done something wrong. But Fr. Tim had done something wrong too. Even if the priest was correct—that Hank wanted what he did to him—what Fr. Tim did was bad. Heck, Hank felt awful when he touched himself for pleasure, and he always confessed it. But having someone else do that to you *had* to be sinful regardless of what the priest said.

How could he have been so wrong about Fr. Tim?

Maybe he should tell Pop.

If he told Ma, she'd beat him because she wouldn't believe him. Ma hadn't beaten him since the day he stole gumdrops from Pearcy's Drugstore. And that was two years ago.

Pop never lifted a hand to Hank or any of his siblings. The memory of what Pop said about Fr. Tim came flooding to the forefront of his mind. His father had said there was something that didn't sit right with him about the priest.

God, I'm sorry for what Fr. Tim did. I know it was my fault, and I must be guilty of a mortal sin. Please forgive me for letting him hurt me. I'll try to go to Confession as soon as possible.

When Hank finally got out of the tub, his body was beet red, he shivered, and his teeth chattered. He wrapped a towel around himself and raced across the hall to his bedroom. Hank dressed in clean pajamas and hopped onto his bed.

The following morning, intense nausea woke Hank before his alarm. He raced to the bathroom door but found it closed, the light on. He knocked. "Pop?"

"Yes, son?"

"I need to—" Hank dropped to his knees and vomited a bit of bile onto the carpet in the hallway.

The door opened. "Sorry, Pop. I threw up on the rug."

"Never mind that. I'll clean it up for you. You better go back to bed. I'll tell your mother you're sick and not going to school."

"Thanks, Pop."

Back on his upper bunk, Hank silently prayed in thanksgiving. Ma might not have been so pleased about the mess on the floor, but Pop always seemed to take things in stride.

Hank stirred when Billy got up, but he fell back to sleep and woke up as Ma ran the vacuum downstairs.

The sun streamed in between the curtain panels, planes landed and took off from the airport, and cars drove by as the world seemed to go on as if nothing had happened. Ma was vacuuming, Billy, Helen, and Tess were at school, and Pop was at work. Nothing had changed, and everything had changed.

Hank still couldn't wrap his mind around what Fr. Tim had done to him. His eyes caught sight of a plastic rosary on the post of his bunk. He picked it up and tried to say a decade of the Rosary. *Mother Mary, help me to forget what happened.*

Chapter 18
Evie
Broken Heart
February 21, 1984

The end of the cheerleading season drew near. The girls waited outside in the frigid cold for their rides home after the basketball game. Evie had her driver's license, but her mother needed the car to go bowling; Mom's league played on game nights.

One by one, the other girls were picked up, leaving Evie by herself. She had told Mom to pick her up at 9:30, but here it was 9:45 p.m., and she could barely feel her bare legs with the icy temperatures.

Why had she ever wanted to be a cheerleader? On the one hand, she had fun with some of the cheerleaders. On the other, several of them snubbed her because she had made the squad while at least one experienced cheerleader— probably a friend of theirs—hadn't made it. Although they never came out and said it, Evie suspected they blamed her.

Worse yet, the guys *hadn't* lined up to date her, so her plan to have the guys notice—and in particular, one basketball player, her crush—had backfired. They *may* have noticed her, but she still hadn't had a date.

All through her high school years, she'd had a crush on this one boy, Chandler. No one called him Chandler, though, not even her friends—no matter how much she protested. They called him by the initials of his full name, Chandler Richard Andrew Paine, aka CRAP.

Evie often daydreamed about him asking her out. In freshman year, he was still short. But between freshman and senior year, he had grown to over six feet tall. She especially liked that he was Catholic and attended the same parish as she did.

A gust of icy wind blew, making goosebumps pop out on her legs. Evie pulled her coat tight at the neck and bounced on her toes. If she could just wait inside the gym for a moment and warm up, she'd be fine.

Evie stepped into the school hallway and stood still, enjoying the warmth. Hearing some of the basketball players talking and laughing, she pushed on the gym door slightly to take a peek. Evie recognized Chandler's voice. "Yeah, I agree. She's the perfect size just to stand there."

Another guy chuckled. "Right. She wouldn't even have to kneel when giving a—"

Chandler's hearty laugh drowned out the rest of the comment. But Evie got the gist of it. *Disgusting*. Her crush said, "Yeah, I can't imagine having *her* as a girlfriend when she looks like a little kid. Evie Gallagher can't be seventeen. She's more like eight years old."

Evie's mouth fell open, and her heart dropped. She let the gym door close and ran outside. The bitter cold smacked her in the face.

Was there a hole somewhere that she could climb into? For four years, she'd had a huge crush on this boy, and he talked about her like *that*? How does a young Catholic man speak in such a way about a girl? And with the other basketball players? Her heart shattered.

As if in answer to a prayer, her mother's car pulled up just then. Evie opened the passenger door to warmth, and the song "Girls Just Wanna Have Fun" by Cyndi Lauper blared on the radio.

Mom said, "Sorry I'm late, Evie. There was an accident near the bowling alley, and I couldn't get out of the parking lot."

Evie nodded. "It's okay." She had to bite her lip to keep from sobbing.

"Are you all right?"

"Yeah, I'll be fine." But Evie wouldn't be fine, not for a long time. Cyndi kept singing, "Girls just wanna have fun." Yeah, Evie would never have fun, not if all guys talked about her like those jock basketball players.

As Mom drove off, Evie burst into tears.

"Okay, honey, what's wrong?"

When Evie tried to spit out the words, she cried so hard that her mother couldn't understand her. Mom rubbed her back.

Finally, she said, "I overheard some basketball players making fun of me."

"Oh, honey."

"They said I looked like a little girl and some crude things about me."

"Aww, I'm so sorry, honey." Mom paused. "Well, you do look like a little girl, but that's what makes you so unique. Don't let it bother you. Someday, you'll be happy you look so young."

"I'm not happy now, Mom."

"Listen, why don't we stop by Dunkin' Donuts and pick up a hot chocolate?"

Even hot chocolate would not make her feel better, but she appreciated Mom's offer. She shook her head.

Her mother pulled up to their house. While she was happy to be home, Evie felt like the world had stopped around her.

Evie would most certainly become an old maid. And, despite Cyndi Lauper's pronouncement that "girls just wanna have fun," she would most likely *never* have fun. It would be best for Evie just to accept it.

***

As she lay in the comfort of her bed, Evie wept. She

thought of her father. Did he also experience this kind of pain? Did kids bully him because of his stature and young looks? He was a boy, so it might've been worse for him.

How would she face those boys again after what they had said? Her former crush was in two of her classes, and the other basketball players in other classes. No way could she face any of them yet.

She wished her father were here right now. Evie missed him so much.

Chapter 19
Hank
Milk and Cookies

During the ensuing two days, Hank did what sick people did: he slept a lot—or tried to—and he didn't eat much. His stomach growled, but he couldn't face eating, not yet. Every time he thought about what happened, it felt like something squeezed his heart so tightly that he could hardly breathe.

The only brightness of those two days was that he could listen to his new transistor radio all day if he wanted. On the evening of the second day, Hank was reading a comic book in bed when the phone rang downstairs. Helen picked it up. "Hello?" she said.

A few seconds passed, then she added, "Oh, certainly, Father. I'll get Mom."

Hank heard his sister calling Ma and then Ma's voice. "Oh, yes, Father. Thank you so much for calling. Hank is doing better today. Yes, I'll tell him. Goodbye, Father."

His mother's heavy footsteps came up the stairs and into Hank's room. "That was that kind Father O'Reilly calling to see how you were doing."

Hank sat up and started to tremble. "Uh...really?"

"Yes, and he said he's anxiously awaiting your return to classes. He said the students miss you. Isn't that nice?"

Hank nodded. "Uh, yes. Nice."

Ma turned around and descended the stairs.

His hands shook, and his stomach turned. How did the priest have the nerve to call his home?

How would Hank endure the next four months of freshman year having to see *him* every day?

Certain his mother wouldn't let him remain home for

another day, Hank prepared for the next day of school and took out his black pants, white shirt, tie, and blazer with the school's logo on it and hung them on the hook inside the closet door.

The following morning, he met his mother in the kitchen. "I feel better, so I'm going to school."

Ma held the back of her hand to Hank's head, even though he'd never had a fever. "You're cool; that's good." She handed him a bagged lunch. "Don't wear yourself out."

"I won't, Ma. Thanks." He kissed her cheek.

"Wasn't it nice to have that priest call about you?"

All he could do was nod.

On the bus trip to school, Hank gripped the handle of his bookbag so hard that his knuckles became white. The boy sitting next to him tried to make small talk, but Hank wasn't in the mood. He just had to get through this day.

The majority of his classes would be fine, but what would he tell Red? Hank would *not* return to the after-school job. Would Red keep the job after school? Would Fr. Tim do something to Red?

When it came time for English class, he tensed and approached the classroom with caution. He glimpsed Fr. Tim through the open door. He sat at his desk, probably marking papers. Only a few boys had taken their seats. Hank stepped to the side but remained in the hallway where the priest couldn't see him. After most of the students had gone into class, Hank finally made his way to his desk, avoiding eye contact with Fr. Tim.

"All right, class, settle down."

Hank kept his head lowered.

"Hank, I hope you're feeling better," Red whispered.

He nodded.

"Welcome back, Mr. Gallagher."

"Th-thank you," Hank said, lifting his head a bit but still avoiding eye contact.

"I certainly hope you're feeling better."

"Uh...yes."

Then Fr. Tim started his lesson on Chapter Six of *Moby Dick*. Hank kept his eyes downward. He listened and took notes, but he couldn't focus. All he kept seeing was the balding top of the priest's head in his lap—and he became sick to his stomach.

The class time dragged, everything moving in slow motion. Then the bell finally rang, and he sprung out of the room like the man shot from a cannonball. Only eighty-five more days until summer break.

Behind him, in the noise of the students racing down the hall, he heard his name. He turned, and his heart practically stopped. It was Fr. Tim.

"Hank, wait!"

"I have to go, Father."

Fr. Tim grabbed his arm and kept him from moving.

Hank lowered his head and stared at his feet. "I'm going to be late for my next class."

"I'll see you after school, right?"

"No. I quit." Hank wrenched himself away from the priest's grip. Not waiting to hear the priest's reply, he sprinted down the stairs to the gymnasium, under the Holy Archangels statues.

How many times had he walked up these stairs on the way to Fr. Tim's class? How many times had he passed under the statues to get to the cellar? Instead of wielding their swords in protection, the angels kept their distance. Shame filled Hank. Was that why the angels didn't protect him? Was it because they knew he was capable of allowing such shameful things to happen?

He'd always thought of Fr. Tim as a kind man who never

lost his temper. Hank winced. How could he *not* have seen the priest's true disposition before now?

Hank neared the open doors of the gymnasium. He'd never thought he would look forward to basketball, but he liked Mr. Romero. Still—maybe there was something wrong with Mr. Romero too? He shook his head. *Being nice isn't an accurate way to judge a person.* Hank would have to be on his guard from now on.

The day finally ended, and Hank went to his locker to get his coat and drop a few books in his bookbag.

He darted out the side door, heading to the bus stop when Red called to him.

"Are you better, Hank?"

"A bit, I guess."

"I was just going upstairs to Fr. Tim's room. Aren't you coming?"

"I quit today, Red. And you should too."

"Why?"

Hank glanced away. "Because you need to, that's all."

"Maybe you can afford to stop working, but I need this money to buy all the extras," Red said.

"Look, Red." Hank turned to face him but avoided eye contact. He didn't know what to say.

Red scoffed. "I thought you were my friend."

Hank heard Red's footfalls become distant.

God, please protect Red. Part of him wanted to add to his prayer: *you know, the opposite of what you did for me.*

When he boarded the bus, his stomach growled. He took one bite of the baloney sandwich Ma had packed for him and thought he was going to vomit.

When he got off the bus, he tossed the sandwich into a trash bin. His stomach growled. Would he ever be able to eat again?

At his house, Hank opened the door and dropped his

bookbag on the coffee table. He tossed his coat onto the chair. Smelling the scent of Gingersnap cookies, he raced to the kitchen. About four dozen cookies lay cooling on the table. He grabbed four and stuffed them in his mouth. He swallowed and took four more. As he chewed, he relished the taste of ginger. *Ma makes the best cookies ever.* He opened the icebox and took a swig of milk right from the bottle.

The floor creaked, and his mother cleared her throat. "Hank? What in the world? Put that milk down. We don't drink from the milk bottle!" She stood frowning at him, a small whisk broom in her hands.

"S-sorry, Ma. I was just so hungry and thirsty."

"And where did half of these cookies go? Did you eat them?"

"Uh...yes..."

She didn't wait for an explanation. Instead, she snapped Hank's backside with the straw whisk broom. "Sorry... doesn't... bring... back those cookies!"

Hank initially drew back as it stung his legs. The rigid steel section smacked against his thighs. Then, resolved, Hank stood straight and didn't try to escape the angry end of the whisk broom. He deserved to be beaten. Maybe if Ma hit him hard enough, he'd forget what had happened.

Finally, she stopped. She stood back and tried to catch her breath. She must've gotten winded from beating him.

"Go to your room and stay there until your father comes home."

As Hank shuffled away, his mother said, "Honestly, a fifteen-year-old acting like someone Tessie's age."

Hank wished he were Tessie's age again because that was before *it* happened.

Chapter 20
Hank
Man-to-Man Talk with Pop

In his room, Hank changed into jeans and a sweatshirt. He climbed on top of his bunk bed and turned on his radio.

Billy barged into their room to change out of his school uniform. "Ma said you ate most of the cookies and drank from the milk jug? You must want a beating or something."

"I was hungry, that's all."

"I'd say. The way Ma tells it, you ate most of the cookies."

"I only had eight."

"Holy cow, Hank! No wonder she's mad."

Billy left the room and pounded down the stairs.

Soon after, Pop stood in the doorway of his room, dressed in his suit, a kind look in his eyes. "Hey, son. Your mother tells me you ate most of the cookies she baked."

"No, Pop. I had eight."

His father smiled. "Ah, I see. Well, that's still too many cookies, isn't it?"

Hank nodded.

"Just wondering, son, if you're feeling better. I know you haven't been well."

"I'm all right, I guess."

"So why did you eat all those cookies?"

"Because they're delicious?"

Pop laughed, which made Hank chuckle. "Well, I can't argue with that reason."

Hank sighed. "I couldn't eat at school. Felt nauseous. When I came home, I was so hungry that I probably could've eaten all those cookies."

"I'm sure you could've." Pop lowered his head for a minute,

then he approached the top bunk bed. "You apologized to your mother?"

"Yes."

"Good. Then that's all I need to hear." Pop stood there a moment and stared at Hank as if studying him.

Hank's cheeks warmed. Could his father tell he had done some bad things?

"Is everything all right with you, son?"

Hank swallowed hard. "Um...no, not really."

"Why don't you tell your old man what's on your mind?" He leaned against the bunk bed.

"I don't know if I can, Pop. It's..."

"You can talk to me about anything, you know."

"I know. But—this—it's personal, and I need to go to Confession."

"Well, I can't help you there. But I can tell you that whatever it is, it'll pass."

You wouldn't think that if you knew.

Should I tell him?

He couldn't even say the words.

From downstairs, his mother's voice yelled, "Supper's ready."

"Well, we better get downstairs. How's your appetite?"

"It's all right," Hank said as he hopped off the bed. "But I have a feeling Ma's not going to let me have any cookies for dessert."

"I think you're right, son."

At supper, Hank listened as Helen told them about one of the new sisters that had just arrived at Hallahan. "She's meaner than Sister Rose Bernadine."

Billy and Tessie gasped. Hank couldn't imagine anyone meaner than Sister Rose Bernadine, but then again, having a nasty nun for a teacher wasn't all that bad.

Tessie whined about a girl tripping her during recess.

Then she droned on about all kinds of things that bothered her that day.

Billy grumbled about his teacher giving too much homework.

The complaints coming from his siblings seemed so insignificant. The little things that once bothered Hank no longer mattered.

"So, Hank, how's the after-school job going?" Pop asked.

Oh, no. "Um...well, I quit today."

"You quit? Why?"

Hank lowered his head, and his hands began to shake. "Um...well, I—" *Please, God, what can I say?* Just then, it came to him. "School is... becoming more difficult, you know, and...well, I just...um...want to focus on my schoolwork."

Pop patted him on the back. "That's very mature of you, Hank, to realize you needed to sacrifice that extra money for what really matters. Is that what you wanted to talk to me about?"

"That was part of it, I guess."

Hank sat frozen in the dark school cellar again. Fr. Tim sat across from him.

The priest touched him on the shoulder. "Oh, Hank! I've been waiting for you. Remember how much you liked it when I did this?"

Hank tried so hard to get away, but he couldn't lift his feet. They seemed to be glued to the floor.

"Hank, Hank, wake up!"

Hank opened his eyes to find Billy smacking his hand. "Gee whiz, Hank!"

Hank gasped.

"All your yelling woke me up."

"Oh, um, sorry, had a bad dream."

"Must've been a real doozy then."

"Yeah, it was."

Hank relaxed against his pillow. He tried to fall back to sleep, but he decided he'd rather stay awake than have that nightmare again. He put his headphones on and turned the dial to the easy listening station. Maybe that would help calm him down.

Chapter 21
Evie
Last Game
February 25, 1984

After taking a day off, Evie felt ready to return to school. She would do her best to ignore the basketball players, especially her former crush. Mom had told her that she shouldn't worry about them and what they thought. The truth was, she hated that they had made fun of her.

As Evie walked to school, she saw a poster about this evening's game, the last home basketball game of the season. She was glad she wouldn't have to "perform" after that.

She reached the school building and headed for homeroom. After stepping into the class, Mr. Bernard approached her. The man was a giant at six and a half feet tall. He towered over Evie and had a low, bellowing voice. "Congratulations, Evie."

"For what?"

"You're on the short list of finalists for the National Merit Scholarship."

"No kidding?"

"No kidding. Well done, Evie."

Evie couldn't believe it. The likelihood of her getting the Merit Scholarship was minuscule, so she *was* genuinely surprised. And happy. It almost made her forget about the basketball players making fun of her.

During the homeroom announcements, the person over the loudspeaker mentioned her name as a finalist in the National Merit Scholarships.

A few of her classmates congratulated her, then she proceeded to her next class, English. Evie was still in the hallway when the English teacher and other students congratulated her.

After Evie sat down, she felt a tap on her shoulder and turned. Mark, the guy who sat behind her, pointed toward Chandler, who sat behind him. Her former crush smiled and said, "Congratulations, Evie."

Her face burned, and anger spiked inside her. Instead of thanking him, she blurted out, "It's amazing what someone who looks like a little kid can accomplish in life, isn't it?"

Chandler's eyebrows narrowed, then he straightened and glanced away.

When class ended, Evie picked up her books. In the noise of the hallway, someone called her name. She turned, and there stood Chandler, all six feet four inches of him. Evie practically had to crane her neck to make eye contact with him.

"Um...you...um...didn't...um...happen to overhear a conversation in the gym on Tuesday night, did you? A few of us heard noises in the hallway."

Evie sighed. "I did."

"Gee, Evie, I'm sorry. We didn't mean for you to hear that."

"I'm sure you didn't."

"If it helps, I don't think that way about you. The guys were making fun of you, and it seemed funny at the time, so I just went along."

"I'm sure it did." Evie's anger softened. "I know I look like a little girl, but I'm not one. I'm almost eighteen."

"Is there any way I can make it up to you?"

"Yes. The next time they make fun of me, stand up for me instead of going along with it."

"I will." He nodded, then turned and walked away.

Evie hurried to her next class, thinking that maybe she liked this guy after all.

***

As usual these days, Evie came home to an empty house. Mom was at the courthouse in Philly, Deb had moved in with her boyfriend, Young Hank was always at a sports practice, and Mitch was working.

She wished Mom were here so she could tell her about the Merit Scholarship.

As Evie flopped down on the couch, she caught sight of Dad's post office award hanging on the wall. Thoughts of him no longer made her cry, but her heart squeezed. *He* would've been very proud of her accomplishments.

Chapter 22
Hank
The Journal

The transistor radio seemed to be the only thing that could take Hank's mind off what had happened. So he hopped onto his bunk and listened to it every chance he got. He could disappear into his own world.

Three different times, Hank thought about telling his father what had happened to him. But when it came right down to it, he just couldn't say the words. When Hank went to Confession last week, he simply confessed that another guy touched him, and he didn't stop him. He didn't lie. Hank knew God would know exactly what had happened.

Now he needed to forget about the whole incident and never think of it again.

Of course, it was hard to forget when he saw *him* every single day.

Since the "incident," he had wet the bed two times. He didn't want his mother to find out about those accidents. Although he'd wet the bed regularly until he was nine years old, he hadn't done so since then. After school, when Ma was out or in the kitchen cooking, he cleaned the sheet as best he could in the bathtub, squeezed the water out, then put it in the gas dryer in the basement. One time his mother caught him carrying the wet sheets to the basement, and he lied. "I spilled a cup of water, just drying my sheets." She seemed to believe that white lie.

Hank was grateful that his parents were well-off enough to own a dryer; most people in the neighborhood still hung their clothes out on the clothesline, summer or winter.

It was essential that his mother *not* find out that he had accidents in his bed.

Hank was watching television Sunday afternoon when Pop came into the living room and sat down beside him. "Son, I'd like to talk to you about something."

For some reason, Hank's mouth went dry, and his chest tightened. "Um, yes, Pop?"

Pop patted Hank's knee. "I get the sense that you want to tell me something, but you're finding it hard to say. Am I right?"

Hank's eyes widened.

"I know it has something to do with your job and why you quit. Billy also mentioned that you're having nightmares."

Nightmare. One. Hank wished that Billy had kept his mouth shut.

"Remember that I bought that journal for you so that you could write anything down, happy things, sad things, disappointing things, scary things. Whatever you've wanted to talk to me about, you can certainly do so. I'm always here to listen. But if you'd rather, you can write about it in the journal."

"That sounds good, Pop. Yeah, I've already written something in the journal, but you're right. Maybe I'll write more."

Pop patted him on the back and pulled him into a hug. Hank was still uncomfortable with anyone touching him, but this was, after all, his father. He loved his father so much. Hank was sure Pop would go straight to heaven because he was the real deal.

After getting into his pajamas and hopping up onto his bunk, he turned on his transistor radio and opened his journal. He flipped to the first page and the entry from Christmas. It seemed like years ago because he had been so happy, but it was only a month ago.

Hank turned to a fresh page and wrote about *that day* and the details. He pushed his pen deep into the paper. His breathing became shallow, and his heart raced. His dinner threatened to come back up. Once he finished writing to the end of the page, he ripped the page out. He couldn't bear to have anyone read this because it was his fault.

Hank turned the page and thought for a moment. He would write a story about an apprentice and a magician.

He started to write, then made a mistake and scribbled over it. Then he turned the page and wrote.

Once he finished, he closed the book.

I'm never going to think about it again. I must forget that ever happened.

Playing Wiffle ball outside in the cool winter air with Billy gave Hank hope that his life would return to normal. As each day passed, he tried to push that horrible incident further and further from his consciousness.

Chapter 23
Hank
An Expensive Habit

The end of the school year finally arrived. Hank watched students get in line to have Fr. Tim sign their yearbooks. That was one priest he *wouldn't* ask to sign his book.

The priest hadn't bothered Hank since the day he returned to school in late January. Hank didn't raise his hand in English class anymore and found it hard to listen to the lessons. And Fr. Tim never asked him any questions.

His report card showed that he received a generous eighty percent from Fr. Tim. He probably didn't even deserve to pass that class. He recited a silent prayer that he would never have to even think about *him* and *it* again.

That incident made him realize that jerking off—which he referred to as a base hit—was not a big deal.

By the end of the school year, Hank had finally grown a few more inches. Either way, he didn't care about the bullies calling him names anymore.

That first week of summer vacation, his neighbor Chet snuck four cigarettes from his parents' drawer, and he coaxed Hank to smoke with him in the alley. *It can't be that bad since Pop smokes a pipe.* But when Hank took a deep puff of the lit cigarette, he was sure he was going to cough up his lung. By the time Hank smoked the second cigarette, he wasn't coughing anymore.

After that, Hank got a job as a paperboy and started spending most of his money on cigarettes. He hid them from his parents, but Pop smoked a pipe and an occasional cigarette, so he probably wouldn't be all that mad at Hank. Instead, it was Ma's response that worried him.

Midway through summer, Hank had his first real kiss, with tongue and all. He'd reached first base. The girl was older and lived on a different block. Some kids were playing outside that evening. The girl pulled him aside and took him by the hand to a secluded corner beside the public school. He didn't even know the girl's name.

Hank stopped having wet dreams because he frequently hit a base hit by himself. He wasn't hurting anyone by doing it, so he didn't confess it anymore. God would understand. After all, He was the one who gave Hank his sex drive. Did God expect him to wait until marriage to get off?

Pop had finally taken three days off that summer. He went with Hank, Uncle Edwin, and Billy down the shore to swim, fish, and stroll along the boardwalk. They stayed at a campground near the bay, pitched a tent, and grilled hot dogs and hamburgers on the charcoal grill.

Of course, with Pop and Uncle Edwin around, Hank tried not to smoke, but he couldn't help sneaking one every few hours. Uncle Edwin finally caught him smoking behind an old, abandoned shed just outside the campground.

"Buddy, you're not smoking, are you?"

Hank dropped his cigarette and stepped on it, but not before Uncle Edwin had seen it. "Uh, yeah, Uncle Edwin, I am." He picked up a smooth stone and turned it over in his hand. "Started at the beginning of summer." He whipped the rock toward the water lapping in the bay.

Uncle Edwin sighed, his gaze dropping to the ground. "Well, you might as well tell your father. He's the one who asked me to search for you. He thought you might be smoking."

"I guess I can't keep too many secrets from Pop."

"No, you can't."

Well, there's one secret I kept from him.

They spent their last day at the beach and on the

109

boardwalk, where they could visit the shops and go on rides.

Hank enjoyed searching for unique seashells and found quite a few that day.

Uncle Edwin took many photographs of Hank and Billy. Pop kept saying, "Make a copy of that one for me, Ed." Hank wondered why Pop didn't own a camera. It was the modern mid-20th century, so most families owned one. Heck, most families in their neighborhood didn't own a dryer, but they all seemed to have a camera.

On the boardwalk, Hank purchased a box of salt water taffies, and Pop let them go on two rides.

It was the best summer ever.

By the time he returned for sophomore year, Hank felt like a real man. He smoked and had some experience with girls. Yes, life was good.

Chapter 24
Evie
No Date for the Prom
May 1984

Here it was, the afternoon of prom night of Evie's senior year. She would've loved to have gone, but no one asked her. No guy wanted to date someone who looked like a little girl. Even her crush, who had redeemed himself, would be taking the pretty—and normal-sized—captain of the cheerleaders.

All of her siblings were preparing to go out on dates—even her mother—and just about every classmate at her high school was getting dressed up for the prom.

She walked up to the Dairy Queen. It was a warm, not-too-hot day. When the server asked her what she wanted, she said, "I'd like a lime float, please."

The girl was younger than Evie. "Now, honey, do you want the kind with ice cream or without?" The server spoke to Evie as if she was a ten-year-old.

"I'd like the float, which has ice cream."

"Okay, sweetie."

She paid the girl, who handed her the float. Evie then said, "Oh, by the way, I'm eighteen. And I know what a float is."

The server's eyes widened. "I'm sorry. I was sure you were a little kid."

Evie sighed. "Well, I'm not." She realized she spoke abruptly, but today was not a day she was happy about being short and young-looking.

She finished the lime float and stopped at the corner store to pick up a few Caramallows to eat later while she was sulking. Chocolate-covered caramel marshmallows always made her feel better.

At home, she popped a frozen dinner in the oven and relaxed on the couch to watch TV. Her heart ached. Not only was she missing her prom, but even Fluffy couldn't keep her company since she had passed away the year before.

At times like these, she missed her father the most. When they were the only ones home, they played Rummy or Parcheesi or just enjoyed old reruns of *Twilight Zone* or *Gomer Pyle*.

Evie's heart ached, and she let the tears flow. She missed Dad so much. Did Dad go to his prom? Evie had a vague recollection of seeing a photo of Dad dressed up in a tux with a pretty girl in front of a Christmas tree.

She turned on the TV to watch *The Love Boat*, took out the Caramallows, and popped one in her mouth. The smooth caramel and chocolate eased her loneliness. If she wasn't going to have a love life, then she could at least watch a TV show about others enjoying theirs.

Chapter 25
Hank
Home Run
December 1957

Hank was now a senior in high school, and he had grown to five feet, five inches. Earlier that day, Hank heard upperclassmen teasing a Negro freshman, so he spoke up for the kid. They just happened to be on the steps under the archangel statues. If the archangels weren't going to help the students at this school, Hank would. Instead of stopping their name-calling, the bullies called Hank an N-lover. He scoffed at their lame attempt. Those names—and bullies—didn't bother him. Hank was now a senior.

He put his hand on the boy's shoulder. "Where are you going?"

"Fr. O'Reilly's class."

Hank tensed. "Um, right." He walked with the boy to the top of the steps. "I hope those guys don't trouble you again."

"Me too. Thanks," said the boy.

Before he turned to leave, Hank said, "Listen, if any teacher asks you to work after school, tell them you're too busy at home and couldn't possibly spare the time."

The young black man squinted. "Um...okay." Then he walked away.

Hank's thoughts shifted to his plans for the end of the school year. Hoping to travel the world, he'd decided to enlist in the Marines. His parents thought it would be a good experience for him.

Tonight, however, he'd settle for a little fun. He worked at Vincent's Market only two nights a week, Mondays and Thursdays, so he had this night, Friday, off. He had been going steady with a girl he met at a game last September, Gayle. He really liked her. She was a bit shorter than Hank, and she was great fun. And pretty, with dark eyes and wavy hair and curves in all the right places. He couldn't see himself married to her because she wasn't Catholic, but they could have fun together.

Hank borrowed the car from Pop. He and Gayle went to the drive-in theater to see *The Blob*.

He and Gayle didn't watch much of the movie because they started kissing, and he ended up on second base. When guilt started to wedge its way into his mind, he dismissed it. Why should he worry about it? He wasn't hurting anyone; he and Gayle were just having fun. They weren't actually having sex, so he wouldn't even need to confess it the next time he went to Confession.

***

Hank took Gayle to his Christmas prom at Archangels on the day after Christmas. When she came down the stairs at her parents' place, his eyes just about popped out of his head. Her dark hair was up off her shoulders, her makeup was perfect and not overdone, and a white furry stole covered her strapless blue dress. He was so proud to have a pretty girl on his arm at the senior prom.

Her parents took pictures of them in front of her family's Christmas tree. Gayle's family was agnostic, so why did they have a Christmas tree?

Back at his folks' house, Uncle Edwin took photos in front of their Christmas tree.

When they entered the hall in South Philly, Hank felt like he was on top of the world. Green garland and red bows and Christmas trees covered in glittering tinsel and lights adorned the venue. Gene Autry's "Rudolph the Red-Nosed Reindeer" played over the speakers. They danced, drank punch, and sang Christmas carols—or at least they tried to remember all the words. He and Gayle never stopped smiling.

He waved to Chet and his girlfriend while Gayle recognized a girl from her public high school and started chatting with her. She held an empty punch glass, so Hank asked if she wanted him to get her another glass of punch. She nodded.

He crossed the room to the refreshment table and ladled punch into Gayle's glass.

While studying the array of cookies and finger foods, someone tapped him on the shoulder. He turned, ready to greet a friend, but then drew back and sucked in a breath. His heart pounded in his ears, and time stood still.

"Hello, Hank. It's been a while." Fr. Tim leaned in close and whispered, "Look at you. You're all grown up and dating a lovely girl."

The priest's aftershave made him nauseous. Hank backed up a few more steps.

"Why don't you introduce me to your girlfriend, Hank?"

Hank couldn't speak. He couldn't think. He glanced back at Gayle, who stood talking to another girl.

"Come on, son."

Son? All Hank could do was shake his head, turn around, and rush back to Gayle. His hands shook so hard that he spilled red punch on his suit. *Ma's going to be mad about that.*

"Here," he said, handing her the glass of punch.

Hank stood beside her, his back to where the priest had been, and he tried to act as though nothing bothered him. He spied a friend not too far from them. "Oh, look, um... there's Chet and his, uh, girlfriend. Let's go talk with them."

"Hank, are you all right? You seem jittery."

That's because I am jittery. "Yes, yes, I'm fine. It's

115

...nothing." In the past three years of attending Archangels, he rarely saw the priest. When he did, he hightailed it in the opposite direction. Why did he have to show up *now*?

Gayle's eyes twinkled, and she smiled. "Why don't we leave and park somewhere?"

Hank nodded. "Yes, that would be great."

They left, and Hank drove to one of their favorite parking spots in Fairmount Park, a secluded area behind the old Centennial Art Museum. Hank had only been to second base with Gayle, but tonight, she seemed to be allowing him to go further. Unable to think rationally, he tried to focus on the pleasure to erase the images of the priest's head in his lap. He couldn't believe it when she nodded for him to go for his first home run. Just before he hit home, Gayle whispered, "Pull out, Hank. I don't want to get pregnant, not yet."

It took every ounce of self-control, but he did as she told him. Still, it was the most exquisite pleasure he'd ever had.

Arriving home after one in the morning, Hank used his key to unlock the door. He hung his coat in the closet and padded up the stairs. After changing into his pajamas, he climbed up to his bunk.

That evening held the most incredible moment, and he'd remember it forever. Still, guilt niggled its way into his heart. He probably wouldn't marry Gayle. They were just having fun, weren't they?

Hank considered going to Confession to confess the sin of "fornication," but he decided not to. He was pretty certain he'd do it again if Gayle agreed. He made a mental note to buy condoms before they went out again.

When his parents tried to wake him for Mass the next Sunday, Hank told them he wasn't feeling well. Without Confession, Hank couldn't receive Holy Communion. Twelve years of Catholic education taught him that if he was fornicating, he was in mortal sin, and he could not present himself for Communion.

His parents didn't try to wake him after that. He overheard his parents' muffled conversation in the hallway one Sunday morning about Hank's "lack of faith practice" (Ma's term). Pop responded, "Let's give him some leeway. Hopefully, he'll return."

Hank enjoyed sleeping in on Sundays, especially since he and Gayle had been out late on those previous nights.

***

Smoke swirled up from chimneys, and a flock of birds took to the sky, greeting the early spring morning as Hank and his father drove back home from the recruiting center. Hank couldn't believe it was April already. He just filled out his paperwork and signed his name. In two more months, he'd graduate, and on July 1st, he'd head off to basic training in South Carolina. He was excited to tell Gayle that there was no turning back.

Later that evening, for their regular Friday night date, Hank took Gayle to the drive-in theater. Bursting with excitement, he wanted to tell her the news before they did anything else. "So, it's official." He twisted toward her and rested an arm on the back of her seat. "I'll be flying out the first of July."

Gayle's eyes shifted away from him, the pleasant smile on her face fading. She made no reply.

"Aren't you happy for me?"

"Where does this leave us, Hank?"

"I don't know. I'll be home on leave at least once a year."

Tears welled in her eyes; then, she covered her face just before a sob escaped.

"Hey, you don't need to cry. You can write to me."

Gayle nodded, pulling a handkerchief from her purse.

Hank made a move to hop into the back seat when Gayle put her hand out to stop him. "Hank, this is all we do together. We don't even talk anymore."

"Well, that's what couples do, right?"

"But we're not married. Either promise to marry me before you leave for the Marines or find someone else."

Hank's mouth fell open. Was Gayle giving him an ultimatum? Hank slumped back into his seat.

"Please say something. You do want to marry me, right, Hank?"

"I-I'm not...I don't know."

Gayle shifted in her seat and turned away from him. "Please take me home then. We're finished."

The drive to Gayle's house was silent, except for her sobs. He felt terrible for her, but he was also angry. Gayle had no right to give him an ultimatum.

As he pulled into the driveway, she flung open the passenger door and exited, just as the car stopped. She didn't even say goodbye or goodnight; she just slammed the door and ran to her house.

Since his night had been cut short, he parked Pop's car back in the alley and decided to go for a walk. He hadn't gotten too far when he heard his name. He turned to find Carlo hanging out of a second-floor house window.

"Hi, Carlo. What's going on?"

"Dino and me are heading into Center City. Wanna come with us?"

Hank shrugged. "Sure." He had nothing better to do.

The three young men took the bus to Center City. On the way, Dino whispered to Hank, "My brother gave me the address of an underground bar that serves beer if you're eighteen and over. And there are girls."

That piqued Hank's interest. "Yeah?"

"Yeah," Dino answered.

Hank had enjoyed an occasional beer at home but never in

public because the age for drinking was twenty-one. That seemed odd, though, since Hank could join the Marines at age eighteen.

They got off at Broad and Snyder, a busy intersection for this time of night, people strolling under red awnings, heading from one club to another. Hank and Carlo followed Dino as he searched for the place.

With the warmer temperatures, the sounds coming from the bars, and the bright streetlights, this evening felt more like summer than spring. When Dino said, "I think the underground bar's over here," Hank wondered whether this bar was actually underground.

They came to a two-story home squeezed between two shops. "This way." Dino led them down a stone walkway and around to the back of the building, where an empty planter sat next to an unmarked door. Dino knocked.

A giant of a man answered the door. "Yeah?"

Dino pulled the card from his pocket and handed it to the man. "My brother gave me this card. You have a bar and girls downstairs?"

Ah, it is underground!

"That'll be ten bucks apiece, gentlemen." The giant held out his hand.

Ten bucks? Highway robbery. That was just about his entire weekly salary. Hank glanced from one friend to the other—both seemed equally bothered by the price—then he pulled out his wallet. Since he was already here, he might as well give it a try. He gave the man two five-dollar bills, and the others did the same.

They stepped inside to another world. Girls were hanging off every guy, and glasses of beer and girly magazines were available on every table. Hank picked up a glass of beer and took a sip. Then he paged through one of the magazines and wondered if he'd be allowed to keep it.

119

A girl with heavy makeup and dressed in a bikini came up to him. "First time?"

"Uh, yes, ma'am."

"You don't have to call me ma'am. I'm Kit. What's your name?"

"Hank."

"Well, I'm pleased to meet you, Hank. Want to go in the back room?"

Hank's eyes widened. Was she a prostitute?

His hand reached into his pocket. "Uh, I don't have any more money. Sorry."

"The first time is free, honey."

"Really?" Hank couldn't resist. He glanced around. Groups of men and scantily clad women filled the small, smoky bar, but he couldn't spot Carlo and Dino anywhere. Had girls lured them away too?

The girl in the bikini led him to a back room. Couples traipsed through the dimly lit room, finding couches and corners but no privacy. Hank found himself with—what was her name? Kit?—on a couch across from another guy and girl. He'd wished he brought more money but accepted what Kit had to offer, then returned to find his friends. Finding them "busy," he decided to leave on his own.

No need to stay. Hank was out of money, but he now knew where this place was, and he couldn't picture himself *not* returning. On his way out, he picked up a girly magazine and stuck it in his coat. No one seemed to care. On the bus ride home, he thought about Gayle. She was right to break up with him, he guessed.

Guilt niggled his conscience. Gayle had broken up with him, so what he'd done tonight didn't matter. And the girl in the bikini didn't have a problem with it. Why should it bother him? He hadn't hurt anybody. The girl had simply performed a service, probably got paid for it by the establishment. And heck, girls like that have been around since the beginning of time. Besides, it wasn't like they'd actually had sex.

When he returned home, he stowed the magazine under his pillow, but he'd have to find a better place for it, so Ma didn't find it—or Billy, for that matter.

He slept in the following morning since it was Saturday. When Billy went out that afternoon, Hank searched his room for a hiding spot. Pulling out shoeboxes, shoes, and boots from his and Billy's closet, he discovered a loose floorboard. He could lift it easily. He shoved the magazine into the tiny, dusty space and covered the floorboard again with the shoeboxes. Hank was pretty sure his mother wouldn't find it. If she did, it wouldn't matter that he was eighteen going on nineteen. It wouldn't matter that she hadn't beat him since the cookie fiasco in freshman year. She'd smack the skin right off his legs.

***

Hank stared at his reflection in the mirror of the bathroom as he shaved. Graduation day. He didn't sleep well last night because he knew he would be attending the graduation Mass but would not be going to Communion. He would likely be the only graduate not receiving. But he hadn't been to Mass or Confession in months, and he wouldn't present himself for Communion in the state of mortal sin.

God will understand, Hank told himself. He thought about the past few months and his visits to the underground bar and going all the way with prostitutes. While the experiences had not satisfied him emotionally, like when he'd been with Gayle, he considered them as essential as breathing. He couldn't explain why, but it took this physical pleasure for him to find satisfaction in life.

In the living room, he fumbled with his tie.

His father, dressed in a suit and tie, came to the rescue. He set a box on the coffee table and reworked Hank's black tie. "Son, you'll have to learn how to do this before you leave for the Marines."

"I know, Pop."

"Your mother and I want you to have this." Pop grabbed the box he'd set on the table and handed it to Hank, a small, gift-wrapped box. He called to Ma in the kitchen. "Hank's opening our gift."

His mother came into the living room, drying her hands with a dishtowel. "Open it, Hank."

Hank ripped the paper and lifted the lid of the box to reveal a crisp twenty-dollar bill and a small fabric case. The case held a sparkling blue set of rosary beads. While appreciating the beautiful rosary, his lack of faithfulness flitted to the front of his mind, and his heart sank for a second. "Thanks, Ma, Pop. This is great."

Pop patted Hank on the back. "We know you don't go to Mass anymore, but your mother and I wanted to make sure you don't forget your faith. It's an important part of your life. And these were blessed by the Holy Father in Rome."

"You don't say. How did you arrange that?"

"A friend of mine went to Rome two years ago, so I gave him money to buy these for you. We didn't realize that you would stop going to Mass...but..."

"Someday, I'll go back, Pop."

"In the meantime, we'll pray to Our Lady to keep you safe, son."

"It's not like I'll be fighting in a war, Pop."

"I know, and we're thankful for that."

At the graduation Mass at Saints Peter and Paul Basilica, his parents and Uncle Edwin sat in one of the far-back pews. When the line formed for Communion, he scooted back to allow his fellow graduates to pass. He was sure he'd seen more than a few of his classmates at the underground bar, but maybe they'd gone to Confession. A few fellows scowled at him as they awkwardly stepped over him. Others snickered as if finding it funny that Hank wasn't going to Communion.

At the end of the Mass and graduation, Uncle Edwin took photographs of Pop, Ma, and Hank in his cap and gown. He wished his parents would buy a camera.

The day passed in a flurry of excitement. They returned home for a luncheon. Aunt Miriam and Uncle Edwin gave him a card with a fifty-dollar bill inside! That was like a month's salary. Hank hugged both of them and thanked them for their generosity.

Hank picked up a bottle of beer from the table and sat in the armchair by the staircase. Aunt Miriam and Ma stood next to the banister and chatted about going to the Korvette's Mall in Audubon, New Jersey, next Saturday to shop.

Aunt Helen, Ma's twin sister, came in with her daughter, Cathy. He liked Aunt Helen and his cousin, but he didn't see them too often.

Cathy and Aunt Helen hugged everyone. When they came to Hank, his aunt kissed his cheek and gave him an envelope. Hank opened it to find a "Congratulations on your graduation" card and twenty-five dollars in cash.

"Thank you, Aunt Helen." Hank stuffed the cash in his pocket, along with the other money he'd received.

Aunt Helen sat down on the other side of Ma, who now sat in the middle seat of the couch, Aunt Miriam on the other side. Cathy, the same age as his sister Helen, joined his sisters in serving people. Hank watched as Aunt Helen whispered a joke to Ma and Aunt Miriam, who then bellowed in laughter. Aunt Helen was quite a personality. Hank couldn't understand how his mother and Aunt Helen were twins. They weren't identical in anything except their birthdate.

Pop stood next to Uncle Edwin. He smoked his pipe as Uncle Edwin took a drag of his cigarette.

He would be leaving these people behind when he joined the service. This was his family, and he was grateful for them.

With the gifts he received today, Hank now had over $300 to take with him into the service. He thought about spending some of it at the underground bar, but that felt wrong. Besides, his plans for the near future promised him more than a dark Philly bar.

Hank hoped that he'd be going to Europe after basic training. He'd heard from Dino's brother that the lifestyle was much freer there, especially in France. Hank could only imagine the pleasures he could attain with those foreign girls.

Chapter 26
New Love
June 5, 1962

Hank peered out the window of the airplane at the ground below. Before enlisting in the Marines, he had never been on a plane. Now, flying was routine. He'd flown to California, to England, to France, and to Germany.

After four years in the service, he'd received an honorable discharge and was now moving back home. Life had changed. He had learned much and had been with more girls than he could count. Although he'd never gotten much leave—or free time—every port had plenty of ladies willing to run the bases with him. A bit of sadness stirred inside him. Yeah, he'd been living a sinful lifestyle, but God understood, right? God knew the strength of his sexual desire.

Maybe one day, he'd get married and settle down. For now, though, he couldn't seem to get enough of girls. Having so many different partners eventually caused him to come down with the clap a few months ago. After a strong dose of antibiotics, it finally cleared up. But he now hesitated to be with loose women. Loose. He scolded himself for thinking of them that way. They weren't playthings.

He cringed as he thought of his sisters. The girls he slept with had families. They were real, breathing human beings who deserved better from a guy.

Hank shook his head. Maybe it *was* time to settle down.

Someday, he'd return to the sacraments. He patted his pocket that held the rosary his parents gave him when he graduated. He hadn't recited many Rosaries in the past four years, but he did say a couple decades when the military

125

airplane he was on experienced mechanical problems, and he thought he might crash in the ocean. Thankfully, the plane landed safely.

All in all, he hoped that once he arrived home in Philadelphia, he would find the right girl, settle down, and get married as soon as possible. Getting married meant being able to run the bases with the girl you loved anytime you wanted.

***

The taxi pulled up to his parents' rowhome. He paid the driver.

Out of his siblings, only fifteen-year-old Tess still lived at home, and when he stepped inside their living room, she squealed with delight and hugged him. His mother was more subdued. Hank kissed her on the cheek. She said, "You look good, Hank. Oh, and make sure you find yourself an apartment. You can't stay here too long."

"Yes, Ma. I told you I'd get a place."

Ma motioned for him to sit on the couch. Then she stepped into the kitchen.

"Hey, big brother," Tessie said. "I've already set up a blind date for you this Friday."

He laughed. "What? With who?"

Tessie sat on the coffee table. "My friend Joan's older sister. I happened to mention that my brother was returning from the service, and she seemed interested. She said she's seen you at church. And she's pretty."

"Do I know her?"

"Probably not." Tessie leaned in and whispered, "You probably haven't been to church since before you enlisted in the Marines."

"When is this blind date scheduled to happen?"

"This Friday. And hey, it's just for a fun time. It's not like you have to marry this girl." She gave him a playful punch to his shoulder.

"All right."

Tess handed him a piece of paper with instructions to meet one Bernadette Marie Shaw at Luigi's Restaurant in Center City at 6:30 p.m. Tessie went on to say that Bernie knew Helen from Hallahan and suggested that Helen and her boyfriend come as well, so it wouldn't be too awkward.

"And did Helen and her boyfriend agree to this?"

"They did."

"Well, I guess that's all right. But you know better than to make plans without my permission."

"Since when do I need your permission to set you up on a date?"

Hank shrugged. Tess certainly had a mind of her own.

His mother brought him a glass of Coke and swatted at Tessie to get off the coffee table.

"Thanks, Ma." He drank it dutifully but wished she would've brought him a beer.

When Pop arrived home, Hank gave his father a bear hug. Out of everyone in his family, he missed Pop the most. He hadn't met many kind men in the service.

"So, how's it feel to be out of the service?"

"Different. I'll probably wake at 5:00 a.m. tomorrow just from habit." Hank lit a cigarette.

"Nothing wrong with that, son." His father sat in the armchair across from him and lit up his pipe. "You said in your last letter that Paris was your favorite place in Europe."

"That's true. I couldn't speak much French, but I learned quickly enough to say important things."

"Like what?"

"Ah, well...." *Voulez-vous couchez avec moi* was not a phrase he wanted his father to know he used. He cleared his throat. "*Qu'est-ce que ç'est?*"

"What's that?"

"Yes."

127

"It means, what's that?" His father let out a hearty laugh.

"Something like that." Hank took a drag on his cigarette then stamped it out in the ashtray.

"What's the Eiffel Tower like? That's one landmark I'd like to experience someday."

"It's wonderful and gigantic. You can take two elevators, one to the second level and one to the very top." Hank had gone there several times, always with a different girl.

"Hard to believe that the people of Paris initially hated it." Pop took another puff of his pipe.

"I enjoyed sitting on the *Champs-Élysées* in the outdoor cafés. The *Champs-Élysées* is the street that leads up to the Arch of Triumph."

"One day, you and I will go to Paris together. What do you say?"

"Absolutely, Pop!" His father's warm demeanor truly made him feel at home.

"As I told you in my letter, you'll be starting work next Monday. We can go to work together."

"Not if I don't live here."

"What?"

"Ma's telling me to find my own place soon."

"Well, she's got a point, but you don't need to rush it."

Hank nodded.

Later that night, he went up to his old room and opened the closet door to find everything he owned in the world. He was grateful that Ma had not thrown out his stuff. He specifically asked her not to do that. Feeling a bit sentimental, he lifted an old shoebox from the closet shelf, opened it, and pulled out his transistor radio. He immediately turned it on to WIBG, and "The Twist" by Chubby Checker roared from the small radio.

Next, he reached into the box and found his seashell collection from down the shore. Every year they went to

Atlantic City, Hank collected seashells, especially those with unique shapes and colors.

Box in hand, Hank sat on the bottom bunk. It hadn't been slept in for some time because Billy hadn't been home since he started college.

He pulled his high school yearbooks from the box. *Good ol' Holy Archangels High.* He flipped through the pages of his senior yearbook then took out the other ones. His journal lay at the bottom of the box. He smiled as he read the first page, an entry from Christmas of 1954. Then he scanned the story on the next page and tensed.

His insides threatened to blow up. He tried to ignore it, but his hands clenched, and he wanted to punch a hole in the wall. The only thing that stopped him was knowing Ma would have a fit if she found a hole in the wall. Maybe he should take up boxing. Then he'd get to punch something all the time.

He hadn't felt such rage in a long time. In the service, he was so busy that he rarely had time to think about anything. He took a deep breath and exhaled but didn't feel much better.

Hank returned the journal and yearbooks to the box, put it away, and went downstairs.

His parents sat on the couch, watching *The Dick Van Dyke Show.* He sat next to his mother. He didn't know who Dick Van Dyke was, but the show was funny, and Hank laughed along with his parents.

Once that show ended, his parents retired for the night, so Hank returned to his old room. He went to the closet and lifted the loose floorboard. All these years, his girly magazine collected dust under the floorboard. He paged through it. Back in high school, this stuff turned him on, but pictures were a poor substitute for the real thing. He returned the magazine to his hiding place and made a mental note to burn it.

When he hopped onto his old bunk bed that night, he was surprised to find that his feet edged off the bed. He remembered so many nights wishing his feet would hit the end of the bed. He wasn't the tallest person now, but five feet, five inches was better than five feet even.

Friday evening came. Helen called and left a message for Hank that she, her boyfriend, and Bernie would meet him at 6:30 sharp at the Italian restaurant.

He stared in the mirror at his reflection and fixed his necktie. His face had filled out a bit over the past four years in the service, probably because of the exercise and the chow. He combed back his hair and checked his watch. 6:00 p.m. He'd better get moving.

"Thanks for letting me borrow the car, Pop."

"Just like old times, son. Bring it home in one piece."

"You bet."

Hank cranked the key in the ignition of the same '51 Ford Squire that Pop had bought ten years ago, still running smoothly after all these years.

He arrived at the restaurant around 6:20 and handed his keys to the valet at the front to park.

Hank strolled into the restaurant and asked the maître d' if the Gallagher party had arrived. The maître d', a tall man with a mustache, indicated that they hadn't.

He stood next to the gigantic marble fountain and scanned the candlelit tables and the grand staircase that led to more tables on the second floor. Luigi's was a fancy Italian restaurant. He wondered if Helen had picked this place out.

He tugged at the sleeves of his sportscoat. Then he lit a cigarette and stood by the window, watching people stroll by. Maybe he could get a glimpse of Bernadette Shaw before she saw him. Three people passed the window. He recognized his sister's short stature. The other young woman towered over Helen. She had to be what? Five feet, eight? Deflated, Hank tried to console himself. What was he expecting? He'd enjoy a nice dinner and friendly discussion.

He turned just as Helen approached him and stamped out his cigarette in a fancy pillar ashtray.

She hugged him. "You look great, Hank. Welcome home."

"Thanks, sis."

"This is Murray, my boyfriend. He's in the Army."

Hank shook hands with the fellow, a slender man with dark eyes and a receding hairline. His smile put Hank at ease immediately.

"And this is an acquaintance of mine, Bernie Shaw. Bernie, this is my brother Hank."

Glancing down, he noticed that she wore two-inch heels.

When his gaze finally met hers, she said, "Nice to meet you, Hank." Her intense, dark eyes seemed to stare into his soul. Tessie wasn't kidding when she'd said that Bernie was pretty. She was *gorgeous.*

"The pleasure is mine." Hank shook her hand. Unlike most girls, Bernie had a firm grip.

The maître d' with the mustache escorted them up the grand staircase to the second floor to a table next to another marble fountain. Murray held out a chair for Helen, and Hank did the same for Bernie. Once they were seated, a waiter asked if they wanted anything to drink. Murray ordered a Budweiser, so Hank did the same. Bernie asked for a Pepsi. Helen asked for a glass of Cabernet.

"One bill, gentlemen?"

Hank and Murray exchanged glances, but Hank had already decided to splurge. "One bill, and I'll take it."

"Thank you, Hank," his sister said.

Bernie took out a cigarette, and Hank lit it with his lighter. Then he took one out and lit it for himself.

"You'll have to pardon these high heels," Bernie leaned close and whispered.

"Pardon your high heels?"

"Yes, when my sister told me about you, she asked if I knew you. I thought I did, but I mistakenly thought I was going on a blind date with your brother. He's quite tall, isn't he?"

Hank sighed. "Yes, he's the tall one, over six feet."

"Well, I wouldn't have worn the heels if I'd known who you were."

"Don't worry about it." Hank smiled to reassure her. He had nothing against tall girls, but he sure did appreciate that Bernie wasn't as tall as she seemed at first. And he liked her voice. It wasn't super high-pitched like most girls. Instead, she had a lower-toned, even sexy, voice.

After a pleasant dinner, Hank asked Bernie if he could drive her home, to which she said yes before he could finish his question. They bid farewell to his sister and her boyfriend, and Hank escorted Bernie down the grand staircase and to the foyer, where he gave his stub to the valet to retrieve his dad's car.

He opened the passenger door for Bernie. When she situated herself, Hank closed the door and proceeded to get into the driver's seat.

"Where do you live, Bernie?"

"South Carlisle Street."

"You mean the South Carlisle Street near South Sydenham Street in South Philly?"

"Yes."

"Then we live pretty close."

"Our families go to the same church, St. Barnabas. Maybe we can go to Mass together."

Hank thought it best not to mention he hadn't been to Mass in more than four years. He *should* start attending Mass again anyway—but he'd have to go to Confession first. "Yes, I'd like that very much."

"What about this Sunday? My mother, sister, and I usually attend the ten o'clock low Mass. Do you want to walk with us to Mass?"

"Sure, that sounds fine."

Bernie made small talk until they arrived at her house at the 3000 block of South Carlisle Street.

"What's it like to be out of the service after four years?"

"Different. I'm not used to sleeping in or having much free time." He paused. "I grew up just around the corner at 29th and Sydenham."

"I'm glad you live close by."

"Me too."

He stopped the car in front of her house, got out, and opened the door for her. "Maybe we can go out next Friday too," Hank offered.

"I'd like that very much."

The two of them stood by the car. He glanced up at the rowhouse and caught sight of a bald man staring out the window behind sheer curtains—*her father. I don't want to give him the wrong impression.* "Well, goodnight," he said, then kissed her on the cheek.

She leaned in and kissed him on the lips. "Here's my phone number." Bernie dropped a small piece of paper into his palm. "Meet us here at 9:45 Sunday morning."

He nodded. Then he waited until Bernie was safely inside. He smiled during the quick car ride back to his folks' house.

Chapter 27
Evie
Someone Just Dad's Size
1987

After achieving her degree in French (with a minor in Creative Writing) at Cumberland State College in only three years, Evie took a well-deserved holiday with her sister. They traveled to Canada, first visiting Montreal and then Ottawa, the capital of Canada. Unlike most Americans, Evie knew quite a bit about Canada.

At twenty-one years of age, she still hadn't had a date or even kissed a guy. Evie had concentrated on her studies to distract her from the likelihood that she would probably never get married. But it hadn't worked. She still yearned to find someone with whom to share her life.

While in Ottawa, Deb nagged her to visit the pub down the street from their hotel, but bars were not Evie's scene. "Why don't you just go yourself, Deb?"

"Because I'm a foreigner, and what if someone speaks to me in French? I need you to come with me."

Evie sighed. "Ottawa is mostly English, Deb. Besides, I don't even drink, and you know they're going to card me."

"Sure. They may even card *me.*"

"Yeah, but you look old enough. You wear makeup, and your hair is dyed blond."

"True."

They approached the pub, and the bouncer waved Deb inside. However, Deb stopped and waited for Evie.

The burly bouncer shook his head. "Uh-uh."

In Ontario, a person needed to be nineteen to drink legally. If the experience with her father's alcoholism taught her anything, it was that drinking in excess was a bad thing.

Sure, a person could drink alcohol and not become an alcoholic, but she figured she'd stay away from it altogether.

That didn't matter to the beefy bouncer who stopped her. "No way you're nineteen."

"Way. I'm twenty-one." She produced her American passport.

The bouncer narrowed his eyes, stared at her passport photo (which Evie had to admit wasn't all that bad), then he studied Evie's face. "All right," he said. "Man, you look like a little kid."

"Thanks," she said without enthusiasm and joined her sister. *And I'm not a man,* she thought.

They settled at a table, and she asked for a ginger ale. Deb asked for a seven and seven.

While a poster outside promoted a live band, they must've been on break. Only the din of tipsy people in conversation filled the air.

Sometime later, a few men hopped onto the stage, and Evie's eyes just about popped out of her head. The lead guitarist, with dark curly hair and dreamy eyes, was gorgeous. As he stepped up to the microphone, she swooned. He sang in a smooth voice that melted her heart and demanded her attention.

Deb whispered, "He's cute."

Eyes glued to him, Evie answered, "Uh-huh."

After each song, Deb and Evie whistled and clapped loudly, with many patrons staring at them. When their set ended, Deb grabbed Evie's hand. "Let's go meet him."

"What?" Evie sucked in a breath. Should she? Could she? She went along willingly as Deb led her to the stage. As they approached, the lead guitarist placed his guitar on a stand by the wall, mumbled something to the drummer, then he noticed the girls, a smile stretching across his face.

After a few drinks, Deb was always more talkative than

Evie. "Hey, you guys are great. I'm Deb, and this is my sister, Evie." Deb had to shout over the canned music.

"Hello, Deb, Evie. I'm Jake." He held out his hand for them to shake it. "Are you American?"

"How could you tell?" Evie yelled. Even his shouting voice made her swoon, but she tried to hold it together.

"Your accent."

Of course, *he* was the one with the accent.

Evie wanted to learn more about this cute guy. He said something else, but she couldn't make it out over all the noise in the bar. "It's so loud in here," she shouted. "Want to talk outside before your next set?" She couldn't believe she just asked him that—would he think her too bold? But she really wanted to learn more about this guy.

As they stood outside, the more Evie talked to Jake, the more she was attracted to him.

They chatted until the next set. Then while she watched him play, it dawned on Evie that she hadn't asked if he had a girlfriend. So on his next break, she asked him, "Um, you don't have a girlfriend, do you?"

"No, I don't. Besides, I don't meet too many girls I'm interested in at these places."

"What kind of girls *do* you meet?"

"You know, partiers and drinkers." Jake paused. "For example, I noticed you were drinking a ginger ale, and you don't smoke." He raised his eyebrows and tilted his head.

"I don't drink or smoke."

He sighed as if he had been holding his breath. "I don't either. Plus, I'm a practicing Catholic."

Evie's eyes just about popped out of her head. Who *was* this guy? "Believe it or not, so am I."

"Really?"

"Yep." She felt a flutter in her stomach. "You don't mind that I look like I'm a little kid?"

Jake laughed. "Well, I have to admit, I thought you might be a lot younger than nineteen, but you have to be at least nineteen to make it past the bouncer."

"I showed him my passport photo." She pulled it out and showed him.

He smiled. "Nice photo. Anyway, I don't mind at all."

"Most guys do." Evie thought it odd that this faithful Catholic man played music in a setting like this. "Why do you play raunchy rock music in a bar?"

"Well, it helps pay the bills. That's the only reason." He took a deep breath of the fresh, warm air. "But I can't stand the smoking and the drinking in these places."

"Me either." Evie paused. "I never go to bars. The only reason I went this time is that my sister bugged me to go with her."

"Well, I'm glad she persuaded you."

"Me too."

"When my bandmates write more music, we're going to record the songs in a studio, and things will change."

"Cool."

When they bid farewell to each other, Jake hugged her, and she remembered her dad saying to her, *You need to find a guy just my size because you fit perfectly to me.*

Yes, this guy fit perfectly to Evie...in every way.

Chapter 28
Hank
Return to the Sacraments

Hank got up at the crack of dawn and fixed himself breakfast. His father came into the kitchen while Hank made oatmeal.

"Morning, son."

"Morning, Pop." He paused. "Hey, Pop, do they still have Confession on Saturday mornings at St. Barnabas?"

"They do. I just went to Confession myself last Saturday. The lines aren't too long."

"I haven't been to Confession since high school. I need to get back into the habit."

Pop patted his back. "I can't tell you how happy that makes me. And your mother will be especially thrilled."

"Yeah. Thanks, Pop."

On his stroll to the church, Hank examined his conscience. He realized that he had no idea how many times he missed Mass nor how many times he had fornicated since his last Confession. He'd have to give a ballpark figure. Perhaps he should even confess that he'd wanted to punch the wall the other day.

Hank decided that he would not visit the underground bar. He wasn't even sure if it was still there. He would try his best not to do a base hit by himself either, but he wasn't sure he could succeed. After all, that's what guys did, right?

However, he wanted to make a good impression on Bernie's family, and to be able to receive the Eucharist was an excellent first step.

He waited in line with the usual penitents, little old Italian widows, hunched and dressed in black, and one elderly man in a suit with his hat under his arm.

When his turn came, he stepped inside the confessional and listed everything he'd remembered. The priest didn't seem all that scandalized when Hank confessed to having sex with girls and visiting prostitutes, but the priest did advise him to increase his prayer life and start coming back to Mass so that he'd receive the graces necessary to lead a more virtuous life.

The priest gave him the penance of saying a decade of the Rosary, then Hank muttered his botched version of the Act of Contrition and thanked the priest.

Hank knelt in the pew, pulled his rosary from his pocket, and quietly recited the first Joyful Mystery, the Annunciation.

As he sauntered back home, he did feel lighter and more joyful, a sensation that he hadn't felt in a long time. Yes, Hank resolved to start attending Sunday Mass again and reciting the Rosary too. It would be a new beginning for him. He didn't know if God wanted him to marry Bernie, but he would have fun dating her to find out.

His alarm screeched at him at 7:00 a.m. the following day, and he went downstairs just as his parents and sister were on their way out the door for 8:00 a.m. Mass.

"Up early, Hank?" Pop asked.

"Yes, I'm going to Mass with Bernie's family."

"The 10:00 Mass?" Ma asked.

"Yes."

"Good for you," said Pop, and he winked at Hank.

Hank dressed in nice slacks and a tie, then he walked the two blocks to Bernie's house and knocked on the door precisely at 9:45 a.m. A chubby, curly-haired teenager opened the door. "You must be Hank. Come on in." She waved him in. "I'm Joan, Bernie's sister. I'm a friend of Tessie's. We're almost ready."

A heavyset woman with salt-and-pepper hair gazed into a framed mirror on the wall as she pinned a mantilla onto her head. Bernie, in a lovely blue dress and jacket, trundled down the stairs and took Hank by the arm.

"Mom, this is Hank Gallagher."

Hank said, "It's a pleasure to meet you, Mrs. Shaw."

The middle-aged woman must've been a looker back in the day because she had a beautiful face even now. She grinned from ear to ear. "You too, Hank. Now, we better get a move on, or we'll be late."

The four of them strolled down Pollack Street toward St. Barnabas Church. It was a warm, sunny day.

Hank had seen a bald gentleman the other night when he dropped off Bernie. To make small talk, he asked, "Where is Mr. Shaw?"

Bernie's mother said, "Oh, he went to an earlier Mass."

"My parents go to an earlier Mass too," said Hank.

Mrs. Shaw and Joan walked ahead of them.

Bernie whispered to Hank, "My father doesn't go to Mass. But that's what Mom tells us whenever we ask. Silly, isn't it?"

"Not really. I understand why she'd want to do that."

"But lying isn't good."

"No, but she's trying to raise you in the faith and protect you from the fact that your father doesn't attend Mass, and she's helping you see your father in the most positive light."

"I never thought of it that way."

They reached the church and went inside. Hank allowed Mrs. Shaw to lead the way to a pew on the right-hand side of the church, and they all knelt to pray. He had forgotten the peace that came with attending Mass. He hadn't realized how much he'd missed hearing the bells and smelling the incense.

He followed along with Bernie's Mass booklet, and if she

140

was as bright as he thought she was, she'd already realized that it had been a while, given his hesitant Latin responses.

At Communion time, he stepped back to allow Bernie, Joan, and Mrs. Shaw to leave the pew, then he followed them to the Communion rail. He knelt between Joan and Bernie. After receiving the Eucharist and returning to the pew, peace settled over him, even though he had trouble remembering the after-Communion prayers.

After Mass, Mrs. Shaw invited Hank to lunch, where she planned to warm up homemade vegetable soup and fresh bread. Hank readily accepted.

At the Shaw home, Hank finally met Mr. Jonah Shaw, who hadn't yet shaved or combed what little hair he had on his head. Hank was sure the man had just woken up.

The soup was tasty, and the homemade bread was nothing like the stuff that passed for bread in the service. It was warm out of the oven, slathered with butter.

Mr. Shaw said little during the lunch, but Mrs. Shaw spoke enough for both of them.

Hank thanked Mrs. Shaw then asked Mr. and Mrs. Shaw if he could take Bernie for a walk. Mr. Shaw said, "Bernie's twenty-one and has a mind of her own. Why don't you ask her?"

Hank stayed silent. Did he offend her father?

Mr. Shaw laughed, and Bernie giggled.

"Jonah, stop teasing the young man. Yes, Hank, I'm sure Bernie would enjoy taking a stroll with you."

Exhaling with relief, he nodded.

Outside, they walked side by side. Hank liked the fact that Bernie wore flats because they were now the same height. "Your parents seem nice."

Bernie chuckled. "Well, Mom's nice most of the time, unless you make her mad, then she'll give you the silent treatment for days. And Dad, well, he's fine when he's not drinking."

"You should meet my parents. You'll like my Pop."

"Won't I like your mother?"

"I'm sure you will, but until you get to know her, she can seem a bit standoffish."

"Do you think she'll like me?" She took hold of his hand and squeezed it, a hopeful look in her eyes.

He squeezed it back. "What's not to like?"

They sauntered along the street in companionable silence. Birds sang in the trees, the cloudless sky was a vibrant blue, and it was a warm, though not humid, day.

Bernie cleared her throat. "So, how long has it been since you've been to Mass?"

Hank tried to hide his grin. "I figured you might notice I wasn't responding too well with my Latin."

"And your knowledge of when to sit, stand, and kneel could use some work too." She giggled.

"Yes. I haven't attended Mass since high school, but I went to Confession yesterday. I'm going to start going regularly."

Bernie nearly jumped at his comment. "That's outstanding! We can attend Mass together."

Her bright expression confirmed that going to Confession and Mass was the perfect first step in getting to know Bernie better.

Chapter 29
Hank
New Job
1962

Hank appreciated having a permanent position at his father's place of employment, Eastman Chemical. Even though he and his father didn't have to leave for work until 8:00 a.m., he woke at 6:00 a.m. that Monday.

He pulled out a dresser drawer for clean clothes.

Hank and his father drove to work together. They chatted about the warm weather, then Pop said, "Tell me more about Bernadette."

"Bernie lives a few blocks over on Carlisle Street. She has beautiful brown eyes and hair and is the prettiest girl I've ever known. I like her, Pop, a lot."

"Is that so? I'd never be able to tell," his father laughed. "Her father's Jonah Shaw, right? I've seen him around the neighborhood. I believe he's a truck driver."

"I didn't ask."

"I've seen Mrs. Shaw and her daughter at Mass. They seem like good people."

"Oh, they are. And Mrs. Shaw is a great cook."

"I bet she doesn't make Gingersnap cookies as good as your mother's." Pop grinned.

Hank suddenly remembered when Ma had beaten him with the dust broom after eating all those cookies—Hank shook his head.

"What's the matter, son?"

"Nothing, Pop. Just feeling different back home again."

"Well, you'll enjoy the fellows at Eastman Chemical. And it's an excellent company to work for."

"I'm sure I'll like it, Pop, especially working with you."

"Well, I won't see you much during the day because I'm the supervisory bookkeeper. But you'll be with a great group of men in the office."

"What sort of work should I expect?"

"Xeroxing, inventory, preparing envelopes for mailing, delivering items to other departments."

"Sounds good."

Once at his desk area at Eastman Chemical, Hank settled in well on his first day. His job wasn't too difficult, and the people seemed nice. Most importantly, Pop was a kind and caring boss who never lost his temper.

Best boss ever. When he thought of the word "boss," he thought of his very first boss and clenched his fists.

Chapter 30
Evie
Wedding Bells
May 1988

When Evie returned home from that first trip to Canada, she began writing to Jake, and he wrote to her. Only two months after the first visit and after receiving beautiful poetic letters and speaking with him on the phone, Evie visited Jake. She had never felt this way about any guy and, as he had mentioned in his letters, neither had he ever felt this way about any girl. During that second trip, Jake declared his love for her, and Evie reciprocated.

After that, they visited each other every two months. After eight months of being apart, Jake got down on one knee and asked Evie to marry him.

In her bedroom a few weeks before their wedding, Evie folded her favorite throw and placed it on top of a few books and decorations in a moving box. With the wedding only a few days away, she needed to prepare for her emigration to Canada. The last item on her closet shelf, a purple blanket that she rarely used, she tossed onto the donation pile on her bed.

Then she sat next to the donation pile for a mini-break and picked up one of the books she'd stacked on her nightstand, a Natural Family Planning guide. Jake had sent it to her. She hadn't even heard of this natural method that couples could use to avoid pregnancy if they had serious need. And Church-approved too! She liked that. She and Jake planned to do everything right. They would not consummate their marriage until their wedding night—Evie sighed, her heart stirring—and they also agreed never to use artificial birth control. *All in God's hands.* That's how they both wanted it.

Next, she uncovered her father's journal and put it in the pile of items she wanted to take with her to Canada. Oh, how she missed Dad and wished he could've met Jake.

On the morning of their wedding day, she woke early. A light rain fell outside. Evie was disappointed that most of the photos would have to be indoors. But the rain brought back the kind of day it was when her father died. As much as she used to love a rainy day, now it just reminded her of one of the worst days of her life.

Evie picked up the small black-and-white photo of Dad and her. She had found it in the box of photos that Uncle Edwin had dropped off after her father died. This was her favorite picture of the two of them together, and she kept it on her nightstand. Dad sat on the grass somewhere, and Evie was safely tucked on his lap and sucking her thumb.

"You know, Eve, you need to find a guy about my size because you fit perfectly to me."

That memory filled her eyes with tears. Her stomach clenched. She was ecstatic to be marrying Jake, but something was missing because Dad wasn't here to share it with her.

"Oh, Dad," she said aloud. "First, I wish you were here right now so I could say these things to you. You would love Jake, Dad. He's about your height, and I do fit perfectly to him. So, thanks for the advice. It's hard to believe that he's never met you. He's introverted like you. In that way, he reminds me of you. But he can be goofy too.

"Second, I wish you could be giving me away today. I know you would've been a proud father, and we could've danced to 'Daddy's Little Girl' at the reception.

"Finally, you may not be here physically, but I know you're here in spirit"—her voice cracked, the tears flowing—"Pray

146

for Jake and me, Dad. I love you, and I miss you."

She put on her wedding dress, then she stuck the photo of her and Dad inside the pocket hidden in the skirt. The pocket was one of the things that sold her on the dress. She also placed her mother's lacey handkerchief in as "something old." Mom had carried that on her wedding day to Dad, and she told Evie she wanted her to do the same.

Downstairs in the living room, there was a flurry of activity. Bridesmaids had gathered, and her brothers were leaving to meet the other groomsmen at the church.

She glimpsed the tower of packed boxes in the corner that she would be taking to Canada. Evie had no idea how she had accumulated so many "things" in her life. But it consoled her to know that her father's journal and his box of treasures would be making the long trip with her.

Chapter 31
Hank
Married Life
December 1962

Absence always made the heart grow fonder. But in Hank and Bernie's case, by December, the couple spent every available moment together. Hank couldn't stand to be away from her.

Hank had presented Bernie with an engagement ring in August, and they planned their wedding for January in the new year. His folks liked Bernie, and Bernie seemed to like them, so all was well.

At Thanksgiving, Hank finally met the rest of Bernie's family: her older sister, Flora (seventeen years older than Bernie), and her brother Jonah Jr. (eight years older).

January had seemed a long time to wait. If it had been up to him, he would have pushed for an earlier wedding, but they couldn't get married during Advent, so he acquiesced.

One reason he wanted to move the wedding date closer: they had already been intimate. He didn't mean for it to happen, but they were at his house while Pop, Ma, and Tess had gone to New York City for the day. They were alone, kissing, and one thing led to another. He should've held back, but Bernie kept whispering, "We're almost married." Hank couldn't argue with that. That and the fact that it had been almost six months since he'd had sex.

And while he felt guilty that they had been intimate—and that Bernie had been a virgin—he was also glad. It made him realize that sex with a girl you truly loved and wanted to spend the rest of your life with was *so* different from "just sex." Hank recognized why the Church and Scripture called for married couples to wait until marriage.

Afterward, Bernie had said, "We'd better go to Confession this Saturday." Hank agreed.

Hank didn't like that they were sinning, even though they had professed their love and commitment for one another.

They'd go to Mass on Sunday after confessing on Saturday. By Monday evening, they were back to finding places to be intimate again. It went like that until just before the wedding.

***

January 19th dawned cold and frosty, but Hank's heart was bursting with warmth and happiness.

The flurries held off until after the reception. They made reservations for the bridal suite at the Fairmount Hotel next door to the reception. The following day, they would travel by train to New York City for a few days.

Hank made Bernie stop at the door to the hotel room. After unlocking it, he picked her up and carried her over the threshold. Though she was the same height as Hank, she was on the thin side, so he had no trouble doing so.

They were both giddy from drinking, but when they consummated their marriage, Hank truly felt like it was a spiritual experience. Afterward, Bernie exclaimed, "We're not sinning anymore!"

"Yes, I know."

After attending Mass at the Basilica in Philly the following day, they boarded the train and arrived in New York City by midafternoon. Hank hailed a cab to the Waldorf Astoria hotel.

Once inside the hotel, they registered, and a bellhop carried their two suitcases up to the eleventh floor. He unlocked the door and went inside. Hank carried Bernie over this threshold here too.

"Hank, you don't have to carry me over every doorway."

"I sure do. It's fun, and I like picking you up."

The bellhop chuckled and waited while Hank fished some coins out of his pocket for the boy's tip.

Their room had a breathtaking view of New York City and Central Park. After they unpacked, they visited the Empire State Building and Times Square before settling in for the evening and ordering room service.

After dinner arrived, they stripped down to their underwear to sit at the little table. That way, Hank surmised, they didn't have too many clothes to take off before being intimate. They ate prime rib, mashed potatoes, and string beans before a dessert of cheesecake.

Bernie ate faster than he did, so when she finished, she sat down in front of Hank and put her head on his lap to—

No! Hank's mind reeled out of control. He jumped up, knocking Bernie to the floor, and then turned away from her. His heart thudded sickly in his chest as he struggled to regain control.

"Hank!" she blurted, then her voice softened. "What was that about? You okay?"

Hank stood silent, his back to his wife. He hadn't meant to hurt her. "I'm sorry, Bern."

"I don't understand, Hank."

He hadn't thought about *that* in a long time. Shame kept him from turning to face her for many moments until he heard Bernie say, "Hank? I love you. Help me to understand why you did that."

Hank felt his wife's hand on his back, so he finally said, "I hope I didn't hurt you, Bern."

"Nah. You'd have to fling me across the room to hurt me." She chuckled.

Hank was glad that she wasn't one of those dainty, feminine girls one could knock over with a breath. He finally turned to face her.

Bernie took him by the hand and pointed to the edge of the

bed. "Here, sit, and tell me why you reacted like that."

Hank sat with his head bowed. He hated thinking about *it*, but he despised talking about *it* more. He'd just have to say it quickly. "When I was young, a priest put his mouth on me down there—"

Bernie gasped. "Oh, Hank, I'm so sorry."

"I don't want to talk about it, though. I just wanted you to know why I reacted like that."

"All right."

Hank eventually finished his dinner, then he and Bernie lay together in the king-sized bed and watched *The Ed Sullivan Show*, *Bonanza*, then *Candid Camera*. Nothing like TV shows to help one to escape from the problems of life. Besides, tomorrow would be better.

***

A few months later, Bernie informed Hank that she was expecting a baby just after New Year's Day. He couldn't have been more delighted.

They started telling people after the fourth month and, by September, Bernie was already wearing maternity tops and dresses. She continued to work part-time at Woolworth's, but she planned to quit just before Christmas.

They lived in a cramped one-bedroom apartment in Philly, about six blocks from his parents' home. Hank was making slightly more than minimum wage at his job at Eastman Chemical. Hank wished he could see more of Pop in their day-to-day work, but Pop was a supervisor working on another floor. He relished their talks to and from work every day.

On November 22nd of that year, midafternoon, Hank's father approached his desk. He rarely visited him during the day, so he wondered what was wrong. Pop's expression was somber. "President Kennedy's been shot, son. We're telling everyone to go home. I'll drive you."

"What? Shot?"

151

"Yes, he was in Dallas and is in critical condition. It doesn't look good."

"That's terrible."

"It is."

For the entire car ride home, Hank and his father quietly listened to the news coverage of the assassination attempt on the radio. Finally, a commentator came on and announced, "The news is now confirmed. President Kennedy is dead; he died at 1:00 p.m. Central Standard Time."

Both he and Pop gasped.

"I don't understand, Pop. How could anyone kill such a fine man?"

"I don't know, son."

Once home, Bernie, large with their first child, collapsed into Hank's arms. "He's dead, Hank. The president's dead."

"I know, hon."

As the two of them sat glued to the television, Hank felt a black rock of darkness in his soul. He didn't even know President Kennedy, yet here he was sobbing as if he'd known JFK his entire life. Maybe it was because Hank related to the young president with two small children. Somehow, though, thick dread squeezed his entire body. He just couldn't make sense of it all.

***

The following January, Bernie gave birth to a son. Hank had already told her he didn't want a son named after him because he didn't want the boy to be a "third." Bernie had pleaded with him, but he stood firm. So their son was baptized Mitchell Henry.

Just four months later, Bernie shared that she was pregnant again. Hank couldn't believe it. They had waited until eight weeks after Mitch's birth to become intimate but hadn't had sex often after that date. The news flooded him with confusion and dread. Now they would have four mouths to feed. Despite this, Hank made an effort to be grateful to

God that they had conceived so quickly.

Just before Christmas, they moved to a new development in Camden, New Jersey, called Fairview Manor. With his father's help, they put a down payment of ten percent toward the asking price of $10,000.

Before they finished unpacking on Christmas Eve, Bernie's water broke. She was six weeks from her due date, so the doctor warned them that if the baby *was* born, he or she might not survive.

Hank paced back and forth in the waiting room until the doctor came out to inform him that he had a daughter. He said, "She's very premature and only weighs three pounds, fifteen ounces. If you're a praying man, I'd encourage you to do so."

Hank headed straight to the hospital chapel, pulled out his rosary, and recited the prayers for his baby daughter and his wife. "Please, Blessed Mother, intercede for us that our daughter may live."

After his short time in the chapel, he took the elevator to Bernie's room.

"Did you see her yet?" Bernie sat up in bed, a tray with food in front of her. She ate a mouthful of mashed potatoes and chicken.

"No, I'm going there next."

Bernie swallowed her food. "She's so small. She's already breathing on her own." His wife smiled. "The doctor said he couldn't believe we had two tax exemptions in one year."

Hank stifled a chuckle. It *was* pretty amazing that they had had two children in the space of eleven months.

He leaned over and kissed Bernie's forehead. "I'll see you tomorrow... *Mom*."

"Merry Christmas, *Dad*."

"Merry Christmas, hon."

Next, he made his way to the newborn intensive care unit. The nurses insisted that he gown up and put on a surgical mask before going in. A heavyset nurse escorted him to the incubator. His daughter's little body had a few tabs on her chest and tubes up her tiny nose. But otherwise, she was perfect.

The nurse said, "She's breathing pretty much on her own, which is an excellent sign."

Hank nodded. He made a mental note to remember to bring holy water next time to bless his baby girl.

It was 11:30 p.m. when he returned home. Sixteen-year-old Tess greeted him at the door, dressed in her pajamas and with cold cream on her face. He couldn't help but laugh inwardly. Tess was only a teenager, and he didn't understand the cold cream on a face with no wrinkles.

Tess offered to spend the night and help eleven-month-old Mitch open his presents in the morning.

"How's Bernie and the baby?" his sister asked.

"Both are doing well, at least for now. The baby's early, so anything can happen. But we're hopeful." Hank paused. "Sis, do you mind if I go to Midnight Mass?"

"Of course not."

"I don't think I could sleep, even if I wanted to. This way, I'll get up with you and Mitch, open presents, then return to the hospital."

"Good plan."

Before Mass at St. Barnabas Church, Hank took a small bottle out of his pocket and dunked it in the holy water font. He then slipped it back into his pocket.

After such an eventful day, Hank had much to be grateful for: a new daughter (*please, God, allow her to live*), a new home, a beautiful wife, and an eleven-month-old son. He offered up this Mass for his family and for his baby girl's continued strength and growth.

Hank had a beautiful life. *Then why don't I feel good about it?*

Chapter 32
Evie
Human Life is Precious
August 1988

Evie was surprised at how quickly she became pregnant. She kept telling Jake that she was carrying twins. In her current cycle, Evie felt ovulation pain on both sides. Also, Evie's grandmother and great-aunt were fraternal twins.

At the first ultrasound, the technician called in the doctor, and they spoke in hushed tones. Evie and Jake exchanged glances. She worried that something was wrong. Instead, the doctor confirmed that Evie was right! It *was* twins! She and Jake couldn't have been more thrilled.

Evie became obsessed with doing everything she could to have a healthy pregnancy. She ate all the right foods and exercised as much as she could. She planned to remain at her job in Ottawa, at least until the end of the pregnancy. Then she would stay at home full-time with the twins.

At the ten-week mark, Evie began spotting, then bleeding more heavily. At the hospital, the ultrasound technician confirmed that both babies had already died. Her doctor recommended a dilatation and curettage to scrape out the "products of conception," but Evie told them that she'd prefer to wait for it to happen naturally.

The pain of losing her twins was more than she could ever imagine. While physically excruciating, the emotional anguish devastated her. When her precious babies finally passed, she couldn't stop weeping.

She slept a few hours a night, only to wake up and begin the process of grieving again. She just wanted the melancholy feelings to go away.

Jake tried to console her. "We'll have more babies, Eve. Just you wait and see."

Grief brought out the worst in Evie. Why had she lost the twins? She'd done everything right. Was it her fault? Could she have done better? Did she lift things she shouldn't have?

That night, Evie fell asleep in Jake's embrace, trying not to sob.

She opened her eyes to find her father sitting in the armchair of her bedroom with two tiny babies in his arms, wrapped in blue blankets.

"Dad?" she whispered, emotion choking off her voice.

"Yes, Eve. I'll take care of your babies until you can."

"Oh, Dad." Her heart fluttered like a hummingbird's wings.

He smiled at Evie then kissed each baby on the top of the head.

"Evie, wake up; you're dreaming." Jake caressed her arm.

She blinked, then opened her eyes. "Yes, I was dreaming." Evie shared her dream with Jake.

"I don't know about you, but I feel better knowing your father is taking care of our babies in heaven."

"Me too." She sighed. "What if we never get pregnant again?"

"Now, Evie, remember that it's all in God's hands. Please try to be more optimistic. We got pregnant with twins on the very first cycle we tried. That tells me God will bless us with more children."

"You're right. I need to be more positive, but it's difficult when my heart hurts so much."

"I know. But remember, since we've only used Natural Family Planning and not artificial birth control, we both understand how your cycle works more than most."

Evie nodded. She had that dream about her father for a

reason. It's the parents' job to help their children get to heaven. She and Jake now had two precious souls in heaven interceding for them. That knowledge—and seeing her father—helped ease the pain in her heart.

Chapter 33
Hank
A Profound Loss
1965-1967

Life with Irish twins proved to be more challenging than Hank thought it would be. Bernie tried not to complain, but little Deborah, at nearly a year old, now needed special braces for her legs, which were growing inward. The braces weren't cheap.

Knowing that the Catholic Church did not approve of artificial birth control, Bernie had tried using calendar rhythm. A few months back, they thought they were in the safe zone. They'd had sex on the living room floor while their toddlers slept. They hadn't had much intimacy since then, so that *had* to be the time their baby was conceived.

Unfortunately, Hank had lapsed a few times and had gone to Philly to be with prostitutes. Since he didn't actually have intercourse—just kind of stood there while they did their magic with their hands—he wasn't actually unfaithful. Right?

He just needed them for release. God would understand that Hank couldn't go that long without sex. He was only human, wasn't he?

Hank tried to remain positive, although Bernie was exhausted. Three children in just over three years. When Hank had asked God to bless them with children, he didn't expect it to happen so quickly. But Hank understood the purpose of marriage: family and children.

Just after they found out about being pregnant again, the phone rang. Bernie picked it up. "Hello? Yes, Hank's here. Just a minute." She gave the phone to Hank. "It's your mother."

"Hey, Ma. What's going on?" He watched their toddlers fighting over a truck.

"Hank, you know those bad headaches your father was experiencing for the past year?"

"Yeah?"

"Well, they just got the tests back. He's got an inoperable brain tumor and only months to live."

Hank couldn't speak. He turned away from the scene in the living room and gazed out the window at the gray day.

"Hank? You there?"

He cleared his throat. "Yes, Ma. I...I just can't believe he has a brain tumor. Pop's always been in great health."

"Yeah, I know. Anyway, they're going to send him home with some medication for pain, but he'll probably have to go back at some point towards the end."

Hank could barely understand what she was saying. "Yes, yes, okay. Um, I want to visit Pop. Would that be all right?"

"Sure, Hank. Not sure what I'm going to do without your father."

He nodded absentmindedly. "Well, thanks, Ma. Goodbye."

Bernie touched his shoulder. "Your father has a brain tumor?"

Hank said nothing. His eyes watered, but he blinked the tears away. *What am I going to do without Pop?* He tried to talk. Instead, he sobbed, and Bernie pulled him into an embrace.

The next day, Hank took the bus to Philly to visit with his father. He and his father hadn't been driving to work together since he and Bernie got married, so he hadn't seen him much, even at work. Hank knocked on the door of his boyhood home and entered.

Pop sat in his armchair beside the staircase. He looked up and smiled. "Hey, son."

"Pop." Hank knelt in front of him. Pop seemed paler than

159

he'd ever seen him. "I'm so sorry to hear about your diagnosis."

"Me too. Of course, it makes complete sense, given the excruciating headaches and the weight loss. I wish they could do something, but they can't."

"Do you want me to get you something, Pop?"

The older man shook his head.

Hank couldn't bear the thought of his father being gone. "I don't want you to die."

"You and me both, son. But if God is calling me home, I'm not going to fight it."

Hank lowered his head and blinked away tears. He had to be strong for his father. *The baby.* He'd tell Pop about their news.

"Pop?"

"Hmm?"

Hank made eye contact. Pop leaned towards him, waiting for Hank to speak.

"Bernie's pregnant again. Due in six months."

"You don't say!" Pop's pale face beamed. "Well, that's a happy announcement amidst my tumor news. Congratulations, son. You and Bernie must be so happy."

"We are. To be honest, we're a bit surprised that we've been able to conceive so easily over the past couple years. We're going to have three in just over three years."

"Children are hard work, son. But they are beautiful gifts."

"I know, Pop."

"Let's see. How many grandchildren do your mother and I have now?" He glanced up as he thought and counted on his fingers. "Helen has two. Billy has one, and you guys will have three. Six grandchildren. It's good to know that the Gallagher lineage is continuing, especially since I'm the only one in my family who's married."

Hank asked, "Why haven't Uncle Edwin and Aunt Miriam ever gotten married?"

"Guess they never met the right person."

"Right."

Pop leaned over and patted Hank on the shoulder. "Don't worry about the unimportant things, son. Instead, focus on the gift of life." He paused. "I've had a better life than most."

Hank nodded. "Well, I'm going to spend the next several months being with you, Pop."

"I'd like that, son."

"Want to watch the game?"

"That'd be great. Who are the Phillies playing today?"

"Cardinals, I think."

Hank turned on the afternoon baseball game and sat down on the couch. Pop's head lolled to one side more than once. *The pain medication must be making him tired.*

His mother came in carrying a bag of groceries. "Hank? Good to see you, son."

"Hi, Ma." Hank got up, took the bag of groceries from her, and set it on the kitchen table.

"Thank you, Hank. Going by bus is not the easiest way to shop."

"I could've driven you in Pop's car."

"Don't worry about that." Ma paused and gazed towards Pop. "He's resting. That's good."

"Yeah, I guess so." *Why did Pop have to be so sick? Why couldn't the doctors cure him?* He tried to keep his emotions in check for both his parents.

Over the next three months, Hank spent every Saturday and a few evenings a week helping his mother with Pop's care. Hank hated seeing him reduced to a mere hundred pounds of skin and bones. But Pop always smiled when he saw Hank. Last week, he and Bernie brought Mitch and Deb to visit. The expression on his father's face was so bright that

161

Hank wondered whether grandkids could be the cure-all to all forms of cancer and sickness. Pop didn't get to see Helen's or Billy's kids often because they lived out of state, so Hank was happy to bring his kids to visit. Running after two toddlers in an older couple's home was challenging. If the kids brought a smile to his father's face, it was worth it.

As Pop got weaker and lost even more weight, Hank spent every moment he could with him. Pop spoke less the weaker he became. At one point, Hank leaned over and kissed his father's forehead. Pop opened his eyes.

"I love you, Pop. You are the best father anyone could ever ask for."

"I love you too, son. You're a good son. Take care of those children of yours and tell them stories about me."

"I will." A lump formed in Hank's throat.

"Son?"

"Yes, Pop?"

Pop had an unusually serious expression and hesitated before speaking. "Something happened to you in high school. I don't know what, but I've been praying that whatever the problem was, it resolved itself."

Hank's heart started to race. He couldn't bear to tell Pop what happened, not this close to his death. "Thanks, Pop. Your prayers have helped."

His father nodded, and his eyes closed again.

Pop was transported to the hospital a few days later. They all knew, once there, it wouldn't be long before Pop entered eternal life. His siblings had visited at least once before the doctors admitted him to the hospital. Now they all gathered in his hospital room.

Pop slipped into unconsciousness, and two days later, he was pronounced dead.

The viewing and funeral Mass passed by in a blur, and when it was all over, as they stood by his father's casket at the cemetery, grief overcame Hank, and he sobbed. He didn't care that grown men were not supposed to cry. He loved his father deeply. How does one ever get over that kind of loss?

The following two months were busy at work, with one temporary boss after another. No one could ever replace his father.

The new baby wasn't due for another five weeks when Bernie's water broke, and she gave birth to another daughter, also premature but breathing well on her own.

His heart was still raw with grief, but when he gazed at their new baby girl, it was the first time Hank felt like he wouldn't always be sad. The name Eve—Evie as a nickname—popped into his head. So they named their second daughter Eve.

Chapter 34

Hank

The Beginning of the Descent

May 1968

At Eastman Chemical, the new permanent boss to replace Pop was hired six months after Evie's birth. His name was John Slade, and he was middle-aged and over six feet tall. When meeting his employees, the first words out of his mouth were, "I don't care who preceded me. Things will be different now that I'm the supervisor." He scowled as if he was disciplining them, even though he barely knew them. His buzzed gray hair screamed "military," and Hank later learned that Slade was an ex-Army major.

Slade boasted about how *he* was brought on board to "save" the company from bankruptcy. "Of course, this will ensure you'll all still have jobs over the next few years." Slade paused. "As you know, the economy is tough right now."

But Hank wasn't prepared to work for such a mean-spirited supervisor. He was the opposite of Pop, whose kindness and gentle manner endeared him to everyone.

Hank nearly allowed his emotions to get the best of him one day when he overheard co-workers speaking about how much kinder Pop was than Slade. His eyes had clouded over, and he thought he might cry, but he immediately blinked to get rid of the tears.

Slade cornered Hank later that afternoon by the water cooler. "I know your father was the previous boss. I don't care about that, and I don't care about you. If you do your job to *my* standards, you'll stay. If you don't do your job to *my* standards, you'll be fired." The man's expression softened. "I'm sorry that your father died, but grief has no place in the world of business. If you can't keep your grief at home, you'll be fired."

Hank opened his mouth, but nothing came out. Had someone told Slade about his emotional turmoil? And what sort of standards did he mean? Of course, Hank would do his best. Wouldn't that be enough?

In Hank's four years in the Marines, he'd never encountered a military officer this cold and unfeeling.

In March, just two months after Slade arrived, Hank made a point of arriving a half-hour before everyone else and staying an hour after everyone had gone home. That way, Hank ensured that nothing was left undone. Slade never explained his "standards," but Hank figured arriving early and staying late would do the trick.

By Evie's first birthday, Slade's dislike for Hank became even more obvious. The man seemed to enjoy tormenting him. He'd bump Hank's desk, and the pens and pencils would scatter all over his workspace. His fellow coworkers told him that the man frequently rummaged through Hank's desk when Hank was on break.

Although Slade was mean to the others, even his co-workers watched with wide eyes as Slade seemed to take particular delight in harassing Hank over the smallest of errors. Last week, Slade tossed an envelope onto Hank's desk. "You didn't put the stamp on properly."

"I didn't?"

"No, look at it. It's crooked."

Again, Hank was speechless. How was he supposed to respond to that?

No one liked Slade, but Slade didn't appear to care. He fired a man for staring at him. He fired another for questioning his requests. And he seemed determined to fire Hank. But Hank had a wife and children to support, so Hank was equally determined to keep his job, no matter the cost.

One of Hank's great joys each day was arriving home in the evenings. His children greeted him with squeals and smiles. They were a cooling balm to the open wounds of working for a tyrant. He played with them while Bernie took a few moments to call her sister, to read, or to go shopping.

The game his kids liked the best was what Hank called "A Guy Walking Down the Street." Hank would hold one child in his arms and say, "A guy was walking down the street and, all of a sudden, he had to scratch his nose." Then he'd lift his hand to his nose and drop the top part of the child's body while he held onto their legs with his other hand. They squealed with delight, even though he did it all the time.

The other great joy of his life was intimacy with Bernie. He hated himself when he sought pleasure with prostitutes. Going to Confession after each occurrence made him feel better. Intimacy with Bernie was on a whole different level: a God-given gift that made Hank forget his problems at work.

With the joy of marital relations came another child. In September, Bernie told him they were expecting another baby in May of the following year.

Hank realized that he needed to double up and increase his efforts to do an excellent job at work. The more Hank tried, though, the more Slade singled him out.

Just before Christmas, Slade approached Hank at his desk. "I hear congratulations are in order, Gallagher." The man never smiled, but now he sneered.

"Congratulations?"

"Yes, your wife has another bun in the oven."

"Yes, sir."

"Well, just remember to stay focused on your work here. You certainly don't want to lose your job with a new baby on the way."

"No, sir."

By January, Hank couldn't sleep at night thinking about what the man would do next. Once a week, Slade reminded Hank that he could lose his job at any moment. From February to April, Hank was lucky if he got an hour of sleep at night.

Hank would come home from work in the evening mentally exhausted, scarred, and reeling from the daily eight-hour battle with Slade, who was getting under Hank's skin and making his blood boil.

As he desperately tried to fall asleep each night, he began to see his father's kind face. He sometimes heard Pop's voice in his head.

On the third Sunday in May, Hank relaxed in the living room. Suddenly, his father sat across from him.

"Pop?"

"Yes, son. It's me."

"Pop, I've missed you so much."

"Daddy, who are you talking to?" Three-and-a-half-year-old Deb patted his hand.

"Oh, um, I'm speaking to Grandpop."

"Where is he?"

"Oh, he's right there."

"I don't see him, Daddy."

"Well, he's right there."

"Okay," her sweet voice responded.

The following week included one business-related crisis after another, and thank God, Slade was preoccupied with other things.

On Friday, after work, Hank didn't take the bus all the way home. Instead, he got off at the intersection of Ferry Avenue and Black Horse Pike, then trekked the rest of the way by foot. He had to get to Cooper Hospital because Bernie was having the baby.

When he arrived, he stopped at the information desk and

167

asked which room his wife was in, but the receptionist told him there was no Bernadette Gallagher at Cooper Hospital. Hank went to the payphone and dialed their home number. Bernie answered.

"Bernie, I'm at the hospital, but you're not here."

"Honey, it's not my time yet. Why did you think you needed to go to the hospital?'

"I was sure it was your time." Hank paused. "I'll take the bus back home then."

"No, no. I'm calling your Uncle Edwin. He'll come and get you. Just wait there, honey."

"All right."

Hank sat on a bench outside the hospital. He was sure Bernie had gone into labor, and the baby was coming.

Uncle Edwin pulled up in his '64 Wagoneer.

Hank opened the passenger door and got in.

"Everything all right, buddy?" Uncle Edwin asked.

"Sure. Everything is fine."

They drove in silence, and when he arrived home, his wife, large with child, greeted him at the door and hugged him. "When you didn't come home after work, I got worried."

"Well, it's fine now."

The weekend passed with Hank still unable to sleep.

That Monday, Hank approached his desk a few minutes early. Slade was waiting for him. As his boss saw him coming, Slade yelled, "You!"

Hank groaned inwardly.

"I told you I wanted those reports on Friday. Where are they?" he screamed.

Hank froze. Slade yelled all the time, but Hank was sure the man hadn't asked him for any reports on Friday.

Slade leaned in and whispered, "You're a pansy-assed faggot just like your father."

Hank was stunned. It was one thing to say that about him,

but about his *father*? He balled his fists, rage building.

When Hank didn't answer, Slade clapped his hands and snarled, "I knew it!"

Hank's pent-up anger came from deep within and spewed out of his mouth before he could stop it. "You're an asshole!" he screamed back at him.

Slade's eyes widened, and he gasped. "What?"

"I..." He froze, rooted to the spot.

"You said I'm an asshole."

"I'm...I'm s-sorry, Mr. Slade. I didn't mean—"

"You're fired."

Hank's heart clenched, and he wanted to cry. In nearly eighteen months of holding back the rage, it had finally come out in one weak moment. He had responsibilities. How would he provide for his wife now?

Slade pranced out of the room, whistling a happy tune.

Slade finally got what he wanted.

As he cleaned out his desk, his fellow coworkers came up one by one to thank him for standing up to Slade. They had wanted to applaud his actions, but they didn't want to lose their jobs. Hank was grateful for their support, but he was still out of a job. The last co-worker gave him a twenty-dollar bill. Hank despised charity, but with watery eyes, he took the money from the man. "Thank you."

The bus ride gave him a chance to get used to the idea of being fired, but by the time he reached home, he couldn't think straight. He wasn't worried so much at what Bernie would say but at the poor prospects of getting another job with his meager high school diploma.

Thankfully, Bernie understood that working for a tyrant could only go on so long. That same afternoon, he went job hunting. Because he had been fired, he had no work references.

By the time he crawled into bed next to Bernie, despair

169

had overwhelmed him, pushing him down so far that his mind became jumbled. "Dear God, please help me," was all he could mutter as he finally drifted off to a restless slumber.

Chapter 35
Evie
A Bittersweet Anniversary
April 1992

Jake and Evie were now the proud parents of two little boys ages three and a half and two, and she was expecting another little one in a few months. Life was busy, and Evie loved it.

The 24th of this month was the ten-year anniversary of her father's death. Evie, Jake, and the children attended daily Mass that morning because the Mass intention was for her father. She was truly thankful that Jake was a self-employed musician and visual artist and set his own hours. This allowed him free time during the day. When Mass ended, he dropped Evie off at home and took their two toddlers out for breakfast at the McDonald's that had a Playplace.

During that solitude at home, Evie took out her father's nearly blank journal and the old treasure box. It had been ten years, but she still thought about him every day. Her heart still ached, but her grief lessened with the busyness of raising a family.

She picked up the journal and reread his entry about his favorite Christmas. Then she reread the story about the apprentice. She remembered reading this in the months after his death. She had wondered what had caused him to write such a melancholy fairy tale. Now, reading it again, she realized that something had happened either to him or to someone close to him.

This story made her sad. Perhaps something had happened that, as an adult, he thought wasn't such a big deal. Much like Evie when she recalled how the jock

171

basketball players talked about her crassly and how that had crushed her. Now, it seemed so stupid. Boys, especially pubescent jocks, made fun of others. That was just the way things were.

Still, she wondered.

Evie called her mother, as she did on every anniversary of her father's death. Mom was in good spirits, and Aunt Flora was with her. They chatted about how much time had passed. They talked about her little boys. Evie could then hear her aunt's voice in the background saying, "Bernie, are you ready to go to breakfast?"

Mom said, "Aunt Flora's taking me to breakfast at the diner, so I better go. Love you, girl."

"Love you too, Mom."

She hung up the phone and picked up the journal again. Her mother rarely talked about her father's breakdown. When she did, though, Evie had always been in awe of Mom's strength when Dad was in the psychiatric hospital. She had been nine months pregnant, and her water broke the day Dad had his mental collapse. Mom had told her that Aunt Flora, Uncle Edwin, and Aunt Tess all supported her during that time. Aunt Flora and Uncle Edwin had taken Dad to the hospital, and Aunt Tess watched Evie, her brother, and her sister.

Evie caressed her large stomach. She could not imagine being large and pregnant with her fourth child and her husband sinking into a world of his own, breaking from reality. Her mother had shown great courage in the face of adversity. Evie loved and admired her mother more because of it.

Chapter 36
Hank and Bernie
Descent into Madness
May 1968

Hank was so happy to be with his Pop again. He couldn't stop hugging his father. "Pop, I've missed you so much. And that tyrant who replaced you, well, he's not half the man you are."

"Well, son, some people can be mean."

"I miss you so much, Pop."

He wrapped his arms around Pop, hugging him tight, but then found his arms empty. No one was there.

He yelled, "Pop, come back. Pop, come back!"

"Hank, wake up, honey," Bernie's soft voice said.

Hank roused. Where *was* he? A cool hand touched his forehead. "Shhhh." He tried to drift back to sleep, but he lay there, eyes wide open, his thoughts a jumbled mess.

The alarm went off as usual. Hank turned to his wife and shook her hard. "Bernie, I'm not going to work today, and I'm not going to call them. They'll know why."

Bernie squinted her eyes but didn't argue. "Honey, why don't I make you some coffee?"

"No, I want a cigar."

***

Bernie sighed and patted her large stomach. This baby was due any day now, and there was something wrong with her husband. How could he forget that he was fired from his job a few days ago?

Last week, Hank walked three miles to Cooper Hospital and called her from there. She'd calmly told him it wasn't her time yet. During the past week, she found him numerous

173

times talking to no one, but Hank assured her that he was speaking to his father.

At first, she had hoped it would all pass. Then she tried convincing herself that it was just a temporary problem.

Dear God in heaven, he's having a mental breakdown. Did I wait too long to get help?

She pretended to give in to his every whim and then telephoned her sister, Flora, and Hank's Uncle Edwin.

Calling Hank's father would've been the ideal choice because Hank and his Pop had been *that* close. Unfortunately, her father-in-law had died two years ago. Bernie understood why Hank still grieved for him. Hank's Pop was the kindest, gentlest man she'd ever known.

Uncle Edwin arrived fifteen minutes after Bernie called him, and in hushed tones, Bernie updated him on Hank's condition and told him that her sister would be arriving any minute. "Where are the kids, Bernie?"

"Down in the kitchen, watching television."

"I'm going to say hi to the kids first, and then I'll see my nephew."

"Sure."

Flora arrived shortly after, and between Bernie, Flora, and Edwin, they discussed the possibility of committing Hank to nearby Pineland Psychiatric Hospital. Bernie tried to keep the conversation quiet, but her sister couldn't help herself. She yelled, "What the heck's going on, Bernie?"

Hank shouted down from the bedroom upstairs, "Is that you, Flora?" And then, "Bernie, what's Flora doing here?"

Bernie didn't respond. She glanced toward the downstairs area, where their three children watched a small portable television in the kitchen. Mitchell was only four and a half, Deb was three and a half, and Evie was two. Right now, Bernie's priority was for her kids' safety and to shelter them from whatever their father was going through.

***

Hank lifted his head from the pillow and heard muffled voices and then footsteps on the stairs. Bernie came into the bedroom and sat down next to him on the bed.

He sat up. "What's your sister doing here, Bernie?"

"Honey, do you still want a cigar?"

"Yes. Where is it?"

"Hank, I'll get it a little later, you know, when the stores open."

With that, she left quickly. Hank could hear them talking but couldn't make out what they were saying. He heard a man's voice too.

Maybe Bernie decided to divorce him and get a new husband. Yes, that's what was probably happening. And he didn't blame her if she did want a divorce. Hank was a lousy husband. Agitated, he sat on the edge of the bed, bent over, and put his head in his hands. He was so very tired. What day was it?

Hank switched on the radio. He turned the dial and stopped when he heard someone speaking about God. The preacher sounded familiar. What was the name of that bishop with the TV show?

"God is the cause of the very being of the universe. An architect looks into his own mind to understand the nature of that which he has designed. A poet knows his verses in his own mind, so God knows all things by looking at Himself. He does not need to wait for you to turn a corner before He knows that you are doing so...everything is naked and open to the eyes of God."

Hank heard the word "naked" and felt a strong urge to take off all his clothes. As the bishop on the radio spoke, Hank was seized with the idea of writing down his feelings about the sermon.

He scanned the room and searched through drawers but found no paper. He did find, however, a ballpoint pen on the dresser. He picked it up and stared at it. Then he glanced down at his naked body and began printing on it. His penis was the primary target, and he carefully printed "GOD" on it. It was no small task writing on the soft skin of his penis.

Then his arms, chest, legs, feet; he hit them all. He shook the pen once or twice to get it to write. Then he refocused on his upper thigh and wrote "GOD" there too.

He put the pen down and stared at his upper leg and penis as a vague memory pierced his brain: a man with a balding head on his lap. He began to weep. *Why am I so sad?*

Suddenly, his wife came in.

"Hank," she screamed. "What in God's name are you doing to yourself?"

Tilting his head, he immediately stopped crying, wiped his eyes, then stared at her, and began to write on himself again with his pen.

She came toward him and tried to take the pen out of his hand, but he gripped it hard. He couldn't give her the pen.

She gently wrestled it from him, and he finally allowed her to take it. She opened the dresser drawer, handed him his underwear, and squeezed his hand tightly. "Honey, put these on and try to get some rest."

"Okay, Bernie, but no sleep. I just can't sleep. You know that."

"Well, then, at least let me take you to the doctor. He can give you something to unwind you—to make you sleep."

"No doctor. We don't have the money. I'll be okay. You'll see."

He still had his underwear in his hands, so he put it on his head. *That's probably where Bernie wants me to put it.*

***

Bernie left, but she returned minutes later with Flora and Edwin. Hank was still naked, now sitting on the floor, his underwear on his head and ink marks all over his body.

Flora gasped, and Edwin stood without saying anything for a moment or two.

Seeing Hank sitting naked without any inhibitions must've been awkward for both Flora and Edwin, who both avoided glancing at Hank. Hank was typically modest. Bernie took the jockey shorts from the top of Hank's head and handed them to Edwin. "Would you mind helping him on with these, Uncle Edwin?"

"Sure." Edwin crouched down and put Hank's feet through the holes, then he slipped the shorts up and over his private parts. "Hey, buddy, what's going on?"

Hank stared at his uncle as if not sure he knew him, but then Hank said, "Uncle Edwin. What are you doing here?"

"I came to help Bernie."

"She's not going to divorce me?"

It took every ounce of self-control for Bernie not to get emotional, but she burst out, "Of course, I'm not going to divorce you, Hank." She paused. "We just want to take you to the doctor."

"All right," he finally said.

Bernie handed Uncle Edwin slacks and a shirt and asked him to dress Hank.

When Bernie turned to leave, she felt a trickling of fluid between her legs. "Damn," she muttered, "as if there wasn't enough going on."

Flora took Bernie's arm and brought her to the bathroom. So far, there was minimal fluid, but her water had without a doubt broken, and she would have to find a way to the hospital. Whether she liked it or not, Bernie would be giving birth to this baby today or early tomorrow.

"What am I going to do?" she asked Flora.

"You're not going to worry. Edwin and I will take care of this. Can you call Tess to watch the kids?"

Bernie nodded.

A short while later, Tess arrived to take charge of the

children. But who would drive Bernie to the hospital? Hank needed to be taken to the psychiatric hospital as soon as possible, but then again, Bernie also had to get to the hospital in Camden to have their baby.

Flora touched her arm. "I'll take you to the hospital now, Bern, and drop you off, then come back here and help Edwin take Hank to the psychiatric hospital."

Bernie nodded. She had no idea how Hank would react to her sister and his uncle taking him to the hospital, but she couldn't worry about that. She had to focus on having the baby.

***

Hank stayed in the bedroom and continued to listen to the radio program. As the bishop related stories from the Bible, Hank's eyes filled with tears, blurring his vision. That memory again, the one with the man's head on his lap. He blinked the tears away. His empty stomach burned, but he had no appetite for food. His whole body ached—crying out for rest—for even a little bit of sound sleep.

He wiped his eyes with his wrist and stretched out on the bed, staring at the crucifix on the wall above the dresser.

At that moment, Hank thought of Christ, of His glories while here on earth, and of His sufferings. His racing mind thought of the many ways he had hurt God. The image of the bald man's head on his lap—no, he didn't deserve forgiveness. He deserved to burn in hell. For eternity.

His father now sat beside him.

"Hey, Pop."

"Hey, son. You don't feel well, do you?"

"Can't sleep. Don't know why."

"Maybe some of your mother's cookies might help."

"Yeah, maybe."

His father no longer sat next to him. Hank wept again. Where did Pop go?

Uncle Edwin came in. "You all right, buddy?"

Hank wiped his eyes and nodded.

"We'll be ready soon to take you to the doctor."

"All right."

Uncle Edwin took a comb off the dresser and combed his hair as if he was a baby.

"I can do that, Uncle Edwin."

"Yes, I know you can, buddy. Just wanted to help. Let's go downstairs." Hank followed Uncle Edwin down the short staircase to the living room. Hank picked up a jump rope hanging on the metal railing and thought it was the most fascinating gadget he'd ever seen. He plopped down on the steps and gawked at it. He would see Pop at the doctor's office, and he wanted to bring him the jump rope as a gift. Pop would like that because Pop could tie knots with it.

Uncle Edwin led him to the couch in the living room and took the seat beside him. "We're just waiting on Flora to return. She had to...well, she had to go out for a little while."

The two of them sat stiffly and quietly as they waited. But the silence made him uneasy. Hank got up suddenly as if pulled from the chair and turned on the television.

The program on the television was a soap opera, and as he watched and listened, the characters' problems became his problems, troubling him deeply. He suddenly realized they were talking about him! Every line spoken had personal significance to him. The show was real. Hank and Uncle Edwin were part of the show.

"Why won't you help them, Uncle Edwin?" Hank sobbed again. Uncle Edwin's hand patted his back.

"Where's Pop? Pop was just here. I know he was."

Uncle Edwin cleared his throat. "Um...well, Hank, he's away."

Suddenly, Hank couldn't see Bernie anywhere. "Where's Bernie?"

"Oh, she went out for a little while too."

Chapter 37
Bernie
A New Baby and Pineland

For the next ten hours, Bernie could think of nothing else other than labor pains and delivering the baby. She gave birth to her eight-and-a-half-pound son early the following day. Gazing at his chubby face, she cried with relief and joy. She couldn't do anything to stop the world from falling apart all around her, but this baby filled her heart with hope.

A few hours later, the nurse came with the papers, so Bernie had to pick out a name. It wouldn't be any use waiting for Hank since he was in no shape to help her pick a name. In previous discussions, Hank insisted that he didn't want a Henry Francis Gallagher III, so she compromised. Little Hank, with the middle name of Jonah, would have to do for now.

Flora picked her and the baby up three days later. While she'd had no choice, Bernie felt like she had abandoned her husband during his greatest moment of need. Now that the baby was born, she desperately wanted to see him at Pineland. Visiting Hank was her top priority.

"After we stop by the house, can you please take me to see Hank?"

"Sure," Flora responded with a look of compassion.

At their home, Bernie hugged her three older children, and then she left the baby with Tess.

Flora drove Bernie to Pineland. One of the staff, a middle-aged woman in a pale blue uniform dress, led Bernie toward one of the wards. "Since he arrived, he's been very agitated. It was necessary to put him in a secured area and on tranquilizers."

"I understand," Bernie said, marching with the woman down a hall that smelled of industrial cleaners. She trembled a bit, anxious to see him. She wanted so much to tell him about their new son—whom she named after him, Henry, but without the Francis so that he wouldn't be the third— and how well the baby and all the children were doing, despite his absence.

The attendant said sternly, "Your husband had to be moved to the locked ward."

Bernie winced. They had locked up her precious Hank like a criminal. Wasn't he just sick?

As soon as the woman unlocked and opened the door, Bernie stifled a gasp.

Hank sat on the edge of his bed, staring straight ahead. He seemed worse than before he was admitted to the hospital. With shadows under his sunken green eyes, uncombed hair, and week-old beard growth, he looked terrifying.

Suddenly, Hank turned toward her. He stared, wide-eyed, and he smiled. "Bernie!"

"Oh, Hank, I missed you." She sat on the cot next to him and hugged him.

He pulled away. "I missed you too." He grabbed her arms and leaned in close. "Listen, Bernie, you need to take me out of this place. I shouldn't be here with all these poor souls."

"I'll talk to the doctor and see what she says."

"All right."

Hank started fidgeting and swatting at something she couldn't see, and then he shouted, "I don't belong here. I don't belong here. Take me home. Now!"

Bernie placed her hand on his shoulder, but he flung it away as if it was an invisible bug.

Hank got up and paced the length of the room, babbling about nonsense, growing agitation in his tone and gestures. Finally, an orderly burst through the doorway and gave him a tranquilizer shot. Then Hank lay down on the cot and fell asleep.

Bernie kissed his forehead. "I love you, honey. Get better soon." *Dear God, please help Hank.*

By the time she met Flora in the foyer, she was sobbing and shaking. Flora consoled her as best she could. Bernie stepped back and wiped her eyes.

"That bad?" Flora asked.

All Bernie could do was nod.

"Well, Hank's doctor wants you to stop by her office. It's next to the hospital. Maybe she can give us some hope."

The two made their way to the office.

"Hello, Mrs. Gallagher, I'm Dr. Charlotte Doyle, the psychiatrist in charge of your husband's case." She shook Bernie's hand.

Dr. Doyle told them that they planned to try electroshock therapy in a week to see if that might work. Bernie didn't know much about electroshock therapy, but it seemed like an archaic treatment. She also didn't like the idea of shocking someone. At this point, however, she was open to trying anything to make Hank better.

Dr. Doyle then asked dozens of questions to try to get at the root cause of his psychotic break. The doctor stated that Hank didn't remember anything from the past five years or so. Bernie shared that his father had passed a few years previous, and he had been particularly close to this father. Also, his new boss at work was cruel to Hank and fired him.

Bernie felt sick to her stomach all the way home and said little to Flora, who respected her silence. When she thought again about the doctor's questions, Bernie realized she had forgotten to mention the abuse Hank suffered from a priest during his freshman year at high school. Could that have something to do with his breakdown too?

Hank had only talked to her about the abuse once.

When Flora pulled up to their home, Bernie was convinced that she should tell the psychiatrist about Hank's abuse by the priest. It could just be the last piece to the puzzle of decoding his mental breakdown.

Chapter 38
Hank
Holly Hall
One month later

Hank balanced himself carefully and then waited anxiously for the hospital attendant to serve him the ball. He took his serve handily, and the game went on, the little white ball tapping the table, sailing over the net, tapping the table again, and the attendant's paddle. Nothing mattered at this moment except this game—he'd even forgotten where he was for a moment. What was important was that he was playing ping pong. And he was winning.

Yesterday, he'd experienced the first of a new treatment called electroshock therapy. He was asleep, and then he woke to excruciating pain in his head, a rubber thing in his mouth, and his entire body shaking.

Someone screamed, and Hank dropped the paddle as the ball came sizzling high over the net toward him. It bounced hard on the table and shot past his head, careening off the wall behind him. It took several more erratic bounces before it came to rest across the recreation room.

The fellow who had screamed was cursing now and throwing punches at other patients. He began to jab and dance about expertly, and as one of the attendants got closer, he landed a beauty of a right hook and sent the white-uniformed attendant sprawling to the floor. It took four attendants, including Hank's game partner, to quiet him down. Then, for a split second, as they led him out, a calm came over the room.

Another patient picked up the ball and motioned for Hank

to play. Hank glanced at him and smiled. The other fellow was shorter than Hank but a bit older. He had light hair and a pockmarked complexion. He wore clean but loose-fitting khaki pants and the same type of shirt that Hank wore. But this fellow's face had a pitifully sad expression that matched his bulgy brown eyes. He didn't speak. He simply held up the paddle and nodded to Hank.

The guy's mournful expression made Hank feel sorry for him, so he served the ball and played a few rounds. He purposefully allowed the fellow to win. Maybe it would brighten his day.

Then Hank ambled out of the room and onto a screened porch with tables and chairs and other patients milling about. Some sat still, and others paced back and forth endlessly. A few went from person to person bumming the most precious commodity here at Pineland: cigarettes.

Hank strolled close to the window, and his legs buckled at the knees. He was weak now, but he would get stronger. He rested his forehead against the screen and stood motionless, gazing out at the beautiful scenery. He didn't know what month it was, but it smelled of summer, and flowers and trees bloomed to their peaks. He inhaled deeply, breathing in the rich, freshly mowed lawn and the flowers in almost every scent imaginable.

"Hey, Hank, tomorrow is Sunday. Will your family be visiting again? I really like them," said a fellow inmate, who could be no more than twenty. What *was* his name?

"I hope so. They're bringing me cigarettes."

"Good, good. You're lucky to have such a nice family."

Back in his room, Hank lay on his cot and drifted off.

Hank woke to someone shrieking. He sat up. He was in a cramped room with a small bed, a night table next to the bed, and windows with bars just above the night table.

The shrieking finally stopped.

185

He craved a cigarette. Was today the day his family was coming to visit him? They usually brought him cigarettes. That always made him feel better.

His door opened. "Hank, time for breakfast in the cafeteria. Better get dressed." A fellow in a white shirt and slacks smiled. "Do you need help?"

Hank shook his head and stood up.

The man in the white slacks and shirt shut the door.

A comb lay on his night table, but where was the mirror in this room? How was he to comb his hair without a mirror?

He opened his door and stepped into the hallway. On the wall above him, he noticed the words, "Holly Hall, Open Ward, Section 2." He followed a few other fellows dressed like he was. The scent of coffee and fried potatoes made him hungry.

In the cafeteria, he picked up a tray and made his way through the food line. He yearned for a cigarette. He was hungry too, but he'd rather have a cigarette.

He sat down at a table with a few other men and ate quietly.

A crashing sound made everyone at Hank's table glance up. Shattered dishes and cups covered the floor near the food line. That'd be quite a mess to clean up. Hank was glad he didn't have that job.

The fellow across from him slurped his food.

Hank kept quiet as he ate.

When he finished, he brought his tray and dishes to the sink near the door and returned to his room.

He lay back down on his bed and dozed off. Hank woke to a loud knocking on his door. He got up and opened the door. It was a big lady with big hair and a tent-like dress. "Come on, Hank. Hurry up. Don't keep your family waiting."

Hank followed the big lady with the big hair and big dress right out the doors and into the sunshine. The sun felt good on his face. He didn't go outside too much.

The big lady with the big hair stopped and pointed. "There they are."

Hank stayed where he was.

"Well, go on. Visit your family." She shoved him, and he stumbled forward.

Near a big old oak tree in the distance, people stood around a picnic table. Mostly adults but a few kids. As he shuffled closer, he saw a playpen and an infant inside it.

All of a sudden, he heard, "Daddy, Daddy!"

Two precious little girls dressed identically rushed forward and hugged his legs.

A woman came toward him. "Hank, I'm so glad to see you." It was Bernie. She leaned in to hug him, stepping in between the two miniature girls.

"All right, Deb and Evie, let go of your dad's legs. He can't walk if you hang onto his legs."

The littlest of the girls pouted, then she cried. "Mama, want to hug Daddy."

"No need to cry, Evie. You can hug him in a few minutes."

Just then, a young woman with big blond hair came up to Hank. "You look good, brother."

He nodded.

Bernie said, "Hey, Tess, can you take Deb and Evie over to the picnic table?"

"Sure, Bern." The woman with the big blond hair took the little girls away.

"Your sister has been a lifesaver, Hank."

"My sister, yeah."

"She's been helping me every day. And your Uncle Edwin has been lending me money to pay the bills."

"Uncle Edwin?"

"Yes," she said, pointing. "He's the older gentleman over there with the cooler."

187

"He looks like Pop."

"He sure does, Hank." She took his hand and brought him to the group. There were a lot of people. A baby in the playpen, a small boy of about five gazing shyly at him, and an older gentleman—Uncle Edwin—and an older lady—Pop's and Edwin's sister. Was her name Mary, Margo?

Uncle Edwin said, "Hank, give your Aunt Miriam a hug. She couldn't wait to see you today."

He nodded and did as he was told.

Then Uncle Edwin said, "Give your mother a hug too."

Hank recognized Ma. She leaned in to hug him.

He kissed her cheek. "Where's Pop? Is he busy?"

Ma's eyebrows rose. Then she glanced at Bernie, who whispered, "Remember, Hank. Your father died two years ago."

Hank's eyes filled with tears. "I miss him so much, Bernie."

"I know you do, honey."

His mother straightened and patted him on the back. "Hank, my dear boy, are they feeding you enough here at this place?"

"I suppose so." Then he remembered the cigarettes. He turned to Bernie. "Where are the cigarettes?"

"Oh, right. They're in here." Bernie reached into her large bag and pulled out a carton of cigarettes.

Hank ripped open the box and pulled one package out. He tore that open then took out a cigarette. Where was his lighter?

Bernie tapped his shoulder, and he turned to see her holding out a lit lighter. He inhaled and immediately relaxed. He missed cigarettes.

He sat at the picnic table as the children ran around it.

"Hey, walk, don't run," Bernie said.

Then the tiniest of the walking children came over to him, patted his leg, then laid her head on his lap.

He began to tremble. Inside, a fire raged in his stomach. He couldn't let her head be on his lap. No, she had to get off! Hank pushed her away, and she stumbled into the side of the mesh playpen. She started to weep. Bernie whispered something to the tiny girl and picked her up. She stopped crying.

"Hank, why did you push Evie?"

"Did I?"

"Oh, Hank."

***

Bernie's heart ached. Hank had no idea what he was doing. At the same time, her children needed to be protected. Hank's mother, sister, and uncle all knew that he wasn't acting right and would have to be monitored. So Bernie made sure at least one adult sat with Hank at all times. Hank would *never* intentionally hurt the children and would be appalled if he understood what he just did.

The meeting with Dr. Doyle didn't give Bernie much hope. The doctor had kept him on tranquilizers to keep him calm. She also confirmed the original diagnosis of psychosis caused by paranoid-schizophrenia and manic-depression, and they'd tried several medications. One seemed promising, even to the point where they moved him out of the locked ward. But he hadn't made any progress since then. At least now, he was able to have visits with family outside.

The following week, Dr. Doyle said, they planned to try two more medications and would utilize electroshock therapy again. It would take at least five more shock treatments to figure out whether that was helping Hank.

Bernie had no idea what she would've done without Flora, Edwin, and Tess. That and the television. It would've been easier if at least one or two of the children were school-aged, but four children had come one on top of the other. They were happy they conceived quickly. But *now*?

Her supportive family had kept her sane for the past month after her husband's breakdown, her youngest daughter potty training, and the new baby up constantly at night. On top of that, she started typing envelopes for a penny apiece. It was a miracle she was still functioning at all.

"Mama?" Evie asked.

"Yes, Eve?"

"Need to go potty."

Bernie sighed. She resisted the urge to tell her daughter to just go in her pants. "Right. Let's see if Aunt Tess can bring you to the bathroom."

***

Hank sat next to his mother. His aunt and uncle took sandwiches and drinks from a cooler and placed them on the table. He felt something pulling his shirt. He turned to find the miniature little girl—was it Evie?—staring up at him. Then out of her mouth came, "Hi, Daddy."

It was so high-pitched that he wondered if the local dogs could hear it. She sure was a sweet little thing.

"Sit wif you?"

Ma pulled the tiny girl onto her lap. "Come here, Evie, and you can sit on Grandmom's lap right next to your father."

Hank stared at her little face. She had the sweetest brown eyes and gazed at him as if he were the only person in the park.

After they finished eating, Hank decided he wanted to sit on the blanket. As soon as he settled himself in a cross-legged position, Tess sat across from him. "Hey, big brother, are you having a good day today?"

Hank thought about the answer to that question. He had cigarettes, so that always made it a good day. And Bernie was here. "Yes."

Just then, the tiniest of the little girls plopped onto his lap, positioned her bottom in the opening of his legs, and snuggled her head against his chest. She put her thumb in her mouth. Hank let her stay there. She wasn't harming anything. He heard a click.

Uncle Edwin said, "That's going to be a precious photo."

When the time came for his family to leave, the little girl in his lap kept saying, "No, no! Want Daddy!"

As the cars drove away, he could still hear the tiny girl crying, "Daddy, Daddy."

He felt so sad for the little girl as she called out for her father. He knew what it was like to miss his father.

Chapter 39
Bernie
Weekend Visit

The phone rang two months later, and Bernie answered it. Dr. Doyle's voice came through loud and clear over the phone.

"I think Hank has progressed to the point where I'd like him to try a weekend visit. Would you be agreeable to that?"

Bernie's heart burst with joy. "Of course, I would love to try that." This meant that the doctor thought Hank was improving enough that perhaps he would come home soon. It was the best news she had heard in a long time.

The following Saturday morning, Flora drove Bernie to Pineland to pick up Hank. He was waiting in the lobby and seemed like his old self. Her heart skipped a beat. An orderly accompanied him outside.

Even after everything that had happened, she was so happy to have Hank back, even if just for a weekend.

She got out and hugged Hank.

"The doctor said I'm better, and I don't have to come back."

The orderly said, "Now, Hank, that's not what the doctor said. This is just a trial visit, right?"

Hank nodded. "Trial visit, right."

Bernie sat in the back with Hank as Flora drove. They kissed and hugged. The joy in Bernie's heart made it seem like they flew, rather than drove, home.

When they arrived at their house, Tess brought the kids outside to welcome Hank home. He kissed each one, including baby Hank, then he hugged Tess. When he turned toward Bernie, Hank said, "I'm the happiest man in the world right now."

"And I'm the happiest woman."

The day went so well that when they went to bed that night, Bernie expected that Hank would want to be intimate, but they just lay together, arm in arm, and fell asleep.

Sunday morning, they woke up to go to Mass. Hank seemed especially eager to return to church. Tess watched the children at home while they attended Mass together. Hank remained quiet the entire time, not responding in the way he usually did before this whole awful breakdown.

By Sunday afternoon, he began to ramble on and on, sometimes making sense, other times not at all.

Then he accused Bernie of having an affair with Uncle Edwin.

"I'm sorry, what?" Bernie couldn't believe her ears. How ridiculous! Face burning as anger rose inside, she tossed the pillow she'd been straightening onto the couch and shouted back at him, "How can you accuse me of such a thing?"

"I can tell. I see the way he looks at you and you at him." Hank pointed at her, then waved his finger wildly in the air.

"Are you kidding me?" she screamed.

The children were now crying.

Tess let off a cow whistle, the shriek getting Bernie's attention. "What's going on here?"

Bernie didn't know how to answer her sister-in-law. Tess calmed Hank down, but Bernie was so disheartened with his actions—and with her behavior as well.

When Flora arrived to take him back to Pineland (early, unfortunately), Bernie felt as if she had failed. By the time they left, Hank was quiet and withdrawn, seemingly in another world.

At the hospital, Bernie told them what had happened. The doctor explained that Hank had suffered a setback and would resume electroshock therapy the following day. When the nurse took Hank upstairs to the locked ward, Bernie's heart was crushed. She wanted to sob, but she had to control it until she returned to the car with Flora.

The entire way home, Bernie bawled like a baby, and Flora tried to calm her as best she could. Just when things started to look brighter, Hank's condition seemed worse than it was months ago. Would he ever get better, or would he spend the rest of his life in a mental institution?

Chapter 40
Evie
One Bad Apple
July 11, 1998

Now the mother of four sons, two to nine, Evie sunk into the sofa and took a deep breath. Most days were non-stop action with four rambunctious, active little boys. It had been a hot day, so Jake offered to take the kids to the park and then to the Dairy Queen. Evie didn't hesitate to say yes. She loved being a full-time mother and usually cherished the chatter of her little boys, but today she felt overwhelmed and needed a half-hour of peace and quiet.

Evie turned on the American news as she wrote out checks to pay bills. She was never one to turn down an opportunity to accomplish two—or three—things at once. At least, this time, without interruption.

Her ears perked when she heard the word "diocese."

"The Diocese of Dallas has agreed to pay 23.4 million dollars to nine former altar boys who claimed they were sexually abused by a former priest. With more on this story, here's Jackson Kelly with the details.

"The Catholic Church has seen its share of sexual abuse cases by former or current priests in the past few years. But no case is more extensive than the one of Rudolph 'Rudy' Kos.

"Kos has been convicted of molesting altar boys and several other youths over eleven years in three church parishes. The victims accused Kos of hundreds of incidents of sexual abuse, beginning when they were as young as nine and usually including drugs or alcohol.

"Kos was not removed from his priestly duties until 1992, years after priests he worked with first complained to top church officials in Dallas about his abusive behavior towards boys. Just this week, the Vatican took the rare step of stripping him of his priesthood status and barring him from any ministry. Jackson Kelly, reporting from Dallas."

Evie shook her head. She had a nine-year-old son, and she couldn't begin to imagine the pain those children endured from someone they should've been able to trust.

Sure, there would always be a few bad priests out there, but why did the news media seem to take particular delight in reporting them?

Of course, one was still too many, and Evie prayed for the victims of that former priest. As far as she was concerned, there was a special place in hell for priests who abused their authority and betrayed the children in their charge.

By and large, though, Evie felt confident that 98 percent of all priests were faithful and holy men. And certainly, 100 percent of the priests that Evie knew were part of that majority.

As Evie finished writing the last check, she heard their van pull into their rural driveway. Their four sons' high-pitched voices were music to her ears.

***

That night, after she tucked the boys safely in bed, Evie shared with Jake the news of the priest in Dallas. "Why does the media make it seem like most priests are pedophiles?"

"I'm not sure they do that, Eve, but you know the words of the Osmond Brothers, 'One bad apple don't spoil the whole bunch, girl.'"

Jake's quirky humor always made her smile. "Well, either way, I'm thankful that we don't know any pedophile priests."

When Evie lay in bed that night, she thanked God again that she didn't know any pedophile priests—except, perhaps, the priest from her parish in New Jersey. But that could've been a misunderstanding. She was thankful that there was only "one bad apple" in the tens of thousands of priests.

Chapter 41
Hank
Treatment and Return Home
November 1968

Hank woke up in his room at Pineland. He glanced at the photo of his wife and children on his bedside table.

Four different medications and many electroshock therapies later, he finally felt like his old self. Not a hundred percent, but close enough that his doctor approved his release today after his family's visit. She cautioned him to take each of the medications faithfully to prevent him from sinking into despair and paranoia. The drugs, she warned, were not a cure but an ongoing treatment.

He glanced at the calendar above his bed. November 4.

The bright sun filled his room with light and warmth. The thermometer outside his window showed that it was only fifty degrees, but it would warm up considerably around noon when his family was scheduled to arrive.

He knocked on the bathroom door to make sure his neighbor, Jimmy, wasn't using it. When he heard no answer, he opened the door and used the toilet.

Then he combed his hair, brushed his teeth, and made his way to the hospital chapel for Mass.

After Mass, he packed all his belongings, his clothes, his toiletries, the photos of his family, and the crucifix above his bed.

Just after noon, the temperature was cool but not cold. He waited at the picnic area for his family to arrive. Everyone would be here, most especially his children. The last time they visited, he just couldn't get enough of his children. The doctor had told him that in that hazy fog of his mental breakdown, he didn't remember he had children, let alone their names. That made Hank sad.

He sat at the picnic table, tapping his foot, and waited. A honk of a car horn made Hank turn to see Uncle Edwin's two-toned Wagoneer and Flora's maroon Cadillac driving into the parking lot near the picnic area. He waved and met them at their vehicles.

"Daddy, I have a flower for you," Deb said as Bernie helped her out of the car.

"Me too," said Evie as she followed.

He hugged both his little girls. Evie said, "Up, Daddy?"

Hank smiled and picked her up. He couldn't get enough of hearing her cute voice.

Baby Hank started to fuss, so Bernie lifted him to her shoulder and patted him on the back.

Nearly five-year-old Mitch hugged Hank's leg.

Bernie asked Tess if she would set up the playpen, which she did. Tess took the baby from Bernie and put him in the playpen with some toys.

Uncle Edwin, Tess, Ma, and Flora were here, but Aunt Miriam wasn't. "Is Aunt Miriam all right, Uncle Edwin?"

"Yeah, she's fine. She just had a bit of an upset stomach this morning and didn't think the ride would be good for her. She said she'd see you when you're home."

"Sounds good."

Evie started squirming, so he put her down. Bernie leaned in to hug him. He whispered, "The doctor says I can go home today."

She embraced him even tighter and kissed him on the lips. "I've been waiting a long time for this, Hank."

"Me too." He paused and stepped back. "The doctor stressed that this isn't a cure, but a treatment. I've got to stay on four different medications for the rest of my life."

"Thank God they found something that worked. You look so good, Hank."

"I feel good too."

When it was time to go, he and Bernie went into the hospital foyer to say goodbye. Hank hugged his doctor. Dr. Doyle never gave up on him and, for that, he was truly grateful. She encouraged Hank to write about his experiences, saying that it would help him to cope with what had happened to him.

Bernie hugged Dr. Doyle too. Then Hank made the rounds, hugging attendants, orderlies, and other patients. Admittedly, he would not miss this place, but he would miss the kind people.

The entire ride home, Evie sat next to him. "I like flowers, do you? You gonna be home freva now, Daddy?"

He tried to keep up, but her questions came out like cannonballs until Bernie said, "Evie, leave Daddy alone."

"No, Bernie, her chatter is like music to my ears. Let her talk."

"All right, but if she bothers you, let me know."

"I will."

***

Bernie was ecstatic to have Hank home again. But the doctor warned her that the medications for Hank's psychosis might have the side effect of a reduced sex drive, at least for a time. So Bernie wasn't surprised that, although they slept together, they weren't intimate. On the one hand, it was probably for the best. They wouldn't be able to handle another child right now. On the other hand, Bernie desperately craved intimacy from her husband.

She told herself that the problem would be resolved when he grew accustomed to the medications.

Chapter 42
Hank
Mentally Ill Need Not Apply

Over the next four weeks, as Hank gained confidence, he went to over fifty job interviews.

He was thankful that his wife was making $75 a week typing envelopes. That meant that Hank could work for minimum wage. Everything was a possibility: milkman, office boy, store clerk, janitor. He stayed away from commission jobs since he wasn't a great salesman.

Hope filled Hank every time he took the bus to an interview. When they asked what he'd been doing for the past seven months, he had to be honest. "Well, I had a nervous breakdown and was in Pineland for that time. But I'm better now."

Each supervisor said the same: "Don't call us. We'll call you," which meant, "We're not going to hire a mentally ill person, even if you're better."

While he felt better mentally, Hank also felt immense pressure to land a job and soon. When despair started to creep in, he brushed it away. He had to maintain hope.

It was now so close to Christmas. How would he and Bernie buy gifts for the kids without him finding a job? The money Bernie earned typing went toward the mortgage and food. *God, I want this Christmas to be happy for the kids. I love them so much and want them to have gifts to open. Please help me find a job.*

Hank also sensed pressure from Bernie. He knew she wanted physical intimacy, but his physical desire was gone. Sapped. Thinking back to the way he had abused sex by visiting prostitutes, Hank was happy. No sex drive meant no temptation for visiting those sordid places. For the time being, he was content with that.

***

A new family moved in next door that week. Hank and Bernie introduced themselves to the new neighbors, Will, Opal, and their dog, Gypsy.

"I feel like we've won the lottery," Opal said after introductions were made. She was a big-boned woman with dark skin. "We've been saving and scrimping for years to move away from that run-down neighborhood we were in."

"You'll love this neighborhood," said Bernie. "We all look out for one another."

"That's good," said Will. "We were a bit afraid, though. Not everyone treats Negroes with kindness." Will was a bit taller than Hank and thinner.

Hank straightened. "I don't think you'll find any of that here. Good people, good neighbors. Anyway, welcome, and if you need anything, please don't hesitate to ask us. We're right next door."

Opal lifted her hands as if wanting to hug Hank and Bernie, but after a moment, she clasped her hands and gave them a big smile instead.

The following day, Hank woke up early, determined to find a job. Music came from the kitchen. Bernie was listening to Dion's "Abraham, Martin, and John" on the radio. When Hank heard the song last week, it moved him, so he bought the record. He listened to it over and over and wrote down the lyrics.

"Morning, Hank." Bernie glanced up from doing dishes. "Would you mind taking the trash out?"

"Not at all."

Hank took the trash bag out to the curb, where he met Will doing the same. "Good morning, Will."

"Morning, Hank." Will sighed. "Makes me sad."

"What makes you sad, Will?" Then Hank glanced down the street. Not one, not two, but ten "for sale" signs had popped up overnight.

Will put his hands on his hips. "You don't suppose they object to us, the first Negro family on this block, do you?"

"Nah, it can't be that. Must be something else."

"You're a very positive person, Hank, and I think, naïve too."

"Naïve?"

"I mean no disrespect, but if I were a gambling man, I'd bet my new house that these people are moving because they don't want a black neighbor."

"Really?" Hank squinted at the sign in the yard of the house two doors down. He couldn't imagine his neighbors moving just because someone with a different skin color now lived on their street.

"It wouldn't be the first time something like this happened."

"I'm sorry, Will."

"You don't need to be sorry. It's just a way of life, I guess." He paused then made eye contact with Hank. "Where do you work? I can give you a ride if you need it. You said you don't own a car, right?"

"Right." Hank averted his gaze then gave Will a sad smile. "I'd take you up on that, but I don't have a job, not yet. I've been searching and applying for over a month now. Nothing."

"Now, why wouldn't somebody hire a fine young man like yourself?"

Hank stared down at his feet. *Would telling Will why people wouldn't hire him make Will not want to be friends anymore?* He decided to be honest. "I suffered a mental breakdown at the end of May. I'm on treatment and doing well, but no one will hire me when I tell them the truth."

"Shoot." Will shook his head. "That's not right. Sounds like some people don't want to trust you. Well, you know what, though? My company's looking for an office boy. They're probably only paying minimum wage, but I'm sure I could get you at least in the door."

"Really?" Did he dare to hope? "That would be great, Will, but I'm not sure the person who's hiring would want a former mental patient working at your company."

"I can tell you that I'm a hundred percent sure you'll get the job."

"I don't know."

"Well, I know the supervisor who's hiring."

"You do?"

"Yes." He straightened and tapped his chest. "It's none other than—me." He laughed. "Go on inside and get me a resume, and I'll have you working today. Now, it's only for the holiday season, so it's temporary, but it'll get you through the Christmas season and well into January."

Astonished at his new neighbor's offer, Hank stood gawking, unable to move.

"Well, get a move on, new employee. I don't have all day!" Will laughed and patted Hank on the back.

Hank raced into the house and to the desk in the living room, where he kept his resumes.

Bernie came up the short staircase from the kitchen. "What's going on, Hank?"

Still processing what just happened, he blurted, "Will next door just hired me for a temporary job at his company. I start now!"

"That's wonderful, Hank." She clasped her hands together. "Do I have time to make you lunch?"

"No, don't worry about it. I had breakfast, and that should be fine." He kissed Bernie goodbye.

He met Will next door, and Will drove them in his

Plymouth Valiant to Center City, Camden.

Hank was so happy to have a job that he did everything he was asked to do—and more.

Will congratulated him on the ride home. "Hank, you're the best office boy we've had. I wish our company had enough money that we could offer you more than a few months' work."

"Will, you'll never know what this means to me that you trust me enough to give me a job."

Will laughed. "Well, Hank, you'll never know what it means to Opal and me to have neighbors who treat us like human beings."

***

The next few months were difficult for Bernie. Hank was better, thank God, but he seemed like a different person, not the self-assured man she married. Bernie could live with that, if necessary. But they might as well have been brother and sister. On the one hand, no sex meant no more children. And since Hank didn't have a permanent job, that made sense for the time being.

But what if they decided they wanted more children in the future? That wouldn't happen without sex.

Maybe Hank was afraid of having more children. They hadn't discussed it, or had any other deep conversations, since his return from the hospital in November.

Bernie resolved to have a heart-to-heart with her husband as soon as she put all the kids to bed that evening.

***

After kissing his kids goodnight, Hank switched the channels on the television to Channel 10 and *Gunsmoke*.

Midway through the show, Bernie sat down on the couch next to him. She said something, but he was listening to Marshal Dillon tell someone to "Get outta Dodge."

"Honey?"

As the show cut to a commercial, Hank turned to his wife.

"We need to talk." Bernie's lips pressed together in a grimace.

"We do?" Her serious expression worried him. What could she want to discuss?

Bernie nodded.

"All right." Hank got up to turn off the TV and sat back down beside Bernie. "What do we need to talk about?"

"Well, we should talk about why we're not having sex."

"Oh." Hank glanced away.

Bernie remained silent.

Finally, Hank said, "This medication, Bern, makes me not want to." He fidgeted with a pillow on the couch. "And that's probably for the best because I can't seem to…"

"What?"

"I've been unfaithful to you, Bern." His heart sped up as he made the confession. Would she hate him now?

"Oh?" Her face remained placid. Maybe she didn't believe him.

"Before my breakdown."

"You had sex with other women?"

"Sex? Not really sex. I…"

"You what?"

"I went to prostitutes so they could give me a…" He couldn't get himself to finish the sentence.

"I see." Bernie sighed, and her shoulders slumped.

"Having sex once in four months…well, I just couldn't do it." He rubbed his forehead. "I'm sorry. But if I got my sexual desire back, I'm afraid I would cheat again."

Bernie lowered her head. When she lifted it, her hope-filled expression made him happy she didn't hate him. "Maybe the doctor can give you a lower dose of whatever medication is taking your sex drive away completely."

"Maybe…"

"How about this? We ask the doctor and see what happens."

"What if we get pregnant?"

"I can buy a box of condoms."

"We're not supposed to be using birth control, Bern."

"I know, but we're living as brother and sister right now."

"Isn't that a good thing?"

"Well, it would be a good thing if we *were* brother and sister. But we're not."

"I know. Maybe just for the time being, we can keep things the way they are." Hank didn't want to risk his being unfaithful again. He loved her and didn't want to hurt her again.

***

As Bernie walked away, she wasn't sure whether the conversation went well or not. Hank seemed so indifferent. Then again, she appreciated his honesty. She didn't want to tell him that she already knew he was stepping out on her. Before she got pregnant with Little Hank, she came down with the clap. She knew *she* wasn't cheating, so she assumed Hank was. Bernie was disappointed, but Hank was still grieving his father's death, and he seemed depressed most of the time. What good would've come from her confronting him? He'd already admitted to being unfaithful.

Bernie respected Hank's choice to wait a while, so six months later, she made an appointment to meet with Hank's psychiatrist at Pineland.

Dr. Doyle didn't think lowering the dose of his medications would do much in terms of his sex drive. "The first priority is to keep Hank on the road to sanity," she said.

Bernie and Hank agreed.

Dr. Doyle turned to Hank. "However, I can give you another medication that could offset the side effect of low libido."

"All right," said Hank.

The doctor wrote a new prescription on her pad and handed it to Hank. "You're doing great, Hank. It's so good to see you again. Have you started writing about your experiences?"

"Yes, in fact, I have, Doctor. Thanks."

"That's good to hear."

Bernie stopped at the pharmacy to drop off Hank's prescription and pick up a box of condoms. It couldn't hurt to be hopeful.

Chapter 43
Hank
No More Disappointments
September 1970

While grateful for whatever temporary jobs he could get for a few months at a time, Hank needed something permanent. A friend urged him to apply for a position at the US Post Office. He did that a few days ago, but they told him it would take months to receive a reply.

Meanwhile, the medications that his doctor had given him to offset the effects of low desire helped. He and Bernie were able to engage in an intimate life again. They didn't get together that often, but when they did, they used condoms.

One thing he appreciated about that new medication was that while his sex drive had returned, it was still much weaker than before his breakdown. Regardless, he was determined to remain faithful to Bernie. All those years, he'd convinced himself that being serviced by prostitutes wasn't being unfaithful. But he now realized he'd only told himself that so he wouldn't feel guilty. But no more. He would remain faithful to Bernie, especially since she had been faithful to him during his breakdown.

The best thing about the past few months was that he had acquired a used manual typewriter so he could now write stories about his time in Pineland and about anything else that might come to mind.

Another topic he could write about was his neighborhood. Will had been correct. His former white neighbors didn't want to live in a neighborhood with black families. One of them said, "If the Negro has the lawful right to live wherever he chooses, then I too have that same right, so I'm moving elsewhere."

Hank learned that bigotry—ably coached by its teachers: hatred and fear—lived on both sides of the fence. Will shared that some of his black friends hated whites, no matter who the white person was.

Hank just couldn't understand hatred. He understood being on the receiving end of bigotry more than the majority of the population, given that most people thought less of Hank because of his mental illness.

While living in this community, Hank was proud that his children blended well with their neighbors, regardless of the color of their skin. As his children grew older, he and Bernie taught them to respect and to treat all people, regardless of creed or color, regardless of what a person looked like or how they acted, like fellow human beings.

In Hank's opinion, his white neighbors left for frivolous reasons. Were they afraid that blacks wouldn't take care of their properties? Many of his black neighbors kept their houses better than some of his previous white neighbors.

Hank and Bernie resolved to stay in their neighborhood.

This beautiful autumn evening, they invited Will and Opal to come over to play pinochle at their house.

When their neighbors came through the door, Evie, now nearly four and dressed in her pajamas, screamed, "Will!" and ran up to him. He picked her up as if she was a member of his own family. Opal leaned over to hug Evie too.

"Opal!" yelled Evie, delighted.

"This girl is such a precious gift, Hank and Bernie."

"We think so," said Bernie.

"As are all your kids—what a blessing they all are to you."

"Indeed," said Bernie.

As if on cue, Deb and Mitch rushed to the older couple and offered hugs.

Bernie said, "All right, kids. Time for bed."

"Awwww," they complained.

"Shhh! The baby's sleeping." Bernie turned to their neighbors and pointed to the card table set with cards and snacks. "Make yourselves at home."

Bernie picked up Evie, took Deb by the hand, and went up the short staircase to the girls' bedroom. Hank went with Mitch to the lower-level bedroom to tuck him in.

Hank pulled the blanket up under Mitch's chin and kissed his forehead. "Goodnight, son." His heart filled with joy when he thought about how much he loved his son.

"No book, Daddy?"

"Sorry, buddy. Will and Opal are waiting on us. Tomorrow night, for sure."

Mitch nodded. "Goodnight, Daddy."

Hank turned off the light and closed the door. He grabbed a couple of beers from the fridge and headed upstairs to the living room.

Opal and Bernie, who drank bottles of Pepsi, teamed up against Will and Hank, who drank cans of Budweiser together.

Will asked, "Did you see the *Flip Wilson Show* the other night?"

Hank said, "Yes. He cracks me up, especially when he dresses up like Geraldine and talks about Killer, her boyfriend."

Will laughed. "By the way, have you heard from the post office yet?"

Hank shook his head. "It'll be several months before I hear from them. However, I just finished a temp job driving an ice cream truck. With it being so close to December, they don't need me anymore."

"Well, I could use you again until you find something permanent."

"Will, you've already done so much."

"Maybe I have, but I've got selfish reasons too. You're one

of the best office boys I've ever had. If I could've hired you permanently, I would have. But we do need you now if you want a few months' work."

"Of course. Thanks." He was grateful to Will for his generosity.

"Until then, Hank, Opal and I will pray that you get the job with the post office. That is, if you don't mind having Baptists pray for you?"

"I'd be honored to have a Baptist praying for me. God is God, no matter which religion you belong to. And I'd greatly appreciate your prayers."

***

Five months later, Hank had still not received anything from the post office. He had been on the lookout for a job since his temporary position with Will's company ended last month.

He kept himself busy by writing stories about his experiences at Pineland. And he enjoyed pecking at his typewriter. If he had to make a living typing—like Bernie— their family would starve. But he'd always enjoyed writing stories, even as a young child.

An article he wrote appeared last Sunday in the parish bulletin. Hank felt he needed to respond to a recent article in last month's diocesan newspaper about apathy in parishioners. The author suggested forcing parishioners to take part in parish life.

New Openness to Truth:
An Observation, Not a Judgment

The hard work and sacrifices that keep a parish functioning are shouldered by a handful of parishioners.

Of course, it's not right. It's downright unfair. But the minute we try to force someone to do something against his will, we have taken the first step toward destroying one of the most essential aspects of human nature: free will.

Free will is one of the greatest gifts from God, and man cannot reach heaven if he is forced to worship or take part in parish life.

When the article appeared in the church bulletin, parishioners came up to him after Mass to express their agreement. Some patted him on the back. "Great essay, Hank."

For the first time in years, Hank was pleased that he had contributed something to society, especially since he hadn't had a permanent job since his breakdown.

Hank tapped at his typewriter in the living room as he composed an essay entitled *Freedom Yesterday* about the similarities of the prejudice that black people experience to the discrimination that the mentally ill face. He read aloud what he had just typed. "In these exceptionally troubled times, can one imagine any day passing without the constant reminder that black Americans remain bitterly dissatisfied with the progress being made toward their complete freedom from social and economic slavery?

"The answer to America's racial ills lies inside the individual, regardless of color."

Bernie called to him from the kitchen. "Hank, can you see if the mail's been delivered? I'm waiting on a check from one of the court reporters."

"Sure."

Hank got up and opened the door. He peeked his head out to see if the mailbox was full. It was. He lifted out the letters. As he scanned through them, Hank noticed the US Post Office insignia on one of them.

His heart raced. He wasn't sure he wanted to open it yet.

Once he opened it, if it was a rejection, he'd have one less job to hope for.

He put the letter on the small table by the door and flipped through the other envelopes. One was addressed to Bernie from the courthouse. He brought the envelope downstairs to her small corner of the kitchen where she typed. "I think this is a check, Bern."

"Oh, good. Anything else in the mail?"

"Just something from the post office."

"What?"

"I'm afraid to open it."

"Come on, Hank, open it. The suspense is killing me."

"What if it's a rejection?"

"Then we'll deal with it." She nudged his arm. "Go get it."

"All right." He went upstairs, and Bernie followed him. He took a deep breath, tore it open, and began reading, "Dear Mr. Gallagher, the US Postal Service has accepted your application for work in its Camden location."

"Hank, you got accepted! Congratulations!" Bernie jumped up and hugged him.

His heart was still beating a mile a minute, but it was the happiest he'd been in years.

He continued reading, "Please present yourself there on March 4 at 9:00 a.m. to begin your training and probation period of five months."

The weight of the world lifted from his shoulders. "You know what, Bernie? They're not going to regret this. I'm going to be the best employee they've ever had!"

***

That first day of work, Hank took the bus early and arrived at 8:30 for his training period. The man in charge said, "I'm sorry, Mr. Gallagher. The person who's supposed to train you has not arrived yet. Would you mind waiting over there?" He pointed to a reception area with chairs.

"Of course not. I'm early. Sorry about that."

"Not to worry."

Fifteen minutes later, Hank met Darrin Stephens, his new supervisor and the person in charge of training him.

"Darrin Stephens?" Hank tried imagining this guy in the show *Bewitched,* but with his round face and trim beard, he looked nothing like Dick Sargent—or even Dick York, the previous Darrin.

"Yeah, yeah, everyone teases me about my name. No, my wife is not named Samantha. And she's not a witch." Darrin chuckled. "And I had the name first. Anyway, ready to get started?"

"Absolutely."

Hank took notes as Darrin trained him in filing letters and all the interior postal worker's jobs.

In three weeks, he'd also be trained as a letter carrier. Then the supervisor would determine where he would be best utilized.

Hank worked so hard over the next few weeks that he practically slept the entire day on his days off so he could be fresh and ready to work.

When he started his letter carrier training at the end of March, he delivered mail in five different neighborhoods and caught on so quickly that the supervisor allowed him to continue the entire week unsupervised.

On the last day of the week, he was surprised to find that one of his routes would be his own neighborhood. So he stopped by his house before he delivered the mail.

"Daddy, you're home!" Evie reached for him to pick her up. He took her in his arms and bounced her up and down.

"Do it again, Daddy!"

Bernie came up the stairs, her head tilted. "Hank, what's wrong?"

"Absolutely nothing! Today, I get to deliver mail to our

215

neighborhood. I was wondering if Evie wanted to join me."

"She won't get in your way?"

"Nah. She'll be fine. Come on, Evie. Want to walk with Daddy?"

"Yay!" Her huge smile and the joy in her eyes made Hank's heart nearly burst.

Evie joined him as he delivered letters and small packages to each of his neighbors. The people that recognized Hank smiled and waved. Of course, everyone loved Evie. Bernie called her a "good-natured slob" because no matter how neatly Bernie dressed her, she always looked like an unmade bed.

As Hank delivered mail, Evie ran alongside him, chatting the entire time. "I like this house, Daddy; it's pretty. Oh, this house has a doggie. I wish we had a doggie. Can we get a doggie? Look at all the toys in that house."

By the end of the route, Evie said, "Daddy, we walked a hundred miles. I'm tired. Can we go home now?"

"Of course, honey. I've finished delivering the mail to this street. Let's go home."

A few weeks later, Darrin came to him with the news that they'd chosen him to be a letter carrier. He was incredibly pleased. Now, he needed to make it past the three-month probation period.

Darrin gave Hank three routes for the first two months. His start time was 6:30 a.m., and his finish time would be 3:15 p.m. However, Hank always got up at 4:30 a.m. to take the bus to arrive for his shift a half-hour early. And he always stayed after his shift to make sure everything was complete.

On August 4th, he found a letter in his personal mailbox at work. He ripped it open and read, "Congratulations, Mr. Gallagher. You've completed your probation period. You are now officially an employee with the US Postal Service. Your medical and other benefits will begin immediately. Welcome aboard!"

Hank had never felt so relieved in his life. His heart was singing. He planned to make sure they would never regret hiring him.

Before Hank started work, he hurried to the payphone just outside the entrance door and phoned Bernie. "You're talking to a permanent employee of the United States Postal Service!"

"Congratulations, Hank!" Bernie said over the telephone line.

"It's time to buy a car! We'll go car shopping on the weekend, all right?"

"Absolutely. Bye, hon. Love you."

"Love you too, Bern."

As he made the rounds and delivered mail on his route that day, Hank shared the news with anyone who greeted him that the post office had hired him full-time and permanently. Everyone seemed excited for him, and some of the older women offered him cold iced tea, which he appreciated because he was sweating up a storm on this hot August day.

At the end of his shift, he could hardly wait to tell his friend Will. After taking the bus, Hank arrived home at 4:30 p.m. and relaxed in front of the television with his kids, all the while keeping an eye out for Will's Valiant to drive up. When he finally saw him, Hank jumped up and met Will at his vehicle.

"I got a permanent job with the post office, Will!"

Will patted Hank on the back. "Oh, that's wonderful, Hank. I bet that feels good."

"It does."

"We should celebrate, Hank! Let's have a couple of beers on me. I have some in my fridge. I'll be right out." He jogged up the driveway to his house.

Hank set up two lawn chairs in the front yard.

A screen door banged shut and Will, dressed in jeans and a tee-shirt, cut across his driveway. Will handed Hank an ice-cold beer. "Congratulations, man."

"Thanks!" Hank cracked open the beer, sat down with Will, and took a long cold swig. Yes, life was good. He was sitting with a friend on a warm summer evening, sipping a cold beer, and he was finally a fully employed, contributing member of society. Perhaps he'd left the scourge of his mental illness far behind him.

He had the next day off.

Last night, he had talked to Bernie about getting a dog. He suggested that he take one of the kids with him and pick out a mutt at the SPCA. Bernie agreed.

They called the children into the living room and shared the news. "We're getting a puppy!"

"Yay," they screamed as they jumped up and down. Hank knew Evie would want to go with him to pick out the puppy. And Hank had just taken Mitch to a Phillies game. But he hadn't spent much time recently with Deb, so he offered this job to her.

"Deb, want to go with me?"

Her big brown eyes and mouth opened wide. "Really? I can go with you?"

"Yes. I need someone to help me pick out the puppy for our family."

"Then yes, Daddy!"

The two went off to the SPCA. Once inside, they were taken to the cages of the dogs and puppies that were available for adoption.

His daughter kept returning to the cage with four black-and-white puppies. Hank watched the four tiny dogs. Three of them were yapping and stepping on the fourth puppy to get attention from Hank and his daughter.

Deb pressed her lips together, suppressing a shy smile, as

if hesitant to believe that he'd agree with her choice. "I...um... like the puppy on the bottom, the one who's being stomped on, the one that's mostly white."

Hank rubbed her shoulder. "Sounds good. I like that one too."

Within a few moments, the white mongrel pup was sitting on Deb's lap in the front passenger seat of the car.

"What shall we name her, Deb?"

"Well, she's white and fluffy, so how about...Fluffy?"

"I can't argue with that."

They arrived home to the squeals of the other children. Bernie nodded her approval. "Cute puppy. Did you pick her out, Deb?"

"I sure did!" Deb exclaimed.

When the excitement died down, Fluffy settled herself on the floor near the couch. Hank turned the TV on and twisted the dial until he got to Channel 48. When he saw Ernest Borgnine beating up Frank Sinatra, he knew the film was *From Here to Eternity*. He had seen the movie before, but he wouldn't mind watching it again. He sat down on his swivel chair.

He glimpsed Evie gently petting Fluffy on the floor. Then she lay down next to the puppy. Yes, Fluffy was just what their house needed right now.

Toward the end of the movie, his two little girls came up to him with hope-filled eyes. Deb said, "Daddy, can we comb your hair? We want to pretend we're hairdressers."

Hank tried to hide his smirk. "Sure, girls. Go ahead."

For the next half-hour, his two girls combed his hair up, down, and to the side. Then they messed up his hair and combed it again. After their second attempt, they stepped around the chair to face him. Then they giggled and returned to their hairdressing. Hank's heart swelled to see his little girls so happy.

Jake and Evie now had five sons, ages eighteen months to twelve years old.

Warmer temperatures, a bluer-than-blue sky, and birds singing sweet tunes greeted Evie that morning. She was preparing to homeschool her boys when her mother called and told her to turn on the television. It appeared that a small plane had crashed into one of the Twin Towers of the World Trade Center.

As they chatted on the phone, a large plane crashed into the second Twin Tower, and both Evie and her mother gasped. Then they were abruptly cut off. When Evie tried to call Mom back, the line was busy.

She watched, stunned at the images.

"Go out and get Dad in the studio. Tell him to come here," she asked her oldest son. Her husband was working on a series of paintings for an upcoming exhibition.

Evie and Jake watched the news coverage, while the four older boys played outside in their yard, and their toddler played with the toys inside. This was a great advantage of homeschooling: she could let the children play outside on such a beautiful sunny day, taking one long recess, which was better than having them see the images over and over again. Jake and Evie sat stunned, watching more footage of each tower collapsing. They soon learned that another plane hit the Pentagon, and another crashed in Pennsylvania. It all felt so apocalyptic. Thankfully, Jake kept his eyes on the four kids outside because Evie couldn't tear her eyes away from the TV. Finally, it was time for lunch.

After making a quick lunch for the family, Evie asked Jake to bring the boys out to the studio to play musical instruments or perhaps paint and draw. Their toddler was napping, so Evie turned the TV on again and soon became riveted to the nonstop story.

And it was odd because anytime something dark and shocking happened in Evie's life or the world, she always thought about her father. What would he think about terrorists flying planes into buildings?

Evie didn't drink, but today she felt like she needed a drink or something to calm her. She could just imagine the impact of today's frightening attack on recovering alcoholics—perhaps they'd be tempted to fall off the wagon.

She kept trying to call her mother in New Jersey, but the lines were all busy. With call-waiting and call-answer, she shouldn't have gotten a busy signal. Mid-afternoon, when she tried to call, a recorded message said that the phone lines to the states had been overwhelmed, and they were working on fixing the problem.

At dinner, the phone rang. It was Mom. "Finally."

"Yeah, that was horrible, wasn't it?"

"I just can't believe it, Eve. What is our world coming to?"

"I don't know. All we can do is pray they find out who's responsible and make sure it doesn't happen again."

Chapter 45
Hank
Assault in Broad Daylight
October 1971

On a fair and sunny October day, Hank arrived home early from his job. Darrin had sent him home because he finished his route in record time. He got into their new car—new to them anyway—a 1968 blue Rambler—and headed toward home via the Black Horse Pike. Not only was this car a good buy, but it only had 40,000 miles on it. Hank felt such freedom in having his own car to drive whenever he needed it. Of course, with the car came gas expenses, insurance, and licensing, but it was well worth it to be able to go anywhere at any time.

As he neared his street, he slowed down, and worry crept in. Police cars with flashing lights blocked the road and wouldn't let him through. So he parked around the block and walked to his house. Two attendants lifted a young girl on a stretcher into an ambulance. People gathered around the end house, and a few police officers went door-to-door asking questions. Hank met a tall, broad-shouldered policeman as he climbed the steps to his house.

"Can I help you, officer?"

"If you're just getting home, no. But if your wife is home, we'd like to talk to her."

"About what?"

"We received a report of a black suspect raping a twelve-year-old girl next to those bushes about thirty minutes ago."

Oh, Lord, the poor girl. Had he heard the officer correctly? "Outside?" The thought sickened him. What if his wife or daughters had been playing outside?

222

"Yes, sir, outside. Now, may we talk to your wife?"

"Of course." Hank invited the policeman inside and called for Bernie.

Evie sat in front of the television with her thumb in her mouth. She turned and said, "Hi, Mr. Policeman."

The officer nodded to her.

Bernie came up the stairs. "Hank, is everything all right?"

"Yes, yes, I'm fine. I just got off early from work. But this officer would like to ask you a few questions."

"Yes, sure."

"Ma'am, did you happen to be outside or look outside this afternoon about thirty or thirty-five minutes ago?"

"Um, no, officer. I was down in my kitchen office typing. But Evie's been home all afternoon if you want to talk to her. She's been watching television here in the living room."

The police officer nodded. "Would you mind asking your little girl to talk with me?"

Bernie said, "Evie, honey, this policeman wants to talk to you."

She jumped up, her ponytail bouncing. "Okay."

Just as the officer opened his mouth to speak, Evie said, "I go to school now—kindergarten. That means I'm a big girl even though I'm little."

Hank still marveled at how high-pitched her voice still was because she sounded so much younger than five.

"That's nice. Now—"

"My little brother goes to nursery school. And I just learned to ride a bike with no training wheels."

Bernie interrupted. "Evie, honey, let the man ask you questions, okay?"

She nodded.

"Evie, did you see anything take place outside this afternoon?"

"Like what?"

223

"Like, did you see anything bad happen?"

Evie pursed her lips, glanced to one side, then tapped her chin. "I saw a big man runnin'. I saw him runnin' 'cause I had just gone to the bathroom and was comin' down the steps."

"Do you remember what he looked like?" the policeman asked. "Was he black or white?"

Evie scrunched up her eyebrows, something she did whenever she thought hard. It was pretty cute.

"Um...he had dark skin like Will and Opal, and he had a baseball cap like my dad's."

The policeman turned to Hank. "First, who are Will and Opal?"

"Our neighbors. They're black."

"All right. And do you have a baseball cap, and if so, which team?"

"Yes, I have a Phillies cap."

"Thank you. Can you get that cap for me?"

Hank reached into the coat closet and grabbed his Phillies hat.

The officer took it and crouched down to Evie's eye level. "Is this the type of hat he was wearing?"

"Just like that."

"Evie, you've been very helpful. Thank you."

"You're welcome, Mr. Policeman."

Bernie and Hank escorted the police officer outside. They stopped and surveyed the scene. There were four police cars on the street, and the road was still blocked off.

"Did he tell you what happened, Hank?" Bernie asked, her tone anxious.

"Yes, he said that a twelve-year-old girl was raped by the bushes over there about forty-five minutes ago."

"What?" Bernie's hand shot to her mouth.

The officer knocked on Will and Opal's door, but no one

answered. Opal had a part-time job at McCrory's, and Will wouldn't get home until later.

Hank called out, "I don't think they're home, officer. Do you have a card? I'll give it to them, and they can call you."

"Thanks again, sir, but if they weren't home, I don't need to talk to them."

"All right."

Bernie and Hank remained on their steps, watching. Hank scanned the neighborhood for the ambulance. "Where's the girl?"

As he walked away, the policeman answered, "She's already on the way to the hospital."

Bernie said, "How horrible. I can't believe...we can't stay in this neighborhood now, can we, Hank?"

"No, not if a rape occurred in broad daylight." And with those words, Hank felt like he had failed his black neighbors because he and Bernie would be moving away just like the rest of the whites.

***

While their home was up for sale, Hank and Will had several conversations about their decision to move out of the neighborhood.

"I know why you've made your decision, Hank, but that doesn't mean I'm going to miss you any less."

"I feel awful about that, Will. You and Opal have been good friends to Bernie and me."

They finally received a reasonable offer for the house, so they accepted it and scheduled the closing for the end of August. Without delay, they began to search for a new home and were confident they would find one before the closing date in August.

***

Hank and Bernie still hadn't found a home they could afford by the first day of August. They both liked a house in

Runnemede, but they didn't have enough for the down payment. They only had $2,000, and they needed at least another $500. At Mass that morning, Hank prayed they could come up with the additional $500 without borrowing money from his relatives.

Hank tossed and turned before he finally got up for work that Monday morning. He felt himself slipping into depression and despair. On the way to work, he tried to think of other possible places his family could move to without the $500 they needed for the house in Runnemede. They could move to an apartment, but they hadn't checked out that possibility yet. If push came to shove, they *could* borrow the money from Uncle Edwin or Bernie's sister Flora, but Hank was determined *not* to borrow any more money from them.

At work, Darrin called him into his office. Hank wondered if he had done something wrong.

Darrin said, "Why the long face, Hank? I've called you into my office because you've received the Exceptional Employee of the Year award."

"I have?"

"You have." Darrin handed him a manila envelope.

Hank opened it to find the award for exceptional employee and a sealed business envelope. He tore it open to reveal a check for $500. Hank's mouth fell open, but he couldn't speak.

"You deserve every penny of that check, Hank. You're here before everyone else, and you stay later than everyone else."

"I'm just doing my job. I'm so grateful for the post office believing in me."

"I know. But you truly *are* exceptional."

"Thank you, Darrin. This means more than you can know."

Before Hank went on his mail route, he made a quick call to Bernie to let her know he had won the award and that they could now make the down payment. "Please call the realtor and tell him to make the offer."

Bernie screamed in delight over the phone. "That's wonderful, Hank!"

While on his route, he decided to celebrate and organize a game night with the kids. Hank tried to have a game night every few weeks, especially in the summer, but he had neglected it lately because of the stressful house-hunting period.

After his shift, he bought four different chocolate bars. Last time, they played Monopoly. This time, they'd play Mousetrap. The winner would have his or her choice of a chocolate bar, and the runner-up would get the next choice, and so on.

Of course, Hank wouldn't play. He would just help each of his children. Usually, Young Hank needed the most help, so that's where he focused his attention. He hoped that he was creating fun memories for them. Hank pictured himself old and gray with his adult kids reminiscing about these good times.

Chapter 46
Hank
One-on-One Time
1972

Hank and his family moved into their new home on August 30th. It was a detached Cape Cod with a spacious yard and gigantic, beautiful maples and oaks in a small town called Runnemede, about fifteen minutes north of Fairview Manor, their previous neighborhood.

The house had an excellent design. The front door opened into the spacious living room. Turning left was a walk-in kitchen that led to a larger dining room and small den, where Bernie would set up her office for transcribing court documents.

At the other end of the living room, a hallway came off the left, leading to a bathroom, the boys' room, and the master bedroom. Upstairs was an attic bedroom for the girls.

The church and school were only blocks away.

The drive to work would take a bit longer, but Hank didn't mind.

And best yet, with the sizeable yard, their dog Fluffy would be able to run to her heart's content once they had a fence installed.

To celebrate their new house, they invited family and friends over for a cook-out the following Saturday, on Labor Day weekend. As Hank barbecued hot dogs and hamburgers over the charcoal briquettes, he watched his kids and their cousins run around and jump through the sprinkler. Someone was mowing their lawn, and the scent of freshly cut grass, along with the intense heat of the charcoal grill, gave Hank a sense of peace. They lived an average life with their average family, and he had an average job. He thanked God for bringing him to this moment. Sometimes he felt like he didn't deserve all this. He took a swig of his Budweiser, a puff of his cigarette, and flipped the burgers over.

After such a joyous day, Hank drifted off to sleep quickly.

A thick cloud of darkness surrounded Hank. Footsteps clicked in rhythm behind him, the sound growing louder and faster. His heart raced. Goosebumps crept up and down his arms. Something was chasing him. He had to run! He turned, but his feet wouldn't move. Whatever was coming after him would soon catch him. Using all his strength and determination, he lifted one foot to step forward. Where was the ground? His foot traveled through nothingness, his body following, and he fell down...down into a black pit.

Hank woke up shaking, his heart nearly beating out of his chest. A black feeling crept its way into his soul, and he couldn't get back to sleep. Giving up on getting more sleep, he got up and turned on the TV. There was always an old movie playing in the middle of the night. He switched the channels. When he saw Teresa Wright and Joseph Cotton, he stopped. *Shadow of a Doubt.* A person could never go wrong with an Alfred Hitchcock picture.

By the end of the film, his eyes were closing, so he returned to bed. Despite his fatigue, he just couldn't settle. A feeling of despair filled his soul, but he willed it away. Besides, it was only five in the morning, and Mass at their new church wasn't until 11:00 a.m.

When Hank woke up, he rubbed his eyes. He stared at the clock on his nightstand. Was it really after noon? Shoot. *Why didn't Bernie wake me for Mass?*

He got up, fixed himself a cup of coffee, and turned the TV on. A few minutes later, Bernie and the kids came through the door. Bernie kissed him. "Oh, good, you're up. You were sleeping so soundly, and you didn't get much sleep. I didn't want to disturb you."

"Thanks for letting me sleep in, but I should've gone to Mass with you." Hank's comment came out a little more abruptly than it should have.

Bernie sighed. "I suppose I'll know that next time it happens."

His wife made breakfast but without speaking to him. He'd never known a more easygoing person than Bernie, but when she was mad, she gave the other person the silent treatment. Hank should apologize—and he would—but an apology always came out better when there were other things to discuss.

Later that night, after the kids were in bed, Hank approached Bernie. "I'm sorry, hon. I shouldn't have been curt with you for letting me sleep in."

Bernie sighed and nodded. "I was just trying to do you a favor. You don't get to sleep in often."

"I know. Thanks for that." He paused. "Bern, I have an idea. I'd like to take each of our kids somewhere, just one of the kids and me. I've already taken Mitch to a Phillies game a few times, but I rarely take Deb or Evie or Little Hank somewhere on their own. I'd like to start tomorrow and take Deb to the Philadelphia Zoo. I know it's Labor Day, but I called, and they're open. It would be just Deb and me. What do you think?"

"It's a great idea. And she'd love the zoo."

"Then it's a date."

The next day when he told Deb he was taking her alone to the zoo, she jumped up and down. Now nearly eight years old, Deb was the perfect age to appreciate the zoo.

When they arrived, he held her hand, and they visited the different inside and outside exhibits. He asked her what her favorite animal in the zoo was. She said, "The giraffes. They're so tall."

So he stopped at a souvenir stand and bought a stuffed giraffe for her.

"Thank you, Daddy. I love it!"

Deb fell asleep in the car on the way home, hugging her stuffed giraffe.

The following week, it was Evie's turn. She was only six, but because of her animated personality, he decided to take her to the Liberty Bell located in Independence Hall in Philly. Then, they'd visit the wax museum. Of course, Evie being Evie, she asked a ceaseless series of questions. "Why is the bell cracked, Daddy? Can I touch it? Is it from a long time ago? Why do so many people want to see this when it's broken?"

He lifted her so she could touch the bell and the crack.

"That's a big crack, Daddy."

"Yes, it is."

He placed her back down on the floor and took her hand. "It's called the Liberty Bell because it was one of the first bells used in the City of Philadelphia, at Congress, I believe."

"What's Congress, Daddy? And why is the bell broken?"

As they exited Independence Hall, the building that housed the Liberty Bell, Hank answered her questions, only to have her ask questions about the answers.

They walked a few blocks to the wax museum. Before entering, Evie asked, "Daddy, remember that *Twilight Zone* rerun about the wax figures coming to life?"

"I certainly do. That scared the heck out of you."

"I know. Will I like the wax figures in real life?"

"Let's go see."

Hank paid the admission fee, and holding his daughter's hand, he escorted her through the museum. They saw wax figures of Franklin D. Roosevelt, Ben Franklin, Elvis

231

Presley, and many more. Evie asked who each figure was, although she knew Elvis Presley and the Beatles, so she didn't have to ask about those. When they came to the scary section, Hank suggested they skip it, but Evie said no. "I'm six now, Daddy. I can handle scary wax figures."

The first figure they came to was Dracula, then Frankenstein, the Mummy, and the Werewolf.

Evie's eyes narrowed as she studied each figure, but she didn't get too close to any of them. Hank held her hand tightly so she would feel protected.

He purchased a small souvenir for her, a wax museum coloring book with crayons, and they left.

It was Little Hank's turn two weeks later. His youngest son was now four, so Hank took him to a petting zoo in nearby Sewell. Little Hank enjoyed the llamas, deer, and goats, especially touching the animals.

Whenever Hank drifted toward despair, these outings with each of his children gave him hope. He kept reminding himself that the medications to treat his mental illness were not a cure but a treatment, and he had to fight constantly to keep from slipping into hopelessness.

Chapter 47
Hank and Evie
Trigger
August 1978

It was twelve-year-old Evie's turn for one-on-one time with Hank, so he offered to take her to a baseball game at Veterans Stadium in Philly.

On the drive there, Hank asked, "Did you know that my Pop, your grandfather, used to take Uncle Billy and me to the Phillies games back when they played at Connie Mack Stadium?"

"That's neat, Dad."

"My father was a gentle, kind man who loved you kids. He seemed so happy when I told him your mother was expecting you. I wish you could've met him."

"Yeah, me too." Evie paused. "How did he die?"

"Brain tumor, cancerous. They couldn't do anything for him except give him painkillers. He wasted away."

"I'm sorry, Dad."

"I sure do miss him."

"Just like I'll really miss you someday when you're gone, hopefully not until I'm old, at least forty-five."

Hank laughed. "That's not old, Evie. I'm approaching that age."

"Well, *you'll* live till you're, like, 70, which is super old."

"I would like that."

When they arrived at the stadium, Hank purchased two yellow-section (or nosebleed) seats behind the Phillies dugout, and when they sat down, Evie asked, "Why don't you and Mom go to Mass anymore, Dad?"

Hank lowered his head. He wasn't going to tell his twelve-year-old daughter that he felt like a hypocrite going to Mass but still using birth control. So he said, "Well, just got into a bad habit, I guess."

Of course, as soon as the game started, Evie plunged full speed ahead with questions about the game. "Why is there an organ playing? Who's the kid handing the bats to the players? Why did that guy catch the ball over there?" Hank had a hard time following the game. Then again, this game wasn't about him; it was about spending time with Evie.

He gave his daughter a scorecard and taught her how to keep score. She stopped asking questions, and for that, Hank was grateful.

"Hank? Little Hank Gallagher, is that you?"

The voice came from behind him. It sounded like an older gentleman. He turned.

Before him stood Fr. Tim O'Reilly in his white-collar and typical modern-day priest attire. For a moment, Hank couldn't move or think.

"This must be your daughter. Oh, Hank, she's sweet. How old is she? Five or six?"

Hank couldn't form words. Thankfully, Evie spoke up. "Excuse me, Father, I'm twelve."

"Oh, well, then please forgive me, young lady."

"Of course, Father."

"So, Hank, what have you been up to? I haven't seen you since high school."

Hank kept his gaze on his feet.

***

Evie watched her father. He'd turned white as a ghost, and he wasn't talking to the loud priest standing behind them. Why wasn't Dad talking to him? And why was he staring at the ground?

"Father, how do you know my dad?"

"I taught him English in high school. He was very gifted in

234

telling stories. Weren't you, Hank?"

The priest waved his hands as he spoke and seemed very showy.

Something was going on with this priest. Evie didn't know what, but something was wrong. Dad never acted like this, at least not since his nervous breakdown. But Evie didn't remember much about that.

Evie pulled on her father's arm. "Dad, I think we better leave."

He lifted his head and stared ahead blankly.

Evie waved goodbye to the loud priest and gently nudged her father down each section until they reached the outside parking lot.

Once there, Dad seemed better. He opened the door to their car, and they got in. But he sat for a few moments with his head bowed and didn't turn the key.

Dad needed cheering up. Evie took her pencil and wrote on the scorecard, "You're the best Dad in the whole world, and I love you so much! Love, Evie." Before giving it to him, she said, "Dad, what's wrong? You look like you saw a ghost."

"That's because I did."

"Here. I hope this makes you feel better." Evie handed him the scorecard.

He read it and smiled. "Thanks, Eve. Love you too."

***

Hank gripped the steering wheel and tried to shake the memory of seeing *him* again. He had lost some memories from the shock treatments. Why couldn't he have lost *that* memory?

Dark hopelessness seeped into his soul.

When he arrived home, he drank all five cans of Budweiser in the fridge. Then he called and ordered two more twelve-pack cases. He needed to blot that face from his memory. Yes, he would drink beer because it made him feel better.

After the tenth can, Hank started to slur his words.

"What's wrong, Hank?" Bernie asked, sitting beside him in the living room. "Evie said you saw a priest who taught you in high school." She leaned in close and whispered, "It wasn't *him*, was it?"

All Hank could do was stare straight ahead and nod.

"Oh, Hank, I'm so sorry. I'm so very sorry you had to see him again."

***

Hank continued to drink, day after day, from the time he arrived home to the time he went to bed. Beer made him feel stable, grounded, but he set limits to his drinking. He only drank when he wasn't working and never until 4:00 p.m. Once in a while, he considered the four different medications he had to take. Each bottle warned against drinking alcohol while on these medications, but beer wouldn't have any detrimental effects, would it?

Bernie told him that he was starting to act like an alcoholic, to which Hank snarled, "No, I'm not. Besides, you can't be an alcoholic and just drink beer." Granted, he did drink every moment he wasn't working.

One day in late August, Hank adjusted the mailbag hanging from his shoulder and gazed up at the clear blue sky. Labor Day would arrive soon. And an extra day off. He'd have to pick up more beer. Just thinking about it made him thirsty for one. It couldn't hurt to have a beer or two at a bar during his route. One beer wouldn't hurt his performance.

Then, after only three beers during his route, he lost consciousness and collapsed on the sidewalk. One of the ladies on his route called 9-1-1, and the ambulance showed up.

"You've been drinking, sir?"

"Just three beers."

"Are you sure that's all you had?"

"Absolutely."

The ambulance brought Hank to a payphone, and he called Bernie. "These guys say I'm drunk, but I only had three beers." He wasn't slurring his words, was he?

"All right, Hank. I'll get Uncle Edwin to pick you up. Where are you? We'll get somebody to go back in for the car."

"Okay."

***

Bernie called the Camden Post Office to report that Hank would be off due to illness for the next few days. She hoped she'd be able to sober him up and get him back to work.

Once again, she had seen the signs: always stopping at the bar after work, drinking non-stop at home. He needed help immediately. Maybe she could convince him to go to Alcoholics Anonymous.

When Hank got up the next day, he immediately went to the fridge. "Bernie, where's my beer?"

Bernie felt like she was disciplining one of her kids. "It's not there, Hank. You can't keep drinking like this."

"It's just beer, Bernie. I only have a few cans a day."

"Actually, no, you don't. You've been drinking so much for the past year or so that you've become an alcoholic."

Hank spat, "Alcoholics become alcoholics on hard liquor, not beer. I told you that."

Bernie took a deep breath and slowly exhaled. "Hank, you have a problem. Please, you need to admit that you have a problem."

"I'd admit it if I did, Bernie. You know that."

"Hank, honey, please trust me. You need help."

"Just get me my beer, Bernie, now!"

Bernie straightened. "No, Hank, I can't let you do this to yourself."

***

After school, Evie plunked down on the couch in the living room. She was now thirteen years old and had just started the eighth grade. She liked her teachers and didn't have much homework yet. That meant she could watch TV all afternoon.

Eve glimpsed movement out of the corner of her eye—Dad? No, Little Hank (who was not so little anymore at the age of eleven) trotted into the room and joined her on the couch in front of the TV.

Her father's strange behavior lately worried her. She knew that he took medications for his mental illness, but Dad was not acting like Dad anymore. He hadn't gone to work for the past two days, and he stumbled around the house like a zombie in his underwear.

Just as the commercial came on, Dad trudged through the living room, stopped, and vomited all over the carpet. Evie and Little Hank exchanged glances. Her brother said, "Eww, Dad." Even Fluffy stared strangely at Dad.

Evie stood up and hollered, "Mom? Can you come here?"

When Mom stepped into the living room, she took one look at Dad and said, "Hank! Dear God." She assisted Dad into the bathroom to clean him up. Evie used paper towels to clean up the vomit on the rug.

Ten minutes later, Mom led Dad from the bathroom and put him to bed. Then she sat down with Evie and Little Hank.

"Sorry that you had to see that, kids."

"What's wrong with Dad?" Evie wrapped her arms around her middle, her stomach churning from worry.

Mom glanced away for a moment, then she made eye contact with Evie and Little Hank. "Your father needs help. He's sick. I'm going to see if maybe Uncle Edwin or Dad's friends from work can coax him to get help."

Evie remembered watching reruns of old TV shows, and

they always called people that drank alcohol "drunks."

Was Dad a drunk?

She sighed. Poor Dad. *God, help my dad.*

Uncle Edwin visited shortly after that. Her mom and Uncle Edwin went into her parents' bedroom to talk with her dad. Muffled voices traveled to the living room, but she couldn't understand what they said. She prayed that her dad would listen to them.

An hour later, Uncle Edwin and Mom came out of the bedroom.

Evie got up from the couch. "What's going to happen to Dad, Mom?"

"He's agreed to stop drinking and go to an AA meeting."

"That's good, right?"

"Yes, that's great news, Evie."

"Your father is going to be fine. He just needed a bit of a push to recognize that he was drinking too much." Uncle Edwin patted Evie's head. At thirteen, she was too old for him to do that, but she didn't mind.

Dad finally came out of the room too. His shoulders were slumped, and he looked like he was trying to hold back tears. Evie and Little Hank ran to him and hugged him.

He returned the hug then stepped away. "I'm going to be okay, you guys. Don't worry."

Mom fixed Dad a cup of coffee, and he sat at the kitchen table and drank it while Dad, Mom, and Uncle Edwin chatted about which AA meeting he should go to. Mom found a group in Haddon Heights. She called the number and asked what time the meeting would be tonight. Evie wondered what AA stood for, but if it would help Dad, she was grateful he would be getting help.

Mom told Dad, "Hank, there's a meeting at 7:00 p.m. I'll help you get ready and drive you there. I'll wait for you too."

Her dad just nodded.

Uncle Edwin stood and put on his hat. "Bernie, let me know if you need anything else."

"I will, Uncle Ed. Thank you."

"Always happy to help. You know that."

She walked him up the short stairway to the living room, then to the front door. "I don't know what I would've done without you over the years."

"We're family. That's why I'm here." He hugged Mom, and then he patted Little Hank's and Evie's heads again. "See you later, kids."

"Bye, Uncle Edwin," they said together.

***

Hank's whole body trembled on the way to the meeting. The last time he shook this bad was when he was delivering mail in minus thirty-five-degree weather.

But he wasn't cold. He just wanted a drink. One beer would do the trick. Uncle Edwin and Bernie seemed to think he needed this meeting, so he said he would go. He would try one meeting, that's all. Then he'd return home and have a beer to get rid of this shaking.

Bernie pulled up into the parking lot of the St. Rose of Lima Catholic Church, alongside a half-dozen other cars. "Here we are, Hank. Do you want me to go in with you?"

He shook his head.

"I'll be waiting right here."

Hank stepped inside and followed another fellow down some stairs to a brightly painted gathering room where a dozen people stood chatting in little groups. He wanted to turn around and go back outside. But he promised Bernie and Uncle Edwin he'd give it a try.

A man called everyone together, and they all took seats in a circle. The main guy, a tall, lean, clean-shaven fellow in his mid-forties, said, "All right, let's get started first with a prayer."

Prayer? They're praying?

When he finished the prayer, the main guy said, "It looks like we have some new people here, so I'm going to ask you all to introduce yourselves. No last names, just your first name and what brings you here. I'll start. I'm Buddy, and I'm an alcoholic."

"Hi, Buddy," everybody except Hank said.

"I've been sober now for five years, but I wouldn't have been able to do it without my sponsor's help."

The next man said, "I'm Jim, and I'm an alcoholic."

"Hi, Jim," everyone, including Hank, said.

"I've been sober for four months."

The next person, a lady, said, "I'm Esther, and I'm an alcoholic. I haven't had a drink in two months."

"Hi, Esther," said everyone.

Hank listened to everyone's stories with interest, and then the time came to introduce himself.

"I'm Hank."

"Hi, Hank," everyone said.

"My wife and uncle say I'm an alcoholic, but I told them I couldn't be because I only drink beer."

Buddy asked, "Hank, how long have you been drinking beer?"

"All my life."

"All right. How long have you been drinking beer constantly?"

Hank hesitated, then he whispered, "A little more than a year."

"Do you want to be sober?"

"Heck, no. I want to drink. I can stop whenever I want to."

"Do you *want* to stop?" asked Buddy.

"Honestly? No," Hank said.

Buddy nodded. "Well, Hank, if you want help, we're here to give it to you. But if you don't want help, there's not much we can do."

***

Bernie spent her time in the car reading *Where Are the Children* by Mary Higgins Clark. However, as good as the book was, she couldn't concentrate. Her thoughts kept drifting back to Hank in the AA meeting. Would he resist their help? Would he even admit he was an alcoholic? She sighed. *God, please help Hank to admit he needs help.*

***

For a few moments, the group remained silent, except for a few people whispering.

"Am I an alcoholic?" Hank finally asked.

"The first step is admitting it, Hank. Once an alcoholic, always an alcoholic. Are you an alcoholic?"

Hank pinched his lips and clenched his fists. He stared down at his feet. He finally exhaled, "Yes, I'm an alcoholic."

"Do you want to get sober?"

"I don't want to hurt my family anymore."

***

Bernie heard people talking outside the car and glanced up to see three people, Hank included, chatting after the meeting. Hank was smiling. *Thank God.*

Hank finally came to the front passenger side and opened the door. "Bernie."

"Hank, how'd it go?" She stuffed a bookmark in her book and closed it, turning her full attention to him.

Hank dropped into the passenger seat and closed the door. "Went good. I've got a sponsor to help me not to drink. I'm supposed to call him whenever I feel an urge to drink."

"That sounds promising. It's always better to have someone support you."

"That's what they said."

Bernie hummed the entire drive home. After all Hank had been through in his life, she was relieved that he had finally admitted he needed help. *Thank you, God.*

***

Hank woke the following day feeling like a new man. At work, his co-workers asked how he was doing, to which he replied, "Much better, thank you."

Of course, "much better" didn't describe how things were going. But Hank wasn't going to tell them that he was an alcoholic. Nor would he share with them that it took every ounce of self-control not to go looking for a beer.

Chapter 48
Hank and Evie
Don't Fall Off the Wagon
August 1980

Mom was working at her new job transcribing daily copy at the District Courthouse in Philly for a two-week trial. Fourteen-year-old Evie missed her mother in the evenings, but her dad came home early enough that they watched the afternoon reruns of *Gomer Pyle* and *Twilight Zone*. Sometimes they played Rummy or Parcheesi.

On this day, Dad arrived home before she did. He stood in the kitchen, staring at the calendar. "Hey, Eve?"

"Yeah, Dad?"

"You know it's been 243 days since I've had a drink."

"Good job, Dad." She patted his back, proud of him and glad that his accomplishment made him happy. "Keep up the great work."

He sat on the couch in the living room, and Evie plopped down beside him. Fluffy joined them and tried to situate herself between Evie and her dad. Evie finally moved over. "You act like you own this house, Fluff."

The two of them watched the rest of *Twilight Zone*. This episode was with Burgess Meredith as a man who loved to read but then lost his glasses and wouldn't be able to read again. It wasn't one of Evie's favorites because the ending was sad.

The eerie music of *Twilight Zone* ended.

"Want to play Rummy while we watch the next show?"

Dad said, "No. Let's just watch the next show. Then I have to fry the bacon for BLTs tonight."

Since Mom started working long hours away from home,

Dad had begun making meals. Bacon, lettuce, and tomato sandwiches were his "go-to" meal, but he also made breakfast for dinner a lot. Not that Evie was complaining, but she wondered when Mom would give them a break from so much bacon.

The music to *The Monkees* came on, and Evie cheered. "Hey, I didn't know this was on now."

"Me neither," her dad said. "Well, I think it's time to start frying the bacon." He pushed himself up from the couch and stretched.

"You don't like *The Monkees*, Dad?"

"Not my favorite show, no, Eve."

"All right."

Dad turned on the news radio station as he fried the bacon.

Evie started the TV show but had seen this episode a few times. "You want me to set the table, Dad?"

"Sure, that would help a lot."

"I think it's only Deb, you, and me for dinner tonight. Mitch is out with a friend, and Little Hank is at baseball practice."

"Okay. I don't have to fry so much bacon then."

"Right." Of course, even when making dinner for three, Dad would still fry half a pound of bacon.

She took out plates and set the table. Before she turned back to the kitchen, something crashed to the floor, and Evie gasped, startled. Dad's glass of iced tea had fallen, the glass shattering and the tea spreading all over the floor.

Dad stood still as a statue and stared straight ahead. Was there something from the news that—

"The new bishop of the Diocese of Allentown will be installed next week. Monsignor Timothy O'Reilly taught English and Shop at Holy Archangels High School in Philly from 1949 to 1959 and St. Stephen's High School in Conshohocken from 1961 to 1969."

Evie touched her father's shoulder. "Dad, are you okay?"

He didn't respond. His eyes filled with tears.

"Dad? Are you okay?"

Still no response.

Evie didn't want to hurt him, so she patted his cheek at first. Getting no response, she shoved him hard on the shoulder. Only then did he blink and breathe and seem to come out of the trance.

"Dad, are you all right?"

"I'm...yes, I'm...I just need to go for a walk."

"Um, okay, Dad. I'll finish frying the bacon for you."

"Yeah, yeah, that's good."

He went out the door, and she watched from the kitchen window as he got in the car and drove off.

Just then, Deb walked through the door and into the kitchen. "Where'd Dad go?"

"I'm not sure. He was just making dinner and listening to the news. Then he dropped his glass of iced tea and stared blankly."

"Weird."

"Yeah, understatement, Deb. He didn't say anything or even move until I pushed his shoulder."

"You pushed Dad?"

"I did, and only then did he come out of his trance."

"That's odd."

Evie turned a few more pieces of bacon over then had a terrible thought. Could Dad have gone out to buy beer? *Please, God, no, not beer.*

When he returned two hours later, he staggered out of the car and into the house carrying a large paper bag with him.

Evie held her breath as she watched him set the bag on the counter. "Oh, no, Dad. You're not drinking again?"

He turned toward her and gave a weak smile. "Uh, no, I-"

"Please don't lie, Dad. I can tell you've been drinking."

"I just had one or two."

"What's in the bag?"

"Just a few beers."

While only a teenager, Evie could tell he had consumed more than one or two beers.

After Dad finished the beers in the bag, he stumbled into the bathroom.

Deb came downstairs. "Dad's not drunk again, is he?"

Evie nodded.

Her sister swore as she was known to do from time to time.

If Evie *was* a swearing girl, she might have sworn too.

The two girls stared at the closed bathroom door. Just then, the sounds of vomiting and retching came through loud and clear. The toilet flushed, and he opened the door. "Hey, girls, wanna wash sum tevelision?"

Deb shook her head.

Evie said, "Dad, I think we better get you into bed so you can sleep off your binge drinking."

"That's a god idea."

"A god idea?"

"I mean a good idea, Eve."

Evie called her two brothers, who were now home and in their room. They opened the door and came into the hallway, questioning looks on their faces.

"Can you two walk Dad into his bedroom, take his shoes, socks, and pants off and tuck him in?"

Seventeen-year-old Mitch gave her a look as if to say, "Who am I? Dad's babysitter?" But he did as she asked.

When they came out of the room, twelve-year-old Hank asked, "Is Dad drinking again?"

Evie's heart clenched. She nodded.

Deb said, "Maybe he'll sleep it off and be better in the morning."

***

247

Hank tossed and turned in bed. Bernie snored beside him. The fog in his brain kept him from remembering how he got into bed. Then it hit him. He'd fallen off the wagon. Bernie was probably angry at him. She would be giving him the silent treatment.

He had to get up. He couldn't drink, he knew that, but then again, he had already consumed every can of beer in the house. Hank eased the covers back, slipped out of bed, and stepped into the kitchen. *Maybe Bernie has some cooking sherry he could drink.*

Then from inside of him, he heard a "No!"

God, I would kill for a cold glass of beer right now, any alcohol, really.

He dialed the number of his sponsor, Buddy, who answered on the third ring.

"Hello?"

"Buddy," he said, trying to keep his voice quiet, "I'm sorry to call right now. I know it's in the middle of the night."

"Hank, you know you can call me whenever you need to."

"Well, I messed up. I had a drink, well, many drinks. I got drunk. What do I do now?"

Buddy said, "I'm sorry to hear that, Hank. But when you fall off the wagon, you just have to get back on again. You can do this. Your family needs you to be sober."

Sadness gripped him, and tears came to his eyes. "I'm sorry."

"You don't need to say sorry to me, Hank. You need to say sorry to yourself and your family."

"Okay."

"We can talk for as long as you need me to, Hank, for as long as it takes for you to jump back on the wagon."

Then Buddy gave Hank three hours of his time, listening as Hank cried and offering him the support he desperately needed.

When Hank finally hung up the phone, he gazed out the kitchen window. The light of dawn was rising. That meant it was around 5:30 a.m.

Bernie, in her robe and slippers, padded into the kitchen. "I heard from the kids what happened." Her voice had more compassion for Hank than he deserved.

"I'm sorry, Bern. I'm not going to drink again."

"You should say sorry to the kids. They don't like seeing you like that."

"I know."

"So why all of a sudden did you feel you couldn't resist a drink? Did something happen?"

Hank nodded. "The news of that priest..."

Bernie drew in a breath.

"He was just appointed as bishop of—I don't remember. Why does he still haunt me now? And why is he being promoted when he..."

"What he did to you was wrong, Hank, horribly wrong. He used his position as a person of authority, as a priest, to gain your trust, and then he broke that trust."

He leaned in to hug her.

She embraced him tightly. "I don't want to lose you, Hank." "You won't."

"Will you be okay to go to work?"

"I'd be better there than here." Hank kissed his wife. "I'll get ready for work."

"I'll make you some coffee. I don't have to be at work until ten."

Hank tossed himself onto his other side in bed, struggling to get to sleep. It was after 8:00 p.m., and he listened to the radio. Tomorrow was Saturday, but he was scheduled to work at 6:00 a.m.

He would be glad when daylight savings time ended later this month because the sun would go down much earlier. Bernie had bought shades for the room to make it dark while it was still light out. Glancing at the glow-in-the-dark clock, he saw that it was now 8:20 p.m.

Someone in the living room was watching television. If he was lucky, it was Evie. She always said yes to coming and sitting with him.

He got up to use the bathroom. When he walked across the hall, he leaned his head into the living room. "Evie?"

"Yes, Dad?"

"I don't like having to go to sleep so early, and I'm having a hard time getting drowsy. Can you come and sit with me, maybe talk with me?"

Evie stared straight ahead, her eyes glued to the TV. "Um, *Love Boat* is almost over, Dad. Can it wait five minutes?"

"Sure. Thanks, honey."

Just after Hank settled himself, Evie opened the door and sat on the side of his bed. He held his hand out for her to hold.

Hank said, "When I was saying the Rosary a few minutes ago, I thought about last year when you said you wanted to be a nun. Are you still considering a vocation to religious life, Eve?"

"Not anymore, Dad. What I want to be is married and have a bunch of kids."

"Well, that's a good vocation too."

"I think so." She dipped her head and smiled. "Now, I just need to find a guy who wants to date me."

"Be patient. The right guy will come along. I promise you."

"Aw, that's because you're my dad."

Hank was silent for a moment. "Am I a good dad, Eve?"

"Sure, you are. Why would you think you're not?"

"Well, because I'm an alcoholic."

"Dad, that just means you can't drink. That doesn't make you a bad father."

Touched to the core, Hank squeezed his daughter's hand. "Do you know how much I appreciate you sitting with me when I can't sleep?"

"I like talking with you, Dad."

"Even though you have other things to do?"

"Well, I do, but if you need me, I'm happy to be here."

Hank put his rosary beads on the nightstand.

Evie gazed at them. "That's such a pretty rosary, Dad. Where did you get it?"

"My parents gave it to me when I graduated high school."

"Cool. I love how you can see them shimmer even with only a nightlight on." Evie hesitated. "Dad, why do you say the Rosary, but you don't go to Mass?"

"I don't know."

"You seem to love being a Catholic."

"I do, Eve." Of course, Hank did love his faith, but he still felt like a hypocrite using birth control. He hoped that maybe the Church would modify its position on the topic. Changing the subject, Hank asked, "What was your favorite one-on-one time with me?"

"Hmmm, that's a hard one. I liked the wax museum. That was cool and a little scary. And the library; do you remember that?"

"Right, it was the first time you went to the library."

"I had no idea that a person could rent books for free."

"And you tried to take out twenty books." He could still picture her walking through the library with that tall stack of books, trying not to drop one on the way to check them out. "You were about seven, right?"

"Yeah. It felt like Christmas." Evie paused. "And you know what, Dad? I still go to the library, but I don't take twenty books out anymore."

Her father chuckled. "You're a good kid, Eve."

"Aww, I bet you say that to all your kids."

"You're right. I do." He patted her hand. "Please stay with me a few more minutes."

"I will."

Hank thought about Evie and about how Pop never got to meet her or Little Hank. Deb and Mitch probably didn't remember him because they were so young when he passed. Hank felt sad about that. Whenever he thought of Pop, his heart still grieved. Someday, God willing, he would see Pop again in eternity.

Chapter 50
Hank
On and Off the Wagon
April 1982

Eighteen months of sobriety, and Hank felt like he was on top of the world. Yes, he still had the urge to drink, but when the temptation grew too strong, he called his sponsor. Hank always said the same things, but Buddy listened patiently every time.

How did alcoholics reach this stage without support, without AA? Hank could not imagine getting through the last year and a half without his family and Buddy.

One beautiful Saturday afternoon in April, he opened the door and lifted the pane to expose the screen. Spring scents of blossoming flowers made Hank linger there.

Bernie and Evie had gone to the mall, Deb was down the shore with her boyfriend, Mitch was in his bedroom watching television, and young Hank was at baseball practice.

Hank turned on the TV to watch the Phillies game at Vet Stadium. He sat back and took a long drink of his iced tea. He wished he could have an ice-cold beer, but he knew he couldn't.

He lit a cigarette, inhaled, and blew out the smoke.

Fluffy pranced over and nudged his hand. While now over ten years old, she still got around easily. Hank rubbed her ears and patted the couch next to him. She climbed up and snuggled against him. He stamped his cigarette out in the ashtray.

During the seventh inning, Bernie and Evie, now back from shopping, came in.

Fluffy hopped off the couch to greet them, jumping on them and licking them.

Bernie said, "Down, Fluff. You'd think you hadn't seen us in a month."

Evie dropped her bags on the couch near the door and stood watching the game on TV.

"Hi, Dad. Who's winning?"

"Phillies, five to three."

"Great."

"Hey, Eve, can you please pour me another glass of iced tea?" Hank held up his empty glass.

"Sure." She took his glass and went into the kitchen.

Hank got up to use the bathroom. When he returned, Evie had placed a glass of iced tea on the end table next to his seat. "Come here, Eve." He pulled her into an embrace. "It's been eighteen months. Not one drink."

"I know, Dad. Good job. We're all rooting for you." She stepped away, but he pulled her back.

"You know what, Eve? You need to find a guy who's about my height because you fit so perfectly to me."

"Dad, if I could just find a guy who wants to date an almost sixteen-year-old who looks like a little kid, I'd be in good shape."

He kissed her forehead. "You'll find someone. Remember I told you, be patient. Whoever marries you will be getting a precious jewel."

"Thanks, Dad, but don't all fathers say that?"

"Maybe, but I *really* mean it."

"I know." She kissed his cheek.

"Love you, Evie."

"Love you too, Dad. I'll be upstairs if you need me. I have some homework to finish, and then I'm going to Confession and Saturday Mass."

"Okay." It made him happy that Evie continued attending

Mass. Only his two youngest kids currently went to Mass.

Evie turned to go up the stairs then stopped. "Hey, Dad?"

"Yes?"

"Why don't you and Mom come to Confession and Mass with me tonight? It's lonely being the only one in the family who attends Saturday evening Mass."

Could Evie have known? The past week he'd increased his recitation of the Rosary from once a week to every evening. The more he did that, the more he craved attending Mass and Holy Communion. "I'll think about it, Eve."

"Okay, Dad."

Hank sat down and took a long swig of his iced tea. He felt an unusual longing to go to Confession and attend Mass. He and Bernie had stopped attending when they'd started using birth control. However, after ten or so years, he missed the sacramental life.

Bernie came into the living room from the kitchen.

"Hey, Bern?"

"Yeah?"

"What do you think about going to Confession and Mass with Evie later today? She asked me to go with her."

"What? We haven't been to Mass in such a long time. I'm afraid the roof will cave in." She chuckled.

"No, I mean it. What do you say we go to Confession then attend Mass?"

"Yeah, maybe. We'll see."

He glanced up just as the mailman delivered their mail. Before the mailman stepped off the porch, Hank got up and opened the door. "Hi, Jack." Jack had been their mailman for the past four years.

"Hi, Hank. How're you doing?"

"Good," Hank said as he pulled the letters from the mailbox.

He returned to the couch and flipped through the

255

envelopes. Bill, bill, bill, junk mail, bill. He put the bills on the end table next to his iced tea, and he tossed the junk mail into the little waste can nearby.

The last envelope was addressed to Henry Francis Gallagher, Jr., and it was from the Holy Archangels Alumni Association. Probably another reunion planned. He had never attended a high school reunion, and he couldn't see himself starting now. Not that he didn't want to see his high school friends again. He just couldn't be bothered. Hank tossed the envelope in the waste can without opening it.

After the baseball game, Hank watched a rerun of *Get Smart* and nodded off to sleep. He woke when he heard the door shut and glanced up to see the time. *Shoot. It's a half-hour before Mass.* Evie had already left. He jumped up and headed for the den, where Bernie sat reading in an armchair. She glanced up.

"Hey, Bern, do you want to surprise Evie by going to Confession and Mass right now?"

"No, you go ahead."

"All right."

Hank quickly combed his hair and dashed out the door. Evie was way ahead of him and probably wouldn't see him coming. When he reached the church, Hank opened the doors and went around to the confessionals. The lights glowed over the penitents' doors, one on each side of the priest's door, and one man stood in line.

Just then, one of the confessional doors swung open, and Evie stepped out. She turned to genuflect toward the altar without looking up. The fellow waiting in line went in and shut the door. Hank would be next.

He kept glancing at Evie to see if she would notice him, but her head was bowed, and, God bless her, she was praying. A lady emerged from the other side of the confessional, so Hank went in and waited until the priest opened the little door.

Hank's heart raced, and his palms were sweaty. After all his rushing, he hardly had time to rehearse what he would say. But he knew it had been at least ten years since he had been to Confession or to Mass, so that part was easy. Also, even though they didn't have sex much anymore, they still used birth control when they did. Maybe the priest would understand that they couldn't have another child right now. Still, he had to confess it.

Although Hank would always be an alcoholic, he had been sober for eighteen months. Better yet, Hank hadn't been unfaithful to his wife in many years. He was sure the Blessed Mother had something to do with that.

If he were honest with himself, Hank suspected that he wouldn't make it to next Sunday without committing a mortal sin, but he felt a strong desire to do this. He only wished that Bernie had accompanied him.

Hank couldn't wait to see Evie's face when he sat beside her at Mass.

The box slid open, and Hank confessed his sins. After the absolution and his botched Act of Contrition, Hank emerged from the confessional feeling better about his life than ever before. He genuflected and moved to sit next to Evie. Her eyes widened, and she gasped. He knelt on the kneeler and leaned over to whisper, "I just went to Confession so I can receive Communion."

"Good job, Dad," she whispered back.

Evie kept turning to him and smiling. Her reaction made him wish he'd gone to Confession sooner. However, he hadn't gone to Confession for Evie. He went because he felt he needed to do so. It had been too long.

Their church had an unusual Greek amphitheater design with a massive crucifix hanging above the altar. He had only attended this new church a few times.

Strangely, the hanging crucifix kind of reminded him of

his high school, where statues of the archangels hung above the school's main staircase. For a moment, his heart clenched. He tried never to think about high school—at least not his freshman year.

At the peace of Christ, Evie leaned over and hugged him. "I'm so happy you're here, Dad," she whispered.

"Me too."

Hank and his daughter walked home from Mass together. When they entered the living room, Evie couldn't stop saying, "Dad attended Mass with me." From her pinched expression, Bernie was annoyed that Evie kept repeating it.

That night, after getting into bed but before turning out the light, Hank's soul felt more at peace than ever before. Some days he still teetered on the edge of sanity, but most days, at least, life was bearable.

Hank took a pen and pad out of his nightstand and started to make a list of topics he wanted to write about.

"A Layman's Guide to Recognizing Mental Illness," he wrote. Then he listed a few things he wanted to write about: inactivity, feeling sorry for oneself, withdrawing from society. Hank wanted normal people, especially his family, to understand how mental illness took hold of a person.

Hank then wrote, "The US Postal System." He had wanted to write an article regarding what a privilege it had been to work for them. So many employees complained and griped, but he had always been so grateful for his job that he wanted to write a positive article that focused on the advantages of working for the USPS.

That would keep him busy for a few months anyway.

As he took out his rosary, a realization struck him. He loved God. He loved Our Lady. He loved his family.

It was only upon receiving the Eucharist after such a long time that he felt overwhelming gratitude to God. So many times over the years—throughout the events leading to his mental breakdown and his alcoholism—the darkness nearly snatched him from this life. His faith in God had saved him. And he was filled with the knowledge that despite his failings—his mental illness, his alcoholism, his unfaithfulness to his wife, or the fact that he and Bernie contracepted—God loved him unconditionally.

***

At work that Monday, he arrived to find that his mail route had changed. A letter carrier from upstate New Jersey had transferred and had more seniority than Hank. The new route was longer and in a run-down neighborhood. He was so disappointed that he nearly cried. He had become friends with many of the people whose mail he delivered. When despair snuck into his soul, he pushed it away and prepared for the day ahead.

***

The following Thursday, after work, Hank was relieved to know he only had one more day of work. He had Saturday off, so he planned to enjoy the two-day weekend. He was still sad about losing the route he'd had for over ten years, but he couldn't do anything about it. He even considered calling in sick one day because the people on the new route complained to him about late mail and other things rather than greeting him with a smile. He didn't know how much longer he'd be able to handle that route, but he would do his best. He would not—could not—have a beer, no matter how bad things got at work.

Evie arrived home after school and complained to her father that the kids in school didn't take her seriously because she looked so young. She didn't like being called "Shrimp."

Hank understood her frustration. He remembered those names well. "Well, sorry, Eve. You're short and probably look young because of me."

"It's not your fault that you're short, Dad." Then Evie told him about this boy she had a crush on named Chandler Richard Andrew Paine. She stared off into space as she spoke about him.

"You like him?"

"I do. He's so dreamy. My friends tease me about him, though. His initials are CRAP. They keep telling me I'm going to be Mrs. Crap."

Hank laughed.

"I'm telling you, Dad, someday, I'm going to get married and have a bunch of kids. I'm going to fill a big house with lots of kids."

It made Hank smile every time she said she wanted many children. Someday, he'd be old and gray and playing with his grandchildren.

"Hey, Eve, I'm going to the Acme to pick up bread, eggs, and milk. Do we need anything else?"

"We have plenty of bacon, so don't buy any."

After buying the groceries, Hank got into his car and turned to the easy listening station (Evie and Deb called it elevator music). "Strangers in the Night" by Frank Sinatra played, and Hank hummed along. Nothing like Frank Sinatra music to make a person feel great.

He returned home to find his youngest son on his way out to baseball practice. The house was quiet, except for Fluffy's excited squeals. She greeted him with the enthusiasm of a hundred people. That was the thing with dogs—they didn't care if you suffered a mental illness or had a relapse or were even an alcoholic. They always showed affection.

While rubbing Fluffy behind the ears, Hank glanced around the quiet living room. He suspected that his oldest son was in his room watching television. And Deb was likely at her boyfriend's house; they didn't see her much anymore. The soft din of pop music came from the attic bedroom, indicating that Evie was home.

After Fluffy settled down, he opened the door to the upstairs bedroom. "Hey, Eve?"

"Yep. Need anything, Dad?"

"Want to watch TV or play a game of Rummy?"

"Sure. I'll be right down."

Hank opened the fridge and poured himself a glass of iced tea. He was craving a beer right about now but shook the thought away. He had been sober for too many months to give up now.

He turned on the television and switched a few channels until he found one that showed reruns of old television shows from the '50s and '60s. On Channel 29, Hoss was talking to Little Joe, so *Bonanza* it was. They watched *Bonanza* as they played Rummy.

The phone rang, and he got up to answer it, taking his iced tea with him.

"Is Henry Gallagher there?"

"You mean Henry the father, or Henry the son?"

"Whoever graduated from Holy Archangels High School in Philly."

"That would be me." Now Hank was annoyed. He wished someone would invent a device that would indicate who was calling before a person answered the phone. Then Hank never would've answered this call. He knew exactly what this was about, and he wasn't interested in attending any high school reunion.

"Henry, we wanted to make sure you received the invitation in the mail."

"I did, but I'm not attending." Hank took a sip of his iced tea.

"So you won't be attending the 30th anniversary then?"

"The 30th anniversary of what?"

"Of Bishop Timothy O'Reilly's ordination to the priesthood."

He sprayed his iced tea all over the table. "I...well—no, I won't be attending."

He slammed the phone down before the fellow on the other end could say goodbye.

Hank felt sick to his stomach. He couldn't believe they were having a celebration honoring *him*. He tried never to even think about *him*.

Suddenly, he was filled with rage. He balled his fists and wanted to pound the table. Hank began to shake. *A beer. No, not a beer.* Yes, a beer was the only thing that would calm him. *No, don't do it.* He shook his head. *But if it's only one beer, it won't harm anything.*

He called his sponsor, Buddy. But the phone rang and rang. "Please answer, Buddy. I need to talk."

But Buddy didn't answer.

"Hey, Dad, what's going on?" Evie stepped into the kitchen from the living room.

Hank avoided eye contact with his youngest daughter. He didn't want her to see his anger. "Nothing." He swiped the car keys from the back of the counter and headed for the door.

"Where are you going?"

"Out."

"But we were watching TV and playing Rummy." Evie followed him to the door.

"Not anymore." He swung the door open and grabbed his jacket from a coat hook, still unable to look at her.

"I don't get it. What's wrong?"

Hank ignored Evie's question. He put on his jacket and stomped outside, the screen door slamming shut behind him. Thoughts raced through his mind as he got in the car and cranked the key in the ignition. *It's not too late. It's not too late.*

Don't go to the liquor store.

Okay, not to the liquor store then. His hands continued to shake as he gripped the steering wheel. He promised himself he would only drink one beer.

He wouldn't get a six-pack from the store; he would have one drink at the bar. Hank parked by Pinky's at Third Avenue and Black Horse Pike. Yes, he promised himself he would only have one drink.

Hank opened the door. It was only four in the afternoon, but he knew the bar would be open. He climbed onto a stool. The bartender said, "Hank, I haven't seen you around here in a long time. What can I get you?"

"A Bud, please."

"Sure thing."

The bartender filled a tall glass with beer from a keg then scraped the foam level with the glass. "There you go, Hank. Enjoy."

Hank leaned over and smelled it. He knew with every fiber of his being that he shouldn't drink even one beer, but it *was* only one. Years ago, he could drink one beer with no problem. Maybe he wasn't an alcoholic anymore.

"You gonna drink that or smell it, Hank?"

Hank cleared his throat. "I'm gonna drink it." He first took a tiny sip—*God, it tastes so good*—then he practically downed the entire glass. He was right. It cured the shakes immediately.

He just had to have another one. *Just one more.* "How about another one?"

"Sure."

Hank downed that one and another then paid his bill and left the bar. Three beers would not be enough to make him forget, so he drove immediately to the beer store and purchased a twelve-pack.

When he returned home, he drank every can of beer and fell asleep on the couch.

"Dad, wake up. Why are you sleeping so early?"

"Huh? What? Oh, yeah. I'll go s...sleep in ...foo mints."

"Dad, you're not drinking again, are you?"

Why did Evie's voice have to be so high-pitched?

He cleared his throat. "No, no." Hank stood up and swayed, nearly passing out. Then he felt along the wall to make it to the hallway, then to his bedroom. He collapsed onto his bed.

***

"Hank? Why haven't you left for work?"

"Bern?"

"Yes?"

"Call work. I'm sick."

"All right."

***

Evie woke to her loud-enough-to-wake-the-dead alarm that morning. Sometimes she wanted to take this noisy contraption and break it with a hammer. But it did the trick and always got her up on time.

She descended the stairs to the hallway. Her parents' door was shut. Evie made her way to the kitchen.

Her mother sat at the table, eating a bowl of cereal.

"Why's your bedroom door closed?"

"Because Dad's sick."

Evie sighed. "He's been drinking again."

"Yeah, I know. But I have to go to work, and I can't babysit him all day. Hopefully, he'll sleep it off and realize he needs to hop back on the wagon."

***

Sometime later, Hank jumped in his sleep and woke to the sounds of thunder and lightning. His head pounded, and the contents of his stomach threatened to come up. He pulled himself up and stumbled to the bathroom, where he vomited.

Hank turned on the faucet and poured himself a cup of water, swirled it around in his mouth, then spit it out. He crossed the hallway and went into the living room. Fluffy wagged her tail but didn't get up off the couch. He glanced at the clock: just after one in the afternoon. Hank was glad no one was home.

More beer. This time, he called the liquor store. They said they could deliver two cases of beer within the hour. Hank just had to survive the next hour without a beer.

He started to get the shakes again. Hank paced the living room until he tripped and landed on the chair by the television. There was a loud knock at the door.

At the front door, Hank paid the delivery boy. Not bothering to put the cans in the fridge, he opened one can and started drinking. He had consumed the first one when he realized that he hadn't taken his medications today.

He reached for the four bottles. "I'm supposed to take some in the morning and some at night," he mumbled, reading the label on one of them. "Maybe I should just take them all at once, so I don't forget." He poured a few pills from each bottle and swallowed them with a beer.

Sometime later, the room was spinning, and he couldn't think straight. *Did I just urinate on the floor?*

Now, as he walked to the bathroom, he felt like he was floating. Weird feeling. He kind of liked it.

Hank squinted, unable to see much of his surroundings. It was a dull, rainy day, and he hadn't turned on the lights. Nausea rose in his stomach, and his head pounded.

He staggered back into the kitchen, where the second case of beer was waiting. As the room tipped, he steadied himself on the table. Then he popped open a can, brought it to his mouth, and guzzled the contents. His head bobbed to the side.

He reached for another beer and felt something dragging on the floor, caught on the hem of his robe. He leaned over and pulled it up. It was his rosary.

Hank stuffed the beads into the pocket of his robe. He

heard a clinking sound on the floor, and then he leaned back against the bottom cupboard.

Hank couldn't remember…had he taken his pills yet? *Pills, I have to take my pills.* He climbed back to the table, opened the bottles, and poured the rest into his hands. Yes, he should take the rest. They would make him feel better.

He felt weak, dizzy, and his head exploded in pain.

He lowered himself back to the floor and fell over sideways. His face hit the beads on the floor. *Mother Mary, help me.*

Hank's world became a black wasteland to which he descended further and further. His last rational thought was, *Dear God, forgive me.*

***

Evie loved the rain, especially on a warm day in April. She usually walked home with Kate, but her friend had stayed after school to attend an Interact meeting. So she journeyed home by herself.

The earthy scent of rain and the flowers-just-about-to-bloom fragrance caused Evie to stop and breathe in deeply.

Before she reached her house, she noticed their car still parked out front. Her mother always took the bus to Philly. Then she remembered that her father had fallen off the wagon and had stayed home.

Hopefully, he was just sleeping it off.

Evie closed her umbrella and left it on the porch. She opened the door and stepped into the living room.

Fluffy didn't greet her. *That's odd.* After tossing her school bag onto the chair, she turned toward the kitchen and found Fluffy on the ground, whimpering quietly. She stopped, unable to move, her mouth open and heart thumping.

There, sprawled out on the floor, was her father in his underwear, the stench of vomit and urine assaulting her nose.

She rushed to his side and pushed his shoulder hard.

"Dad? Dad, wake up! Wake up!"

But he wouldn't rouse. She shoved him harder. That usually brought him around but not this time. Nothing. *Call 9-1-1.*

Evie reached for the wall phone in the kitchen and dialed 9-1-1. The person who answered asked her, "Emergency, ambulance, or fire?"

"Um, ambulance. My dad's passed out on the floor, and I can't wake him."

"Stay on the line with me. What's your name?"

"Evie."

"Okay, Evie. What's your address?"

Evie gave her the address. "Please send them now!"

Fluffy nudged Evie's arm and whimpered.

"It's okay, girl." Evie stroked the dog's neck.

"Is someone there with you, Evie?"

"Just my dog."

"Okay. The ambulance is on its way, but stay with me on the line until they get there."

"All right."

"How old are you, honey?"

Evie gritted her teeth and clenched her fists. This was not a time she wanted to sound young. "Almost sixteen."

"All right. Just stay with me, honey."

Evie knelt by her father and kept pushing on his arm to see if she could wake him up. Nothing she did roused him. He was warm. *He can't be dead.*

The lady from 9-1-1 rambled on about something, but Evie just wanted to wake her father. Finally, she heard the sirens of the ambulance getting closer. "I think they're here now."

"Yes, all right. Can you make sure the door is open for them, Evie, and also take your dog to another room?"

"Yes, ma'am." She grabbed Fluffy by the collar and put her in the boys' bedroom.

Next, Evie went to the door and waved for them to come in. The paramedics burst through the doorway and immediately started working on her father. They asked her to wait in the living room, so she did. Evie sat on the chair across from the kitchen's entrance so she could watch what they were doing. Should she call Mom at the courthouse?

Evie had watched enough of the shows *Emergency* and *Quincy ME* to know that the paramedics performed CPR on her dad. *Dear God, please don't let him die.* Next, they used some sort of machine that made a popping sound. They tried that a few times, then one of them glanced at his watch. "Time of death, 3:42 p.m."

Behind the paramedics, Evie screamed, "No!"

One of them tried to calm Evie, but she cried so hard, she began to hyperventilate. When she glanced back at where her father lay, a sheet now covered his body.

She pleaded with the paramedics, "Can't you keep trying? He's only forty-five. Please. He's so young. There must be something you can do for him."

"I'm sorry, but we've done all we can."

Evie dropped to the floor, her head in her hands. All rational thoughts vanished. Her father was dead.

"We've called the coroner, hon, and he'll be here shortly. Do you want to give your mother a call?"

Evie stared at them blankly. "W-what?"

"Do you want to call your mother?"

"Yes, I'll do that now."

"All right."

Evie glanced toward the kitchen, where her father's covered body remained on the floor. She couldn't use that phone. Evie raced upstairs to her and Deb's room to use their phone. She called the courthouse and asked for her mother. When Mom finally got on, she said, "What's up, Eve?"

"Daddy...he's dead. Please come home."

There was a split-second of silence, then her mother said, "Wait, what?" Another pause, then Mom asked, "How do you know? Did you call 9-1-1? Are you sure?"

"Yes, Mom, the paramedics are here. He's dead."

Her mother's pained voice screeched through the telephone, "Dear God, no!"

Chapter 51

Evie

Accusations From Boston

January 2002

Shortly after the beginning of the new year, Evie had a free evening without her boys. Jake had been encouraging her to take some time for herself, so he brought all five of their children to the movies to see *Monsters, Inc.* Their second oldest had been begging them to see the film ever since it was released the previous summer.

Evie watched the nightly news, a glass of ginger ale and a bowl of sour cream and onion chips on the coffee table. A story entitled "Church Allowed Abuse by Priests for Years" aired. Evidently, a journalist uncovered the story that many pedophile priests in the Boston area were allowed to continue in parishes where abuses were reported. And, the story suggested, Boston wasn't the only diocese that allowed this sort of behavior.

She went to the computer and did a search. As she read the stories of survivors of clergy abuse, one thing seemed prevalent among most: secrecy. When the abuse happened, rarely did the victim tell their parents, and many kept the abuse secret for years.

Some reliably accused priests had been moved from parish to parish instead of being removed from ministry.

More than one survivor spoke of struggling with alcoholism, drug addiction, and mental illness. They talked about desperately trying to forget the abuse, only to be reminded when their abuser was promoted, contacted them, or was in the news.

Evie straightened as her memory brought up an incident

that had never sat well with her. *The baseball game!* That loud priest had spoken to Dad, but Dad hadn't even wanted to look at him. What was the priest's name? Fr. O something? She wished she could remember. At the time, she thought he was too showy for a priest. The priest didn't seem to care that her father had gone pale and was not responding to his questions.

Evie's stomach turned. Could it be? *Was...my father abused?*

She remembered another time when Dad fell off the wagon. When *was* that? Yes, he was frying bacon for dinner and listening to the news on the radio. Was that news about a priest? *That* priest? Evie couldn't be sure. Maybe she was just letting her imagination run wild.

One thing was certain. Evie had some of her father's items. She racked her brain, trying to remember where she kept her father's treasure box, journal, printed essays, and freshman yearbook. Evie felt compelled to find Dad's things. Maybe they could help her understand what, if anything, happened to him when he was younger.

Chapter 52
Evie
The Journal's Hidden Message

Evie had no time to search for her father's items before the kids came home with her husband.

The sound of laughter and many footsteps outside meant that Jake was home with the boys. Evie put the littlest boys to bed and directed the older boys to read in bed. This was the time of day she usually hit a brick wall, too tired to do anything else but sleep. Besides, she would search first thing in the morning, when she was fresh and energetic after a night's sleep.

Before the children woke up the next day, Evie scoured two different storage areas for her father's items. It only took about ten minutes to find what she was searching for: his treasure box, stories, yearbook, and journal were all in one place.

She picked up the journal. Its musty scent made her sneeze, but it appeared to be in excellent condition. Evie opened it and flipped through the pages, finding everything just as she remembered.

Little footsteps above meant that her youngest two sons were probably awake. The older boys always slept in, even on homeschooling days. She clapped the book closed, picked up the rest of the items, then went to prepare breakfast for her toddlers.

That night, after a full day of homeschooling, Evie read *Snowed In at Pokeweed Public School* to her two youngest. They pleaded for one more book, so she read *Miss Nelson is*

Missing, then she tucked her two precious boys into their beds and kissed their foreheads.

Their three older boys watched television in the downstairs rec room. They'd go to bed in about an hour.

In her bedroom, Evie clicked on the overhead light, then sat in the armchair and opened the treasure box to find seashells, baseball cards, and other valuables her father had saved.

Next, she paged through the essays and the yearbook. Not too much there either, although the stories he wrote about his time at the psychiatric hospital were depressing.

She picked up his journal, wondering what sort of information she could glean from it.

Opening to the first page, Evie recognized her father's cursive writing, although it was somewhat neater than she had remembered.

The short entry about his favorite Christmas and receiving his transistor radio made her smile. She turned the page. Scratched-out words were at the top of the page and nothing else. The following page contained a story entitled *The Apprentice and the Magician.* She read it quietly.

There once was an apprentice and a magician. The young apprentice trusted the magician with his very life. He worked with the magician every day, assisting him and helping him come up with magic spells.

Not everyone in the kingdom liked or admired the apprentice. In fact, he had many enemies.

The magician protected the apprentice whenever his enemies were nearby.

One day, the magician invited the apprentice to the dungeon of his castle. When the apprentice arrived, the magician gave him a cup with a secret potion. The apprentice didn't know what the secret potion was, but the magician

273

said, "Drink up, son, and my powers can be yours."

So he drank and drank and drank.

"Do you want to learn a new spell, apprentice?" the magician asked.

The apprentice could barely respond as the potion was mesmerizing.

"Say these words after me," said the magician.

While confused and under a spell from the drink, the apprentice repeated the words of the spell.

Suddenly, the apprentice was entrapped in a dark dungeon with dust so thick he could barely see out the two tiny windows. Wooden stairs led to a locked door. An ancient statue of St. Michael perched above him, half its face missing.

For years and years, he suffered in the darkness. Only short glimpses of beauty and light appeared. The apprentice lived out his life in this hopeless, lonely prison.

Evie remembered reading this years ago and thinking it was a depressing fairy tale. Something had definitely happened to him or someone close to him, but what?

Evie turned back one page to the one with the scribbled words. Her gaze shifted to the binding. It appeared as if the page before the page with the blacked-out title had been ripped out. She tilted her head, curious. Evie held the book up to the light. Squinting, she could see indentations from whatever he'd written on the page with the blacked-out title.

After shutting the book, she got up. She told her older boys to head off to bed, and then she searched for her husband. At this time of night, he was likely in his arts/recording studio working on audio engineering or painting. She put on her coat, made her way across the yard to his studio, and opened the door.

Jake stood in front of an easel, painting. He looked up. "Hey, everything okay?"

"Yeah, I think so. Do you have any dark pencil crayons I can use?"

He cocked an eyebrow. "Why?"

"Because I think my dad may have written something in his journal but then ripped out the page. I can see the indentations on this page that's blank except for one scribbled word. I was wondering what he might have written." She paused. "Of course, it could be nothing."

"Oh, okay. You're probably going to need a piece of charcoal." He set down his paintbrush and turned to a box, which he shuffled through before producing a piece of dark charcoal. "I'll help you."

"Sure."

Evie opened the book and pointed to the page with the indents.

Jake smeared a bit of charcoal across his index finger then lightly passed his finger over the indents, side to side. Soon, words appeared.

I thought Fr. Tim was the best priest in the world. But a few weeks ago, when we were working after school, Fr. Tim told me he was rewarding me for a job well done. So we sat on two armchairs facing each other. He brought out a bottle of whiskey, and he kept giving me gulps. He talked and talked and talked. Finally, the room spun, so I closed my eyes and rested my head on the back of the chair. As the room was spinning, I felt my zipper being undone. When I opened my eyes, Fr. Tim's head was in my lap and on the most private of places. I froze. I should've pushed him off me, but I froze. When he was done, he tried to get me to do that to him, but I pushed myself away. He came after me as I staggered away. He said that's what people who love each other do, and he only did it because I wanted it. I know it's my fault, but Fr. Tim did something bad to me.

275

Chapter 53
Hank
It Was Supposed to Be a Normal Day
January 1955

Fr. Tim sat in the chair facing the stairs and motioned for Hank to take the other chair in the basement of Archangels High School. The priest reached under his chair and pulled out a bottle and a small bowl of chocolates.

"This, my boy, is a reward for all your hard work."

Hank took a few pieces and consumed them. They were rich, peppermint-flavored chocolates.

Hank looked over Fr. Tim's head to a corner shelf, where an old statue of St. Michael stood, its face gone. He'd never noticed that creepy statue before.

As Hank chewed, he squinted to read the label of the bottle. *Jameson Irish Whiskey.* It kind of looked like a big bottle of the stuff Ma gave him when he was sick. What was that stuff called? Paregoric? "What's this?"

"It's the finest whiskey this side of the Mississippi."

"Whiskey?"

"Yes, son. And I've seen how well you work, how conscientious you are, and how grown-up you are, regardless of your stature." He paused, opened the bottle, took a swig, and handed it to Hank. "Wouldn't those boys who call you names be green with envy right now?"

Hank had no idea how to respond to that, although those bullies might be envious. He gripped the bottle but hesitated. What would be wrong with taking one sip of whiskey? His father let him taste his beer a few times. He brought the bottle to his lips then took a small sip. It burned his mouth and tasted like gasoline.

"Hank, come on, take a manly gulp."

He nodded. This time, he took a long, hard gulp but then nearly spat the liquid out, coughing and choking. His entire throat and mouth were on fire.

Fr. Tim laughed. "Believe me; someday, you won't cough like that."

The priest offered another swig, then another, all the while throwing a few words in. "What about our Varsity Basketball team winning five games in a row? Mackey scored 44 of the 94 points in that last game. That's almost half of the winning score."

Hank's face numbed, and he felt lightheaded. He and Red had only attended one basketball game. When Hank recognized two players as the bullies who called him names, he had no desire to return.

Fr. Tim rambled on about *The Lone Ranger*, a dog, and sledding, offering Hank another swig of whiskey.

The heater went on and drowned out whatever Fr. Tim said next. But the priest offered him more whiskey, and he obligingly gulped it down.

The priest's words became a jumbled mess of strange phrases he'd never heard before. His head lolled to the side. When Fr. Tim offered another drink, he pushed the bottle away. He thought he was going to throw up.

Now the dank cellar was spinning. He slumped back in the chair, closed his eyes, and rested his head, everything spinning around him like on that spinning ride at Willow Grove Park.

As the world spiraled around him, he heard something about "magic" and "love." It felt like someone was unzipping his trousers. What the—he lifted his eyelids open enough to see Fr. Tim's head in his lap—*oh, God, what's happening*? He squeezed his eyes shut.

He froze. Well, not every part of his body. For a moment,

Hank couldn't think straight. This *had* to be a nightmare. This couldn't be real. Fr. Tim was a priest, a holy man of God. And a man of God would *never* do this.

When the priest finished with him, Hank finally opened his eyes.

"See, Hank, your body responded to me. That proves that you liked—and wanted—what I just did. You obviously like boys, not girls."

No, you're wrong. I like girls. Hank squeezed his eyes shut until he felt the priest's hands on his shoulders. His head floated toward Fr. Tim and downward onto the priest's lap.

"Now, it's your turn."

No! Hank clumsily smacked the priest's arms away, and he stood up, only to fall back against his chair. Hank staggered toward the staircase. He reached it and grabbed on, leaning against the banister of the rickety wooden steps.

Fr. Tim's hand on his shoulder startled him, and he pulled away.

Didn't Fr. Tim say that masturbation was a sin? What he did *had* to be worse than *that*.

As if the priest knew Hank's thoughts, he said, "Hank, my boy, remember that when you give yourself pleasure, you do it alone. But when you are showing love to someone, it's perfectly fine. Don't you love me?"

Hank remained with his chest leaning against the railing, everything tilting around him. He didn't want to look at the man. He opened his mouth, but no words would come. He wanted to say, *Not like that.* His stomach heaved.

"Don't worry, Hank. The next time will be better. You'll get used to it."

No, no, this wasn't right. Next time? No, there wouldn't be a next time.

"Here, let me help you, Hank."

The priest scooped Hank up as if he was a baby. Hank

twisted and turned, panicking, desperate to escape, so the priest finally put him down.

"I'm...I'm going...home," Hank finally sputtered.

"Suit yourself, Hank. Don't tell anyone our secret. I wouldn't have done what I did if *you* didn't want it. I love you. We weren't doing anything wrong."

Hank swallowed. "But...." Was he right? Did Hank *want* it? No, he didn't. And his body betrayed him by responding. Hank should've been smart enough and strong enough to push him away from his lap. *This is my fault.*

As he stumbled to the wooden steps, he heard Fr. Tim say, "Remember, don't tell anyone, Hank. You don't want those senior bullies hearing about what we just did. No one would understand but you and I."

Hank gripped the wooden railing. His legs felt like jelly. He tripped up the stairs, praying that Fr. Tim wouldn't follow him. Finally, he reached the top of the stairs and felt around for the doorknob. When he finally found it, he twisted it, but it wouldn't turn. *Please!* He pulled and tried to turn it, but it wouldn't open. He banged the door.

"I'll unlock it for you, Hank. No need to get upset," the priest said from behind him on the stairs.

When the priest got close enough to touch him, Hank flinched and squeezed his eyes shut until he heard the click. The door swung open. Hank burst out of the cellar like the bit of puke that had just spit out of his mouth. *Please, God, don't let him come after me.*

As he staggered away, he heard the priest say, "Don't worry. I'll clean this mess on the floor."

Gotta make it to the door. He tripped and fell, but he half-crawled and half-stumbled the rest of the way across the foyer. The main office was to his right, but he wouldn't be able to ask for help. He couldn't tell anyone what had just happened.

Finally, he pulled himself up and held onto the side wall as he inched toward the outside door.

The cold, fresh air helped him to regain some awareness of his surroundings. It was close to dusk. He could barely put one foot in front of the other, let alone walk with ease. He leaned against one of the exterior columns. *Just need to rest for a bit. Please, God, don't let him come after me.*

After a moment, Hank staggered along with his hands out in front of him, feeling his way to the metal fence of the school's parking lot. The way the earth seemed to slide under his feet reminded him of being on one of those modern moving walkways in Jersey City that Pop had taken him and Billy to last year.

He collapsed against the fence, the cold metal seeping through his coat. The air was freezing, so he stuck his hands in his pockets. Hank wouldn't make it to the bus stop four blocks away until he could at least walk straight.

Hank's mouth tingled, and he retched again on the sidewalk. *Maybe I shouldn't go home.* What other options did he have, though?

A touch to his shoulder made him jerk and yell out.

"Mr. Gallagher, are you all right?"

Hank sighed with relief. It was Brother McCallum's voice. "Just feeling sick, that's all."

"Why don't you let me take you home then?"

No, he could not get into a car with a priest—or a brother—not now. "Um, no, thank you, sir, I mean, Brother. I'm just going to take the bus home."

"Well, how about I assist you to the bus stop?"

Hank didn't respond immediately. He had to think. They were outside. It was dusk, but there was enough light out. He wouldn't be able to walk without assistance. "I guess so, but you shouldn't get too close to me. I just threw up."

"Don't worry about that. I have a pretty resilient constitution."

Whatever that means. "Thank you, sir."

"Which bus do you take, Hank?"

Hank pointed. "The South Philly bus. It's four blocks away, at Broad Street." The almost-priest took Hank's arm, and he shrunk back. But he gave in and allowed him to hold onto his arm.

As they walked, Hank prayed that Brother McCallum wouldn't tell a stupid joke. Thankfully, he didn't. They shuffled slowly along the street. Hank tripped a few times, but when they finally made it to the stop, Hank mumbled, "Thank you. I appreciate it."

Brother McCallum responded, "Next time, only take one sip, Hank. I hope you feel better soon."

Hank nodded.

Chapter 54
Evie
The Name of the Wolf

Evie stood next to her husband, stunned as the words in her father's journal became visible. Her father must have written this all down and then ripped out the page and thrown it away. It seemed that this Fr. Tim had abused Dad, and Dad had kept the horrible incident secret his entire life. Worse, Dad had blamed himself, at least in part, for what had happened to him.

Her eyes filled with tears. Her heart ached for her father as a young boy, for the wounded man who carried this secret for so many years, and for the innocence lost. And—rage bubbled up inside her—he'd not seen justice in his lifetime.

Now so many things made sense: Dad's nervous breakdown, his alcoholism, his troubled life, the way he died.

Evie tossed and turned all night but couldn't sleep. She kept imagining a pedophile molesting one of her boys, and her heart clenched.

Her eighteen-month-old toddler climbed into bed and snuggled next to her at some point during the night. His warm little body and soft breathing consoled her, and she managed to sleep for a few hours.

The following day, Evie called her mother. Mom answered on the first ring.

"Have you been watching the news?" Evie asked her.

"You mean about the pedophile priests? Yes. And the whole sordid scandal just makes me sick."

"I know what happened to Dad."

Her mom was silent on the other end. "How?" she sounded defeated.

"He wrote it down one day after it happened and ripped out the page from his journal. But Jake and I were able to use charcoal on the indentations on the following page to read the words."

"Oh." Her mother paused then said, "I'd like you to read it to me, Eve."

"All right." Evie read the outlined words, her heart clenching all over again. When she finished, Mom was silent on the other end of the phone.

"Mom?"

"I'm here. So the name of the priest is Fr. Tim?"

"That's what it says. I don't know his last name, though."

Her mother stayed quiet.

"You don't seem surprised, Mom."

"Well, I'm not. Your father told me what happened to him, mentioning it only two or three times but not giving any details. Seeing how it made him feel, I never brought it up again."

"So you knew all this time? Why didn't you tell us?"

"Because you guys were all kids when Dad died."

"Yeah, but we're adults now."

"I know, but like your father, I tried to forget that happened to him."

"Well," Evie said, "after a night of crying, I'm furious. How could his abuser and all these other pedophile priests get away with it for so long?"

"I don't know, but it makes me angry too."

"Angry is an understatement. Oh, Mom, I wish he would've told *somebody*." Evie sighed. "Everything about Dad's life makes so much sense now."

Mom said, "Well, there's not much we can do now. Dad is dead and hopefully at peace in heaven."

"What if this Fr. Tim is still alive? There must be something someone can do."

"What if he's dead?"

"Then I hope he's burning in hell." Evie was surprised at how hateful she sounded, but that priest had ruined her dad's life and had severely altered her mom's and siblings' lives. She hoped that priest was suffering as much as he made Dad suffer.

***

As the busy mother of five young children, Evie couldn't spend much time researching the whereabouts of Fr. Tim on the internet. Besides, she didn't even know his last name. In light of what happened to her father, Evie and Jake were inspired to read the tale about the apprentice and the magician again. Evie said, "This sounds like an abuse story as well, doesn't it, Jake?"

"Yeah, so a magician tricks an apprentice and winds up in a dungeon? Maybe being trapped in a dungeon is like being trapped in secrecy. Perhaps it was his way to express what he couldn't say in any other manner."

The following weekend, her husband took the boys out sledding for the afternoon. A blizzard in Eastern Ontario had just yielded an accumulation of forty centimeters, and the boys were bugging their dad to go sledding on the big hill nearby.

Two deadlines loomed for articles Evie had to write. So she worked on those, then she glanced at the coffee table, where her father's items had remained since the discovery of the hidden words in his journal. She picked up his freshman yearbook. It occurred to her that she might find out the last name of the priest from this book. Dad's abuser might have been a parish priest, but priests also worked at the high school. Could he have been a teacher instead? She paged through the book and found only one Fr. Tim: Fr. Timothy O'Reilly, OP. As she studied the man's face, she had a realization. The incident at the Phillies' game with the loud priest—this very well *could* be that priest.

After getting that name, she spent all available free time searching the internet for information about Fr. Tim O'Reilly. Over the ensuing months, she learned that he was a retired bishop, still alive at eighty-nine and living at a convent near Allentown, Pennsylvania.

She found nothing on the internet accusing him of abuse, at least not yet.

***

Evie read through her father's journal again. There were, after all, pages left to write in. Perhaps she could finish writing in the journal that her father had started. It could be a way to keep Dad present to her. It could also help her to connect with him as she tried to put the puzzle of his life together.

Conflicting emotions swirled around in her mind, and she had to let them out.

Starting a few pages after the page with the story of the magician and the apprentice, she jotted down words in a free writing exercise, like the one she used when she had writer's block.

Rage

Sadness

Anger

Grief

Outrage

With each word, Evie pressed the pen harder into the page. She realized that she had been grinding her teeth and stopped.

Then she studied the list. It didn't surprise her to find rage as the predominant emotion right now.

Evie turned the page.

I wish I could go back in time and stop that priest from abusing my father.

Just the other day, Jake asked her why she had to micromanage everything he or the kids did. "Sometimes," he had said, "you have to let things happen naturally." Or, as he reminded her, "Hope for the best, but be prepared for the worst."

Evie rarely hoped for the best. She was a glass-half-empty kind of gal, as opposed to Jake, a glass-half-full guy.

The open journal lay in front of her. She wrote the title, "Evie."

Teenage girl finds her father dead.

Hope for the best, be prepared for the worst.

Actually, expect the worst.

Before her father died, she always hoped for the best. But Dad's sudden death had turned Evie into someone who ramped up the "be prepared for the worst."

The best way to be prepared for the worst was to always expect the worst. When she and Jake became pregnant with the twins, she had deluded herself once again into hoping for the best—by believing that those babies would be born. And, of course, the worst happened, and her babies died.

That's just the way life was. She would face tragedies in her life, whether she was prepared for them or not. Hope didn't really change anything. And she'd just have to accept that, just like she'd have to come to terms that her father had been abused.

***

In May, Evie and her husband visited nearby Pembroke for a session with their spiritual director, Fr. Arthur, a short, middle-aged priest. During her time in Confession, she shared her anger and rage with the knowledge of her father's abuse by a priest. Fr. Arthur listened patiently and said nothing until she finished her tirade on the injustice of this priest never being arrested but instead being allowed to continue his abuse of other victims for so many years.

When she finally finished, Fr. Arthur sat back in his chair. "Evie, can you pray an Our Father with me?"

"Of course."

Together, they recited the Our Father. "Our Father, Who art in heaven, hallowed be thy name. Thy kingdom come. Thy will be done on earth as it is in heaven. Give us this day our daily bread, and forgive us our trespasses, as we forgive those who trespass against us."

The priest stopped there, so Evie did the same. Then he continued, so Evie prayed it along with him. "And lead us not into temptation, but deliver us from evil. Amen."

He remained silent for a few moments to the point that Evie was about to start asking questions if he didn't say something.

"Evie," he said. "What your father went through is the worst thing imaginable. That priest needs to be held accountable, and, yes, you need to seek justice, if possible. There's no worse tragedy than being betrayed by someone to whom you have entrusted your well-being. Clearly, this priest was a wolf in sheep's clothing."

Evie nodded through all this, while inside, she was raging. She was still so angry at the abusive priest for ruining her father's life.

"Please keep in mind that whether he receives justice in this life or the next, he will receive God's firm justice."

"I believe that, Father. But I'm just so angry. My dad was a kind boy who had his innocence taken away by this monster."

"I understand, Evie."

"How could God allow something so awful?" Her voice trembled, but she couldn't stop now. The questions poured out. "And the memory of coming home and finding him dead on the floor? The effect on my mother and siblings? I still can't get all of that out of my mind."

"Well, God allows it because He allows free will. But you must know that God was crying along with your father and along with you when you discovered him dead and when you found out about this abuse."

His words rang true about God being with them in their suffering, even though she didn't always feel it. But she struggled to understand why God allowed free will when so many ugly things happened because of it. "The only thing that keeps me going right now is this compulsion to get justice. I want that man to suffer." Her eyes filled with tears.

"Look, the anger you feel is normal and is justified to a certain extent. But it tells me that you haven't forgiven your father's abuser yet."

"Forgiven? How can I forgive such a vile man who probably doesn't want forgiveness?"

"Evie, I know this isn't easy to hear right now because your pain is so raw. But you need to do your best to forgive this man."

"Why should I? He's not asking for forgiveness!" Rather than glare at the priest, she shifted her gaze, her eyes snapping to the crucifix on the wall, to the corpus of Christ hanging morbidly on the rough wooden cross, and her heart wrenched inside her.

"Evie, you don't know that. He could be. I just asked you to recite the Our Father with me."

"Yes."

"If we want Our Father in heaven to forgive us our sins, we *must* be willing to forgive those who sin against us."

Evie slumped in her chair. In these past few months, her outrage about what Fr. Tim had done to her father seemed to have taken over her life. Now Fr. Arthur was telling her she had to forgive this monster. "Father, how can I forgive him?"

"Pray for the grace. Forgiveness doesn't just come

overnight, especially forgiveness for someone who commits a heinous act against someone you love. I understand that. But you must try. Spend time in front of the Blessed Sacrament. Pray to Jesus for the grace to forgive this man. Pray for his soul."

Evie remained quiet. In the rational part of her mind, she knew Fr. Arthur spoke the truth. He remained their spiritual director precisely because he always offered so much insight. But she had to admit that ever since her father's death, she'd had a problem with trust: trusting God, trusting her husband, even trusting the Church. But Jesus wouldn't give us a prayer that called us to forgive if it wasn't essential to do so.

The priest continued, "In an exorcism, the exorcist must name the demon. Once he can name the demon, he's closer to expelling him." He paused. "You've already named the priest—and I'm not calling him a demon, but evil is often influenced by demons. Now you have a unique opportunity to stop the effects of the abuse because you know what happened. However, you won't be truly successful in whatever you do if you do it out of anger...wishing ill on another." Fr. Arthur hesitated before continuing. "Another thing I'd like you to think about is that from the Cross, Jesus said, 'Father, forgive them for they know not what they do.'"

Her gaze shifted back to the crucifix on the wall as Father continued.

"Jesus petitioned for unconditional forgiveness as He suffered unimaginable pain." Fr. Arthur smiled sadly. "No matter how much this hurts or how much pain you're in, you're still called to forgive."

Evie realized that everything Fr. Arthur said was true. She would have to pray for the grace to embark upon this journey to do the impossible: forgive her father's abuser.

Chapter 55
Evie
The Scene of the Crime
July 2002

Before their scheduled summer trip in July to visit the family back in New Jersey, Evie called Holy Archangels High School and asked if they might be open during the summer. The receptionist indicated that they would be open the entire month of July and closed during August.

Jake asked her why she wanted to visit the school.

"Because I want to see the 'dungeon' from my father's story, that's why."

"It could all just be symbolic, Eve."

"I understand that. But you know this is going to bother me until I get to the bottom of this. I'd like to see the place for myself."

***

Jake drove most of the way from Ontario to Jersey. Having departed on a hot weekday, the whole family was grateful for the van's fully functioning air conditioning.

After the initial excitement of their arrival at Mom's home, Jake played with the kids in the living room while Evie spoke to her mother in the kitchen. Evie rinsed off the plates and handed them to her mother, who loaded them into the dishwasher. Mom stopped. "Hey, Eve, are you standing in a hole?"

"Funny, Mom." It was an old joke, to be sure, but since Mom was so much taller, Evie felt like she *was* standing in a hole. *This is a good time to tell Mom about my plans.* "By the way, Mom, I'm going to visit Dad's high school tomorrow." She rinsed off another dish and handed it to her mother.

"Why are you doing that?"

"I want to visit Dad's school because something bad happened to him there, and it's part of Dad's history. It's like, you know, if one of our relatives had been in a concentration camp in Germany, we'd want to go there out of respect, right?"

Mom scowled. "Why don't you just leave that in the past, Eve? Why do you have to dredge that all up again?"

Evie turned away from Mom and stared at the fridge plastered with photos of her kids, her nieces and nephew, and the same smiley face magnet that Evie brought home from school in eighth grade. "Because I feel compelled to see where it happened, Mom."

"Look, it was a long time ago. What can be done about it now?"

"I'm not sure, Mom. I'm still trying to figure it all out." *Mom's clearly uncomfortable.* To change the subject, Evie asked, "When is Little Hank coming over with his kids?"

"He and his family will be here for dinner."

Evie chuckled. "I can't believe we're still calling him Little Hank after all these years when he's nearly six feet tall."

Mom laughed.

***

Her mother had already made plans to spend the following day with the kids, having a picnic in the backyard and playing on the slip and slide. Evie and her husband kissed the children and her mother goodbye.

She and Jake took the PATCO speed line, a partially underground train that transported them from New Jersey to Center City Philly. They got off at 8th and Market Streets and walked the six blocks to Holy Archangels High School.

Once they reached the school, Evie turned to her husband. "Do you want to go in with me?"

"I think I should."

Evie stopped in front of the entrance and peered up at the St. Michael statue. A tall clock tower loomed above that.

Jake opened the door for her, and Evie stepped inside the cramped, stuffy foyer of the clock tower, her husband following behind. A steep staircase gave access to the tower, but it was closed off with a locked iron gate. There weren't too many of these sorts of 19th-century school buildings left in the United States.

They walked through an open entranceway to get to the school lobby. It had no air-conditioning, but, at least here, several standing fans blew hot air around the lobby. A receptionist's desk sat off to the right, and a winding marble staircase rose up in the center of the lobby. Above the grand staircase hung statues of the archangels: St. Gabriel, St. Michael, and St. Raphael.

Evie stared in awe. She had never seen such beautiful statues, and the way they hung straight down from the ceiling reminded her of the church she used to attend in New Jersey with the hanging crucifix, the same church where she and Jake were married.

Her husband pointed her to the receptionist, a middle-aged lady with short, salt-and-pepper hair, who looked at Evie over her glasses.

"Hello," Evie said.

"Hello. What can I do for you?"

"We just wanted to walk around the school if you don't mind. My father attended here many years ago."

"I'm sure that would be fine. Here"—she slid two blank name tags toward them—"write your names on these and check with me before you leave."

"Of course."

They stuck the nametags on their shirts.

"Where to first, Eve?"

"Let's go upstairs."

They proceeded up the wide marble staircase, Evie leading. She stopped under the sculptures of the archangels and gazed upward. From this angle, with the light shining through the windows, the statues gleamed with ethereal reflections.

Evie continued up the stairs to the classroom in which Fr. Tim O'Reilly had taught during her father's freshman year, 1954-55.

Reaching the room, she tried the knob, not surprised to find it locked. She'd just wanted to see the door and to take the same steps her father took when he attended school here.

After gazing at the door for a moment, she peered each way down the dark, quiet hallway. An eerie feeling came over her. She shuddered and took her husband's hand. "Let's go back downstairs."

The two started down. Again, Evie stopped under the hanging sculptures and stared at them. Any student taught by Fr. Tim would've walked under these very statues before stepping into the classroom of a predator.

Her body tensed, and she caught herself grinding her teeth. Yes, she was on the road to forgiving Fr. Tim O'Reilly for his abuse, but the thought of him violating her father still infuriated her.

"You're allowed to be angry, Eve. This is righteous anger. There's nothing wrong with that."

"I know."

Jake took her hand and smiled. "But you don't need to grind your teeth."

"It's a hard habit to break. But I know."

They descended the rest of the stairs and strolled around the lobby.

Evie noticed an old door under the staircase. She approached the receptionist's desk.

"All done?"

"That door over there under the staircase"—she pointed—"does it lead to a closet or a basement or cellar of some kind?"

The middle-aged lady's eyebrows lifted. "It's the basement."

"Would we be able to go down there?"

The woman stared over her glasses at Evie. "Um, well, the janitor would have the key. Let me call him on the intercom and see if he will unlock the door for you."

"Thanks so much."

A few minutes later, an overweight, well-worn man, his shoes thumping against the floor, came toward the desk.

"You the folks that want to see the cellar?"

"Yes, please," Evie answered.

"It's a mess down there, but I'll unlock the door and take you down myself. I want to make sure you don't get hurt."

"All right."

The janitor led them to the door under the stairs. He unlocked and opened it, then pulled on a chain for an old-fashioned light bulb.

"The stairs are the only thing new down here, so you'll need to be careful when we get down there."

Evie stepped on the new stairs, and her husband followed behind. As they descended, the scent of hardwood and varnish lessened, and the moldy, stuffy, old cellar stench took over.

At the bottom of the stairs, the janitor turned on another old-fashioned lightbulb.

Two small windows that bordered the ceiling were so filthy that they allowed minimal light to come in. Everywhere she turned, she saw cobwebs and a thick layer of dust, even on the dim hanging lightbulbs.

When her eyes adjusted to the dimness, she took in the cellar. The layout seemed to be precisely the way her father had described the "dungeon" in his tale about the apprentice.

And there, on a corner shelf beside one of the dingy windows, stood an old broken statue, much of its face shorn away. It held a sword in one hand, and the devil was under its feet. *St. Michael.*

The hairs on the back of her neck prickled. Now Evie knew without a doubt that this was where the priest abused her father.

Suddenly, Evie couldn't breathe, as if someone was strangling her. She gasped for air. "Can't breathe…"

She heard her husband say, "Come on, Eve, let's go upstairs."

As she climbed the steps, her breathing started to return to normal.

Once back in the lobby under the massive marble staircase, Evie was able to take a long, deep breath.

"As I said…" The janitor cleared his throat. "That room hasn't been used much in the past ten years or so since the school installed electric baseboard heaters. The school had to replace the wooden stairs a few years ago when two students stepped right through a rotted piece of wood. Both were hurt. One boy's leg was ripped from ankle to thigh and—"

Evie interrupted. "Um, thank you, sir. You've been very helpful."

They gave the receptionist the name tags and stepped outside into the heat of the late morning.

"There's something eerie in that cellar, Jake. I'm not sure how to explain this, but it felt like some…*thing* was strangling me."

"Yeah, that place gave me the creeps too."

"That's definitely the place my father described in his tale of the apprentice and the magician, right down to the St. Michael statue with half his face missing."

As they walked away from the building, the warm sun felt hot on her head, and Evie chided herself for not wearing a hat. They passed by a Catholic church, the Italian market, a few shops, and rowhomes.

They stopped at a pretzel vendor and bought two soft pretzels and a 7-Up. When she grabbed money from her purse to pay for the pretzels, she noticed a tiny bottle of holy water at the bottom of her purse. She should've given that cellar a healthy sprinkling of holy water. It was a good thing the school kept the room locked and didn't use it much.

They had one more stop before returning to Mom's house in New Jersey, a visit she didn't tell her mother about.

***

As the train whisked them to the Haddon Heights station where they began their journey this morning, Evie said, "I need to visit Fr. Tim, Jake."

"What?"

"I need to talk to him."

"Why?"

"Maybe to confirm what I think is the truth?"

"Are you asking me or telling me?"

"I'm asking if it's the right thing."

"It depends on your motivation."

"Yeah, I'm working on that." She paused. "If I decide to visit him, I'm not going to tell Mom, at least not yet. She seemed upset that we were visiting Dad's school."

They remained quiet, both of them watching the New Jersey countryside pass by as the train went underground for the next stop. Then Jake said, "Gosh, the boys would love this underground train. How about we go home, get the boys, and bring them for another trip to Philly?"

"You want to bring five young boys to Philly?"

"Sure. Why not? And they'll love the speed line."

"All right, then. Let's bring them to see the Liberty Bell. My father brought me there when I was little. I couldn't understand why a cracked bell was so special."

Jake laughed. "Well, you're still little."

"Haha." She feigned a chuckle at his facetious poke.

They returned to her mother's place and shared with their sons that they wanted to take them on a surprise trip. Their squeals and shouts of joy were music to Evie's ears.

The boys asked questions about where they were going, and all Evie and Jake would say was, "It's a surprise."

Once inside the PATCO building, they paid for their tickets and then waited on the platform for the train. When it loudly pulled up, she and Jake escorted their boys onto it. Jake and Evie managed to get two seats together, with Evie holding onto their fourth son and their fifth son on Jake's lap.

The boys could hardly sit still in their seats. When the train went underground, their second-oldest son said, "Wow, cool, it's dark and fast like we're flying the Millennium Falcon."

When they finally reached the Liberty Bell, they had to stand in line for half an hour, but it was worth it to Evie.

Back when Evie was a child, kids and adults could put their hands on the crack of the bell. Now, though, the bell was behind glass. Their boys seemed to be more impressed with the glass enclosure around the bell.

"Why is that bell so important, Mom?" her oldest son asked.

"Because it symbolizes freedom."

When she said "freedom," tears welled in her eyes. She thought about her father's story of the apprentice locked in the dungeon. Her father indeed had his freedom stolen by the trauma inflicted upon him.

Chapter 56
Evie
To Visit or Not to Visit

Evie and her family attended Mass that Sunday at St. Maria Goretti Parish in New Jersey. Afterward, Evie asked her husband to take the children back to her mom's place while she remained in the church to pray.

Evie prayed for her father's soul. Then she prayed to discern whether she should visit the bishop, whose actions had complicated her father's life in so many negative ways—and, by default, Evie's family's life as well.

When Evie recalled the trouble she'd had breathing in the school's cellar, her hands trembled. How would she react to coming face to face with the person responsible for the evil that occurred there? Maybe she *should* just leave it all in the past instead of dredging it up, as her mother had recommended.

Just thinking about meeting Bishop O'Reilly made her heart race. She shook her head. It would probably be too painful for Evie to meet her father's abuser. She tried to dismiss the idea of visiting the priest, but then she felt an internal tug pulling her back to reconsider it.

Lord, what do you want me to do? What could I accomplish by visiting my dad's abuser?

She continued to pray, but each time she thought about coming face to face with her father's abuser, her whole body shuddered, and her heart pounded. How would she be able to actually visit Dad's abuser if she couldn't even *think* about it without such physical reactions?

Evie stared up at the massive hanging crucifix and the representation of a broken and beaten Jesus. *Now, that was a horrible crime.* Here Evie was trying to get justice for her father. What kind of justice did Jesus ever receive? Why did Jesus have to die such a tortuous, painful death?

Suddenly, Evie felt an overwhelming obligation to follow through and visit with the bishop. Yes, she needed to do this for her father. While seeking justice and confronting her father's abuser were good reasons, she now understood that she had a much more important purpose for visiting the bishop.

When she returned to her mother's house, she logged onto the internet to find the phone number of the Allentown convent, the retired bishop's current residence. Evie called them, and they verified that Bishop O'Reilly did live there and that he accepted visitors.

Evie found Jake sitting outside on a lawn chair, watching the boys and their cousins playing. She told Jake that she had decided to visit the elderly priest.

He said, "All right. Do you know why you feel this urgency to visit him?"

"I need to hear him say the words, Jake."

"You know he may deny it, right?"

"He'll probably deny it, but I need to try."

"Do you want me to go with you to meet him?"

"No. I need to do this alone."

"Really?"

"Yes. A small woman is less intimidating than a small woman backed up by a man."

"All right then. Since Allentown is on our way home, why don't we do it then?"

Evie sighed, not satisfied with his suggestion.

"Look, Eve, I know. Now that you've made this decision, you want to go as soon as possible. But if we swing by there on the way home to Canada, then we'll have no need to mention it to your mother, in case she gets upset."

"You're right, I guess."

"And you can take the next week or so to continue to pray and discern what you'll say to him."

"Sounds like a plan."

"Then, after you've met him, you can tell your mother."

"All right." *Besides, maybe I'll chicken out and not actually go through with it. Then there would be nothing to tell Mom.*

During the week's activities, everything was shadowed with dread. She tossed and turned during the nights. She just wanted the visit with the bishop to be over and done.

After Mass the following Sunday, she and her family said goodbye to her mother. Jake navigated their way to the convent in Allentown, where Bishop Emeritus O'Reilly lived.

They pulled into the convent lot and parked. Run by the Immaculate Heart of Mary sisters, the convent, probably built in the '60s, was of modern construction.

Their oldest son asked, "Hey, why are we stopping here?"

Turning in his seat, Jake said, "Well, Mommy needs to visit somebody who lives at this place."

"Who are you visiting, Mommy?" their second oldest asked.

Evie was taken aback by her son's question. "Um, well, I'm visiting an elderly man."

"Why?" he asked.

She sighed. "Well, remember I told you about Grandpop?"

"Yeah, that's your dad," said her oldest.

"Well, this man taught Grandpop in high school."

That seemed to satisfy their curiosity. Jake and Evie then said a prayer for her to have patience and for the priest, who had no idea he was about to have a visit from one of his victim's daughters. While still in the process of trying to forgive her father's abuser, she hoped she would be able to talk with this man without losing her temper or her composure.

Evie checked her pocketbook to ensure she carried the

photocopied pages of Dad's story and the traced journal entry. She kissed her husband goodbye, and he gave her a comforting hug for support.

Evie then blew kisses to her kids, and her husband drove away to a local park to allow the boys to stretch their legs.

After taking a deep breath to steady her resolve, she strode down a long sidewalk, simple landscaping on either side, and stepped into the foyer of the convent. The foyer ceiling was an octagonal dome with windows, making the area very bright.

She had to will her hands to stop trembling before she approached the information desk. Then she asked if she could visit Bishop O'Reilly, to which the young sister responded, "Yes. He's in the parlor, I believe. Are you family?"

"Um, no, ma'am, I'm not. I'm...um...just a visitor."

"Would you like me to announce your visit?"

"Um, no, I don't think you need to do that."

"Well, the bishop enjoys visitors. He loves sitting outside, but it's too hot today, so he's in the air-conditioned parlor. It's just around the corner," she said, pointing. "Your second left. You can't miss it."

"Thank you, Sister."

The octagonal shape of the room caused Evie to have to maneuver around the wide reception desk. She then followed the hallway to the second room on the left. There was no door, just an entranceway. The parlor consisted of two contemporary couches, an armchair, and a recliner, all around a modern coffee table. Tall windows lined one wall, while religious artwork decorated the other walls. The room was empty except for an elderly man in a wheelchair by the window. *Bishop Timothy O'Reilly.*

Evie stood in the entranceway, unable to move. The silhouette of the man in the wheelchair gave her a heavy,

301

dark feeling. Her throat tightened, and she could barely breathe. In her mind, she again descended into the darkness of the school cellar. She prayed that God would give her the courage to confront her father's abuser. *Lord, give me the right words.* She willed her breathing to return to normal and tiptoed closer.

Her hands still trembled, and her heart pounded so loudly she thought it might come out of her chest.

The elderly priest must've sensed her presence because he immediately turned from the window and glanced at her. "Hello, my dear. Are you lost?"

Yes, this is the priest from the photos. Except now he is totally bald.

"I...um... don't think so. You're Bishop O'Reilly?"

"Yes, dear, I'm Bishop O'Reilly." He paused. "But you can call me Fr. Tim."

At that suggestion, she cringed. *I'll keep it formal, thank you.* "Do you have a few moments to speak with me?"

"Of course." He wheeled his chair over by the sofa. "Please have a seat, dear."

Evie sank into the sofa, not sure where to begin.

The wheelchair-bound bishop was now gazing down at her. "Do I know you? You're a cute little thing. You're kind of young to want to visit an old priest. You can't be out of high school yet."

"The last time we met, you thought I was six years old."

"We've met?" His eyes widened.

"Yes. And actually, I'm thirty-six."

"Oh, go on, my dear. There's no way you can be thirty-six."

"With five sons."

Bishop O'Reilly clapped his hands. "That's marvelous." His voice wasn't as loud as she remembered, but they were outside back then. He glanced away then asked, "What is your name, dear child?"

"Evie—well, Evie Gallagher is my maiden name."

"Gallagher, huh?"

"Yes, sir. You taught my father at Holy Archangels High School for Boys in Philly." Evie took a deep breath and exhaled. She placed one hand over the other to hide the trembling.

"Ah, the 'Angels,' of course. I remember my time there. What did you say your last name was?"

"Gallagher."

"Gallagher, hmmm."

"His first name was Henry, but everyone called him Hank."

Wide eyes told Evie that the old man remembered her father. "Short little fellow. You must take after your father. You're such a wee thing." He smirked.

Evie's pulse sped up and her body tensed. *He must know now why I'm here.* For one brief second, she wanted to smack that smile off his face. *Lord, give me courage.*

"Yes, I do take after him."

"So, how is your father these days?"

Sensing that less information might be the right strategy, she responded, "He's doing well now, I believe."

A moment of awkwardness hung in the air.

Evie opened her pocketbook and lifted out the papers. "I'd like to read you a tale my father wrote in February of 1955. You might find it interesting, seeing that you taught my father English and encouraged creative writing."

"Oh, do read it. I love a good story."

Evie proceeded to read the tale of *The Apprentice and the Magician.*

When she finished reading, the bishop said, "Interesting fairy tale."

She cleared her voice. "You...used to do magic tricks, correct?"

303

"Excuse me?" The bishop tilted his head.

"Well, this is not just a story. I'm here today because my father... 'told me' what you did to him when he was a freshman, and this story is part of the proof. You're the magician."

As she spoke, a slight twitch of his eyes indicated to Evie that he realized she knew what he had done. But the arrogant grin remained.

He shook his head and said smugly, "My girl, first, that story is proof of nothing. And if your father told you that I acted inappropriately, he's lying. I was probably the only teacher in that school who didn't hit my students."

Her heart thundered in her chest. "I'm... not talking about physical abuse or discipline, Bishop. I'm talking about sexual..." She drew out the word sexual to make sure he heard what she said. "...abuse."

Bishop O'Reilly lowered his head. When he made eye contact again, Evie was confident he would admit to it. He said, "The truth is, I loved those boys, and I loved your father. I would never have done anything to harm them."

"Well, my father says differently." She paused. "And why would my father lie about such a thing?"

"Little Hank was very good at telling stories and likely still is. My dear young lady, with the whole *Boston Globe* story, every priest is being blamed for abuse. I understand why you're here."

"That's *not* why I'm here."

"Young lady..."

Evie's heart was now pounding so loudly, she was sure he could hear it. She straightened. "I'm here because you hurt my father. He had a nervous breakdown thirty-four years ago and had problems his entire adult life. I hold *you* personally responsible for what happened to my dad."

Bishop O'Reilly straightened in his wheelchair, his chin

lifting defiantly. "Well, if you think you know the truth, then why do you want to speak with me?"

Evie gritted her teeth. If she sat any longer, the sofa might swallow her up, so she stood. The cool air from a nearby vent reached her now as she looked down on him. "Because the truth will set *you* free, Bishop." She paused a moment to give him an opportunity to come clean. "You say you 'loved' those boys. However, true love calls us to love as God loves. What you did to my father was the opposite of love, and it affected every member of my family."

"I assure you—"

Evie cut him off. "Look, you can rationalize all you want. Whether it's an assassin murdering JFK, or extremist Islamic terrorists flying planes into buildings, or supposed men of God betraying boys who trust them implicitly, these are all tragedies committed by those assuming power over others—they are the *opposite* of love."

The bishop sat there with that stupid smirk on his face, as if he was just humoring her and couldn't wait for her to leave.

"Your grace?"

Evie turned toward the voice. The sister from the registration desk stepped into the room.

"Would you like your late morning tea?"

"Thank you, Sister." He turned to Evie. "Would you like some tea, my dear?"

Evie shook her head. She couldn't believe the respectful way he addressed the sister, with a voice that could melt butter. Maybe he had convinced himself that he didn't do anything wrong all those years ago. But she knew better. She was just starting to make out what was behind his arrogant grin.

When the sister disappeared from the doorway, Evie said, "Oh, and my father died twenty years ago."

The elderly priest's body seemed to relax.

"However, he wrote about what you did to him. She held up the certified copy of the traced sheet from the journal and read part of it. "I opened my eyes to find Fr. Tim's head on my lap."

When she glanced at the priest, his already pale complexion was now blanched, but the smile remained plastered across his face.

"Remember, the truth will set you free, Bishop. I name and accuse *you* as the abuser, and I name my father as the victim." She paused. "I've already brought a certified copy of this story and this journal entry to the Pennsylvania Attorney General's office. I asked them to open a case against you for abusing my father."

Finally, thank God, the smirk disappeared and was replaced by an open mouth. He quickly closed it and said nothing. His eye twitched again, and he turned his head away from her.

As angry as Evie had been during these past few months, now she felt sorry for him. He was just a pathetic, prideful wolf whose world as a respected member of the clergy was ending. "Look, I'm not doing this because I hate you. In fact, I'm trying to forgive you for what you did to my father. But the only way you'll ever be free again is if you admit what you did to my father. Admit it to yourself, to God, and to any other victims who may come forward inspired by this evidence."

He sat with his head lowered, his entire body sinking deeper into the wheelchair. But he made no reply, no acceptance of his guilt, no statement of regret, no apology, nothing. He even avoided eye contact with her.

"I'll pray for you, Bishop." With that, Evie left.

***

When Evie returned to the parking lot, she felt lighter. She hadn't expected Bishop O'Reilly to admit that he abused her father. Evie hoped for it but, in the end, was not surprised. By the different nuances in his voice and eyes, Evie could tell that the bishop knew she had discovered the truth and that there was no point in maintaining the wall of lies that had fueled that smirk of his.

Ten minutes later, Jake finally pulled up in the van, and Evie got in. Their boys greeted her with the enthusiasm of a large crowd, and, for that, she was grateful. It was good that Jake had taken them for a run at a nearby park before climbing back into the confines of the van. They would only stop a few times during the rest of their eight-hour trip.

Jake asked her how it went, but it had all happened so quickly and with so much turmoil, that Evie didn't quite know how to recount the event. Hours later, when the boys were all quietly napping in the seats behind them, Evie shared with him her conversation with the bishop and the fact that the arrogant man seemed surprised that she had already handed over the certified copies of the story and the traced page from Dad's journal to the Attorney General's office.

That night, after unpacking from their trip, Evie opened her father's journal to the story about the apprentice and the magician. Her eyes watered. It truly *was* a sad story.

***

Three years later

Mom called that morning to tell her the "news" that there were allegations against Bishop O'Reilly for abusing eleven minors. If she didn't know better, her mother sounded relieved. Of course, Evie already knew about the allegations. She'd received an email earlier in the week from the

Attorney General's office, indicating that the Grand Jury report from 2005 had finally been published. She couldn't believe it when she read that Bishop O'Reilly had been accused with credible evidence of the sexual abuse of eleven minors. When confronted with the evidence of his abuse of eleven former students, the Attorney General said Bishop O'Reilly finally confessed, asked for forgiveness, and gave them the names of other boys he had abused. She was thankful that the bishop had finally "come clean." At least there was hope for his eternal soul.

She continued to pray for Bishop O'Reilly. She prayed for all the "Angels," living and dead, who had passed under those statues and directly into the arms of a wolf in sheep's clothing. She prayed fervently for her beloved father, whose pain and secrecy kept him from living life to the fullest.

Despite the abuse, her father's life was one with tremendous value. Her efforts to find justice, to forgive his abuser, and to give his abuser a chance to tell the truth had been a heartbreaking prayer for the healing that her father may have still needed after his death, and she held great hope for his eternal salvation.

Chapter 57
Evie
September 2018

Evie stared in disbelief at the news program. Cardinal Theodore McCarrick had been accused of sexually abusing seminarians and at least one underage boy. Not only that, Archbishop Carlo Maria Vigano, former Vatican nuncio in Washington, released a statement indicating that the present Holy Father knew of the allegations against McCarrick.

Evie had thought the whole clerical sex abuse scandal was over years ago. Not only was it *not* over, but the very people in charge of making sure that young people were safe from pedophile priests—bishops and at least one cardinal—were guilty of the same behavior.

All through the following month, since the accusations had been made public, Evie felt sick to her stomach. How could so many bishops allow these predators to remain in positions of authority?

It was no wonder that many Catholics were leaving the Church. Anger, confusion, disappointment, disillusionment, and distrust were rampant among the faithful.

Despite Fr. Tim's abuse, her father never left the faith. Her mother—now deceased—never left the faith either, so Evie would follow their example and remain in the Catholic faith.

Still, anger at what her father and so many others experienced at the hands of these wolves in sheep's clothing resurfaced. Evie tried to remember that anger was justified, but she couldn't dwell on that. She had already forgiven her father's abuser. She prayed for all victims of sexual abuse.

Now she would pray for those abusive priests who were clearly not acting *in persona Christi*.

Evie glanced at the photo of her second oldest son and his fiancée on the fridge. Her heart rejoiced when she thought about his upcoming wedding and the prospect of grandchildren in the future. There was so much for which to be grateful.

These new allegations about McCarrick had exposed old wounds. But Evie was determined not to allow the anger to rear its ugly head again. Although it was painful, she used these new allegations as an opportunity to heal any lasting effects that never quite got dealt with many years ago.

And that was a necessary thing.

Epilogue

The Apprentice and the Magician
By Henry Gallagher

There once was an apprentice and a magician. The young apprentice trusted the magician with his very life. He worked with the magician every day, assisting him and helping him come up with magic spells.

Not everyone in the kingdom liked or admired the apprentice. In fact, he had many enemies.

The magician protected the apprentice whenever his enemies were nearby.

One day, the magician invited the apprentice to the dungeon of his castle. When the apprentice arrived, the magician gave him a cup with a secret potion. The apprentice didn't know what the secret potion was, but the magician said, "Drink up, son, and my powers can be yours."

So he drank and drank and drank.

"Do you want to learn a new spell, apprentice?" the magician asked.

The apprentice could barely respond as the potion was mesmerizing.

"Say these words after me," said the magician.

While confused and under a spell from the drink, the apprentice repeated the words of the spell.

Suddenly, the apprentice was entrapped in a dark dungeon with dust so thick he could barely see out the two tiny windows. Wooden stairs led to a locked door. An ancient statue of St. Michael perched above him, half its face missing.

For years and years, he suffered in the darkness. Only short glimpses of beauty and light appeared. The apprentice lived out his life in this hopeless, lonely prison.

Ellen Gable

The Apprentice and the Fair Maiden
by Evie Gallagher

A diminutive fair maiden heard about an apprentice who disappeared years ago without a trace. His disappearance at such a young age greatly saddened her. She traveled the kingdom to discover what had become of the apprentice by speaking to those who were acquainted with him.

Finally, the fair maiden arrived at a magician's castle and asked the magician if he knew where the apprentice was. The magician denied ever knowing the apprentice, but the fair maiden knew he was lying. Many had already informed her that magician had instructed the apprentice many years ago.

On her way out of the castle, a cryptic symbol appeared above the doorway, and she committed it to memory.

She continued to travel throughout the kingdom, showing all she encountered the hand-drawn version of the symbol. Eventually, a shepherd boy pointed her to a stone cave with the very same symbol she'd found above the doorway of the magician's castle. The fair maiden opened the door to the stone cave, expecting to see the apprentice. All she found, though, were chains and bones. The apprentice had already died.

The fair maiden wept for the unfortunate apprentice. "I've done everything to find you and to release you, and now I'm too late. I've spent all this time trying to help you, and I've failed."

An ethereal light illuminated the stone cave. The spirit of the apprentice said, "Thank you for your rescue."

"I don't understand," said the fair maiden. "You're dead."

"I am, but my spirit was still imprisoned here. Your search for me and your discovery of this cave will free my spirit from this prison."

"You've been through many terrible experiences, and some

of those were not your fault," said the fair maiden. "I pray you will be at peace in eternity."

With that, the spirit of the apprentice disappeared from the cave. And the fair maiden wept, partially from sadness, but mostly from joy.

Afterword

The story you have just read is based loosely on the actual events of my father's life, though it's a fictionalized account. Names, timelines, and places have been changed and are used fictitiously.

The following is an article I wrote just after the allegations against McCarrick came out.

The Forgotten Victims of Clerical Abuse
By Ellen Gable Hrkach

August 21, 2018

"He heals the wounds of every shattered heart." Psalm 147:3

The recent revelations about Cardinal (now Archbishop) McCarrick, and the newly published Grand Jury report from several dioceses in Pennsylvania, are disturbing, especially to the most devout Catholics. Some members of the Church are leaving in disgust. I haven't yet read the PA Grand Jury report, but from what I can gather through social media, it will take someone with a strong stomach to endure the entire document.

The most recent announcement that homosexual networks existed within seminaries and dioceses has caused some Catholics to have a crisis of faith because numerous seminarians tried to alert higher-up prelates, to no avail. It's unacceptable that a bishop—or as in the case of McCarrick, a cardinal—would be complicit. Pope Francis has now made a public statement promising justice for the victims.

For every abuse that was reported, there are likely hundreds, maybe thousands over the past 70-plus years, that were not—and have never been—reported. There are many victims who will never see justice.

Whenever I hear a story about clerical sex abuse, it opens a wound, not only because I'm Catholic, but because my father was abused over seventy years ago. He is one of many who never reported the (likely ongoing) abuse.

My father's abuser was indeed a priest, who happened to be one of his teachers in high school. This information was something that my siblings and I didn't find out until after my father died, as he had only told my mother about the abuse.

Back in the 1940s, priests were placed on a pedestal. My father couldn't go to his parents or other teachers or anyone because he was ashamed, and he didn't think anyone would believe him. At the time, my father was discerning the priesthood. To say the abuse confused him is an understatement. I can't imagine having to attend school and see your abuser every day and not be able to say anything.

Dad later met and married my mom and tried to settle down into married life. But his troubles were far from over. He dealt with depression and other mental illnesses on and off for a few years before he had a mental breakdown in 1961 and was committed to the local psychiatric hospital. I remember visiting him there and, despite the odd surroundings, I was always happy to see my dad.

He was eventually diagnosed with paranoid schizophrenia and manic depression (now called bipolar disorder) and was prescribed a regimen of medication.

My dad continued to battle with mental illness for the rest of his life. He eventually became an alcoholic and died tragically at the age of 49. His life ended not unlike many other abuse victims.

It wasn't easy to lose my father. But the first time I saw him in the casket after he had passed away, he looked more at peace than I could ever remember. I felt confident that God would take care of him.

When I first found out my own father had been abused, I was angry, but my father's troubled life made a lot of sense in light of his abuse. Of course, I wanted to strangle the priest who traumatized him.

There are many like my father out there, some living, and some already deceased, who are/were unknown victims of clerical abuse.

But we as a family were (are) victims too. As a family, we watched my father's struggles and suffering. We watched him go through drunken stupors and depressive episodes. We watched him get on and fall off the wagon too many times to count. It wasn't unusual for him to break down and cry. I know that there are many factors that cause someone to have a mental breakdown or become an alcoholic, but I believe the abuse contributed substantially to his ongoing despair.

So with the recent allegations, what is the way forward? First, I'd like to pass on encouragement to the many faithful and virtuous priests with the words of Dr. Janet Smith when she said: "To all you wonderful, faithful, chaste, devout, self-giving priests out there, my heart goes out to you. Thank you for answering the call and thank you for staying. The temptation to leave will be great. Please stay. We need you now more than ever. And please know I am praying ardently for you!"

Second, many of the links below give detailed ways the Church can move forward. One thing is for certain: leaving the Church is not an option.

Did my father ever leave the Church of his youth? No.

Following his example, I will do the same. Why? Because my faith is not dependent on the pope, any priest or any human being. I'm Catholic and will remain so because of the

Eucharist, because of Jesus Christ and because I believe God's Word. My faith also tells me I must forgive: the priest who abused my father, anyone who tried to cover it up, and any past and present priests, bishops, and cardinals who have been guilty of any wrongdoing.

As Frank Sheed said in the early '60s: "We are not baptized into the hierarchy; do not receive the Cardinals sacramentally; will not spend an eternity in the beatific vision of the pope. Christ is the point. I, myself, admire the present pope (Paul VI), but even if I criticized him as harshly as some do, even if his successor proved to be as bad as some of those who have gone before, even if I find the Church, as I have to live with it, a pain in the neck, I should still say that nothing that a pope (or a priest, bishop, cardinal) could do or say would make me wish to leave the Church, although I might well wish that *they* would leave."

And there is always hope. I believe very much what Fr. Joseph Ratzinger (Pope Benedict XVI) predicted in 1969: "From the crisis of today the Church of tomorrow will emerge — a Church that has lost much. She will become small and will have to start afresh more or less from the beginning. She will no longer be able to inhabit many of the edifices she built in prosperity. It will be hard going for the Church, for the process of crystallization and clarification will cost her much valuable energy. It will make her poor and cause her to become the Church of the meek... But when the trial of this sifting is past, a great power will flow from a more spiritualized and simplified Church."

As we pray and make reparation in the days ahead, I ask you to pray for all those forgotten victims (like my father) who never reported the abuse and for all families of abuse victims.

Let's continue to pray and fast for all victims and their extended families. As much as we yearn for a renewal of the

Church and the defrocking of any cleric who chooses not to live a chaste priesthood, let us also continue to pray and fast for the conversion of the abusers. As difficult as it is, we are all called to forgive.

Resources

Grand Jury Report https://www.attorneygeneral.gov/report/

Survivors' Network of those Abused by Priests (SNAP)
https://www.snapnetwork.org/

Bishop Accountability.org (list of credibly accused priests)
https://www.bishop-accountability.org/accused

Clergy Abuse Survivors Face a Lifetime of PTSD
https://www.catholicnews.com/clergy-abuse-survivors-face-a-lifetime-of-recurrence-of-ptsd/

Courage International *(A Roman Catholic Apostolate for those who experience same-sex attraction and those who love them)* https://couragerc.org/

Acknowledgments

It takes a village to raise a child, and in the same way, it takes a group of people to help an author to write, create, research, edit, and everything else that comes with crafting a difficult story like this.

A huge thank you to my one and only, James, for developmental editing, for designing the beautiful cover, and for composing the poem that appears at the beginning of the book. I would not have been able to write this book without his expertise.

Special thanks to my brothers for sharing incidents about our father. And to my youngest sister, Laurie, thank you so much for sharing honest feedback with me.

A huge shout-out to Theresa Linden, whose superior editing skills made this book the best that it could be. To Carolyn Astfalk, Ann Frailey and Nick Lauer, proofreaders, whose keen eyes catch the most minor typos. Thank you!

To my dear friend, Ann Frailey, whose wonderful pep talk gave me the push I needed to finish this book. As well, I appreciate your feedback and comments regarding the story.

And finally, to my late father, who, in many respects, was my co-author for this book. I used his stories, essays, and articles when writing some of adult Hank's dialogue.

About the Author

Ellen Gable (Hrkach) is an award-winning author (2010 IPPY Gold medal, 2015 IAN finalist, 2020 International Book Awards Finalist), publisher (2016 CALA), editor, self-publishing book coach, speaker, NFP teacher, Marriage Preparation Instructor, Theology of the Body teacher, and past president of the Catholic Writers Guild. She has written twelve books and has contributed to numerous others. Her books have been collectively downloaded over 730,000 times on Kindle and have nearly three-quarters of a million pages read on KDP. She and her husband, James, are the parents of five adult sons, seven precious souls in heaven, and grandparents to one adorable grandson. In her spare time, Ellen enjoys reading on her Kindle, researching her family tree, and watching live-stream classic movies and TV shows. Her website is located at www.ellengable.com.

Ellen enjoys receiving feedback from her readers: please email her at fullquiverpublishing@gmail.com

Published by
Full Quiver Publishing
PO Box 244
Pakenham ON K0A2X0
Canada
http://www.fullquiverpublishing.com/

56885771R00191